The Ballad
Of
Huey Tate

by
Mick Hare

To my sisters, Sheila and Mary.

Also by Mick Hare

The Sean Colquhoun wartime espionage series

A Pious Killing

A Noble Killing

The Ben Franklin Private Investigator Series

The Flashwater Murders

Behind The Mask

Promise Broken

"I follow him to serve my turn upon him." Iago.

One

They are standing face to face. From fleeting moment to moment, she sees changing emotions in his eyes. Or thinks she does. Surprise. Pain. Shock. Sadness. Regret. Shame. At any given moment it could be any of those. Or it could be fear. She looks for love but cannot be sure it is there. In her left hand the piece of paper. He glances at it, then looks straight back into her eyes. Is that understanding she sees emerging within him? She hopes so.

Two

Alabama 1939

Jesse had assured Huey that everything would be fine.

"I don't know about that," Huey had answered. "Mapleville is way off my beaten track. I appreciate your offer, but I don't know. It could cause a lot o' trouble for the both of us."

"Heck, Huey, you ain't got no need to be worried. You'll be with me. Them old hicks down in Mapleville, they ain't had no band touring through in months – maybe a year past since they seen one. You'll be fine."

"Jesse, in case you ain't noticed, I'm a coloured guy. Them country music hicks don't like the likes o' me."

"Okay, I'll pay you double what I did last time you filled in for Joe."

"That was in Ohio, Jess. There's a world of difference between Ohio and Mapleville, Alabama."

"I'm still offering double. What do you say?"

In the end it had been the money that swung it. And so here was Huey riding south on the battered old tour bus of The Country Music Coasters – Jesse's band. The guys hadn't said much when Jesse had stopped the bus outside Huey's place and brought him on board.

"Heads up, guys," he called out to the other seven members who were variously, dozing, smoking or playing cards. "Y'all remember Huey. He stepped in on guitar for Joe several months back on the Ohio tour. Well, I'm mighty pleased to tell you that he's joining us for the gig in Mapleville. By the time we hit Montgomery, Joe should be back with us."

"Hey, Huey," a long-legged wire of a man under a Stetson called. "You bin practising them country tunes we showed you? We won't be playin' any of your blues music in Mapleville." This brought a few guffaws from the other members, but Huey was pleased to see the man they all called Stick. He played fiddle in the band and had spent a lot of spare time during the Ohio trip sharing musical ideas with Huey.

"Good to see you Stick, and you guys. I hope you got room for one more." The guys went back to what they had been doing and Huey, without being told, automatically went and sat at the back of the bus. He stashed his guitar box under the seat and opened the sheaf of music Jesse had given to him, in order to refresh his memory. It wasn't his favourite musical style but there was plenty in it to intrigue him. The slight variations in the riffs and the country scales, as compared to the blues, interested him as much as the similarities and overlaps.

As the bus rattled along most of the men got some shut-eye. But Stick came down the bus and sat with Huey to chat about the set of tunes they were going to play. Difficulties started on arrival. The dance was taking place in the Mapleville High School gymnasium and Jesse led the way in. They were met in the entrance area by the janitor who shook Jesse by the hand and welcomed him back to Mapleville.

"We sure bin lookin' forward to your return, Mr Dwyer."

"Our privilege," Jesse replied. "Now if you'll just show us the way backstage we'll get ourselves ready."

The janitor suddenly bristled when he looked over Jesse's shoulder and took in the rest of the band. Right at the back, carrying his guitar case and a snare drum for Reg the drummer, was Huey.

"Er, hold on there just a minute, Mr Dwyer. Uhnm. I don't exactly know what to say. Could you please all just wait here while I go and find Mr. Saul?"

"Why?" Jesse asked. "You got a problem?"

"Oh no, Mr Dwyer, it's nothing like that. Just hold on here for me. I won't take more than a second."

The guys turned and looked at Huey. Stick winked and shrugged his shoulders. He turned to Jesse. "Don't take no shit from these hicks, Jess," he warned. "They ain't gonna turn down a night's dancing just 'cos we got Huey with us. I bet they ain't had a night out since the last time we was through here."

The musicians found some place to lean against and practiced what musicians have to become expert in the world over; waiting. Saul and the janitor hustled through into the entrance. Saul walked up to Jesse and they shook hands.

"Chrissakes, Jesse, what you playing at?" but he wasn't speaking in an angry tone. It was more like a father chastising a playful child.

"You know me, Jake. I never go on stage without a guitarist. Joe's laid up and Huey's stepped in. Take it or leave it."

Saul shrugged and released a world-weary sigh. "Okay. But make him keep a low profile. Sit him well in back, behind the drummer if possible."

"Now you're being ridiculous. But we'll do the best we can. Now, can we come in?"

"I'll lead you through. Come on."

Saul pushed open the double doors into the gymnasium and led the band through to the backstage area. The few revellers who had turned up early followed them with their eyes. Excited chatter erupted as their eyes fell upon Huey.

That long walk across the dance floor turned out to be the worst of the evening until the interval. Huey spent the first half in a seated position behind the front four of mandolin, fiddle, banjo and double bass. The steel pedal guitar player sat directly opposite Huey on the other side of the drummer. The hall filled up with the townsfolk all dressed in their best togs; ladies in gingham dresses and the men in cowboy boots, vests and Stetsons. Only soft drinks were served at a side hatch and hot dogs were to be dished out in the short interval. Something crackles in the air when a Southern belle finds a young black man extremely attractive. Even a dirt-poor Southern female has to be treated like a belle by Huey's kind. Huey was a handsome young man with a strong build for his five-eleven height. It is a moment of forbidden excitement for the Southern belle but a moment of lethal danger for the black man. As they left the stage for the interval Jesse mentioned that Saul had laid on hot dogs and coke for them at the side hatch. Huey was heading for the cramped dressing room they had shared earlier when Stick took his arm and said, "Come on brother, I bet you's as hungry as the rest of us."

"Ah, I don't know," Huey began, but Stick was already pulling him across the gym to the hatch. Huey kept his eyes to the floor but couldn't help a glance around as they neared the hatch. He immediately locked eyes with a young woman who was staring at him. As that happened, she smiled. Before Huey had been served his hot dog, she had wandered over. She moved close to Huey and reached her arm across his to pick up a bottle of Coke.

"Hello," she said. "My name's Veronica. What's yours?"

Huey didn't answer. He looked around for Stick or one of the other guys to help him out of this situation. But they had wandered off towards backstage to eat their dogs. "I've been watching your playing. You're very good. I'm learning to play the guitar too. I love it. I like country music but I really love the blues."

This comment made Huey turn and look directly at the woman. Girl is what he would have said if he'd seen her in the street. She was barely eighteen. She was very pretty in that Southern belle tradition; big brown eyes, deep brunette hair, rolling down her shoulders in a ponytail and thin, red, impudent lips. As soon as he had looked at her he knew it was a mistake. He looked away immediately and reached out to accept his hot dog from the woman serving behind the hatch. But it was too late. From above the silence that had fallen over the hall, he heard the clacking of cowboy heels on the wooden floor.

A voice called, "Hey, hey! Goddammit, Vee! What you doing now?" A youngish man, around twenty, twenty-one or so, five-eight, wearing his papa's moustache, came steaming across. He reached out and grabbed Vee's arm, jerking her round to face him. He was struggling with embarrassment and the humility of having to reprimand his date in public. How far should he go? Too far or not far enough? Not knowing, he swung and slapped her on the cheek. She let out a squeal and pushed him hard in his chest, so that he stumbled. Huey knew he had no role to play in this conflict and so he took his chance to scoot back to join the other guys in the band.

"Hey Jess," he said when he could grab his attention. "I'm not sure I should come out for the rest of the set."

"Why the hell not? What's happened?"

Huey briefly explained. "Holy shit. Did you touch her?"

12

"Hell no!"

"Did you speak to her?"

"Not one word. It was over in a second. She was interested in the guitar. But her man didn't see it that way."

"Okay," Jesse muttered. "I'm going to have a word with Saul. Give me a minute."

He disappeared. Huey looked around at the others. Most of them wore an 'I could have told you so' expression. Stick looked around too. "Goddammit guys," he yelled. "Give the guy a break."

The double bass player said, "Nothing against Huey, Stick. But this could be trouble. If it's trouble it's Southern trouble. And Southern trouble is real trouble."

Jesse returned after a few minutes. All the guys looked at him hopefully. "Saul's going out to have a word with the couple. He'll come in and speak to us before we go back on."

Sure enough Saul came in a few minutes later. Sweat was beading across his wrinkled brow and his bulbous nose shone under the feeble light. His white crumpled suit bore the stains of sweat and a misplaced sliver of onion from his half-eaten hot dog.

"Remind me to give up this promoting game. It's not good for my heart. Anyway, I think we're good to go. The young man seems calm now. His sweetheart has said she's sorry and she didn't mean nothin' by it. We should be okay. To be safe we'll finish at ten not ten thirty. Okay?"

The second half was interminable for Huey. He sat well back, tried not to look into the crowd at all. But occasionally he couldn't help himself. Each time he did he glimpsed a couple of guys staring or pointing at him. Or thought he did. Maybe he was running a bit too scared. The sweat on his fingers did not help with his playing and he got one or two sharp looks from Jesse.

Having wished the evening over a million times, when it came to the last song, he suddenly realised that, if anything was going to kick off, now would be the time. Maybe he wanted this last song to go on forever.

Ever the wise man, Jake Saul had slipped out halfway through the second set and persuaded the Baptist minister to accompany him back to the school. He explained the situation and hinted that the school might stop all groups renting out the gymnasium if a ruckus kicked off and it got reported in the local paper. The minister, a Canadian by birth, was a regular user of the school's facilities and allowed Jake to convince him that his presence would calm everyone down. Spending time in between dances to wander around and chat with the revellers he had had the desired effect. Veronica and her beau were wrapped in each other's arms for the last waltz and the minister walked with the band to their bus as they prepared to depart.

It was the drummer's turn to drive so Jesse sat at the front popping open bottles of Bud with that unique fizz. "Step up boys. You done great tonight. We got booked again for next year. Montgomery next stop."

As Huey collected his Bud, Jesse handed him his pay packet.

"Hey Jess," yelled Stick, "Whatsay we double back and fix our new guitarist up with that Southern beauty?"

The bus broke out into raucous laughter. Huey blushed as he rolled his way back to his seat with his beer and his pay. He could afford to laugh as well now.

Stick rolled down the bus like a sailor in a storm. "These damn Confederate roads!" he cursed. "Huey, come up here."

Huey put down the sheet music he was reading and followed Stick up the aisle to the front seats. Stick pushed him in beside Jesse and sat himself down across from them. "Hey Jess," he said reaching across Huey to nudge Jesse awake. "What now?"

"Here's what now. I reckon you should take Huey on full time. And some of the boys agree with me. Permanent."

"Where's this coming from?" Jesse said looking at Huey. It was a complete surprise to Huey who shrugged in embarrassment.

"Like I said, it's coming from me and a few of the boys. Huey's the best damn guitarist we've ever had and you know it."

"And what about Joe?"

"Ah come on Jess, you know he's as good as finished. He's too in love with the bottle. How many more times is he gonna let us down? How many more excuses you gonna take?"

"Stick," Jesse said, sitting up and putting a hand on Huey's arm. "Heck I know how good this boy is. But you saw the trouble tonight. Hell, seventy-five per cent of our gigs is in the deep south. If we have Huey with us full-time permanent it's as sure as goddamn we ain't gonna get out of it. No. I'm sorry. Huey, if all our gigs were in Chicago or Detroit you'd be my first pick every time. But I can't do it."

"Ah come on Jess."

"Never mind come on. I told you the truth. And Huey knows it. And you shouldn't of put Huey in this position. Huey, go on back to your seat and get some shut-eye. And you, Stick, think your big ideas through before you go and raise a fella's hopes like that.

Three

Paris 1940.

"Stand back!"

The gendarme pushed Marc in the chest, making him stumble backwards.

"Why?" Marc retaliated. "And what are you doing here anyway? This is Paris. The gendarmerie has no business here. Get back to your rural military duties."

The gendarme ignored him. But Marc wasn't finished. The tramp of military boots thundered in their ears as the parade went on.

"These are our streets, not theirs. What's a Frenchman like you doing protecting them?"

"You'd better ask the generals that, not me. And get back!"

"Traitor," Marc snarled. The gendarme sneered and turned away.

Clara saw Marc ahead of her through the surging crowd. She pushed her way towards him. "What happened?" she asked.

"Nothing," he shrugged. "Just some French Nazi throwing his weight around."

It was the day of national humiliation. The Wermacht had routed the French army and a triumphal parade was being held along the Champs-Élysées and through the Arc de Triomphe. Hitler was rubbing their noses in the dirt today. His revenge for the Treaty of Versailles. Parisians stood in silence as the naked display of military might marched past. Swastikas waved from every building, the Tricolour having been torn down. The young couple stood on the corner of Rue de Tilsitt, wondering who, amongst the onlookers would seek to ingratiate themselves with the invader. It was 14th June,

17

1940 and Clara was hoping to begin her studies in the Sorbonne at the end of this year but those hopes were now up in flames. Marc was twenty-four years old and coming to the end of his own post-graduate studies there. He had studied philosophy and political history. He knew that the college records would identify him as an enemy of Nazism, much more so than the normal Parisian.

Marc and Clara turned away from the parade and walked back along Rue de Tilsitt. Movement around the city had already been curtailed by the invaders. Car usage had been restricted to the German military or those French men and women who had already curried enough favour with the Germans by seeking to administer their regime for them. Halfway along Rue de Tilsitt they collected their bicycles and headed along towards the left bank, following the Seine towards the 5th Arrondissement. Their task had been unofficially sanctioned by the college department head. They stood their bikes together at the bottom of the steps below the statue of Montaigne and walked towards the politics building. There were two students sitting on the steps smoking. They were immersed in each other's company and they paid no attention to Marc and Clara. The rest of the campus was deserted. Parisians were, for once, not self-assured about how they should behave. With the copied keys they had been given, they let themselves into the building. Once inside Marc attacked the lock with a hammer and a chisel to make it appear that there had been a break in. He did the same at the door to the central office and then used a wrench to open all the filing cabinets. Clara began lifting all the files out of the cabinets and threw them onto the floor. Marc joined in until all files formed a large mound in the middle of the office. Before setting the mound ablaze they made sure no personal details of course members and lecturers had been overlooked. With a gentle sprinkling of paraffin and a fusillade of burning matches the mound was soon alight.

They stood by the door, their mouths and noses covered with scarves, until they were certain that the whole bundle had caught. Then they ran back through the building and across to their bicycles. At the corner of Rue des Écoles they entered Café Soirée and telephoned the fire service. It was their first act of resistance – but not their last.

Four

Paris 1940.

Almost nineteen years old and not long since arrived in Montparnasse from her parents' home in Saint Denis, Clara waited at the bottom of the steps leading up to the cathedral of Sacre Coeur. She wore a headscarf tied tightly around her head and neck. The long tail of her red wig flowed over her collar and down her back. The sunglasses were an unnecessary fashion affectation as the sun had long since gone down below the skyline. An evening Mass was just ending and emerging first through the great double doors into the Paris night, was a group of uniformed Nazis. Hitler's concordat with Pius XII had ensured that practising Catholics could balance their Nazism with their religion. The officer she was waiting for was at the rear of the group. They had met three evenings ago. It wasn't hard for Parisians to know where to go to meet German soldiers. They headed straight to the obvious areas, like peacetime holidaymakers. It had been strolling around the gardens below the Eiffel Tower that Clara had drawn her Captain into conversation. It wasn't difficult for a young French woman to attract a German officer. It was what they were there for. Hitler's promise to his faithful troops – at least one visit to experience the delights of Paris; one of those delights being young French womanhood. He had been easy. If he hadn't been an invader she might have liked him. He didn't force himself on her and readily agreed to meet up a few days later. Those few days would allow Clara to make the necessary preparations. His brother officers stared at her as they passed and called jeeringly to their blushing comrade. He peeled off from them and took Clara's arm. She led the way down into the nearby streets. As they reached a corner leading to a narrow alley he took her arm and pulled her to him. Her schoolgirl German was enough for them to communicate. He stooped to kiss her. She succumbed for several seconds before gently pushing at his chest and whispering, "Not here. Come on. I have a room waiting."

His excitement rose and he pulled her closer, kissing her as his hand explored her breasts. They moved on and entered an alleyway halfway along a quiet street.

"Where is the room?"

"It's just through here," Clara reassured him. "This way is more discreet for me. Some of my countrymen do not like us to associate with someone like you. To them you are the enemy."

"The fighting between France and Germany is over. Our Fuhrer will forge a peace treaty beneficial to both our countries."

"I am sure you are right."

He pulled her to him. She made no move to prevent his hands from reaching inside her skirt. His behaviour did not offend her. She recognised his inexperience and felt a pang of sorrow that this would be the extent of his awareness in matters of love. She took his hand and led him along to where the alleyway opened out onto a patch of waste ground. As they moved out of the alley, two men stepped from the shadow of the wall and fired a bullet each into the young soldier's head. He fell like a stone.

Blood splattered across Clara's headscarf and cheeks. She removed her scarf and wig and stuffed them into the pockets of her mac. Jean-Paul was already making his getaway across the open ground to where his bicycle was stored. Taking Marc's hand, Clara stepped over the dead Nazi and they hurried into the street where their own bikes were waiting. In moments they had disappeared into the Paris night.

Ten months earlier.

Clara opened the unlocked door to her parents' house. This had been her home since birth and it had been a happy childhood. But recently the arguments had become endless and home life had become difficult. Her parents had provided a loving home for their only child but they were now profoundly unsure about her plans for university. It was something unknown to them. No-one before in their family had ever studied at university. Her father had worked his way up to a respectable middle management position with Saint Denis Bank. He had secured a position for Clara there; a front of house teller, and it would be perfect for her until she married. She stubbornly refused to take the post and remained adamant about moving to central Paris and attending the Sorbonne. The arguments were ongoing and tiring for both sides.

Clara turned before leaving and saw the disappointment in her mother's face.

Waiting outside were Michelle and Jolie Beck. Michelle was eight and Jolie six and they lived with their parents further along the street. They jumped up from the pavement when Clara appeared and ran to take her hands. The girls always made her smile. They made her think of her happy childhood – before the arguments had begun. Walking towards them were her parents' friends – an elderly couple amongst those her parents had invited for the evening

Where are you going?" Michelle asked. "Can we come?"

"No you can't," laughed Clara. "I'm going out with a friend. You can walk with me to the end of the street."

The three 'ladies' swung their arms as they walked along. Passing the Beck's house Clara saw Mr Beck in his front garden. He was working hunched over a bench, cutting a length of timber.

"Hello Mr Beck," Clara called. "Who is your latest cabinet for?" Mr Beck, a short, dark, thick-set man paused in his labour and straightened up. When he saw that it was Clara and his two daughters his face cracked a smile.

"Mlle Bisset. Bonjour. This one is for Monsieur Brodeur."

"Ah, the chief inspector at the local gendarmerie. I'm sure he will be pleased with your workmanship." Monsieur Beck was famed for his expertise in most parts of the city.

"The very same. I'll be glad when it's finished. He's not an easy man to please. Where are you taking my two mischievous imps to? Or are they pestering you beyond distraction?"

"They are accompanying me to the end of the street. And if they are good," she added turning to look down into the two faces beaming up at her, "I will bring them back a surprise from the town."

"Oh, thank you Clara," the girls sang in chorus.

"What will you bring us?" Jolie asked.

"Don't be silly," Michelle teased. "How can it be a surprise if Clara tells us?" Seeing Jolie's disappointment at being outsmarted by her sister, Clara knelt down and hugged her. She reached out and pulled Michelle into the embrace and the two little sisters laughed.

"You shouldn't spoil them," Mr Beck chided. "They will become unmanageable." Clara began to run towards the end of the street, gently tugging the two girls breathlessly along with her. Their giggles echoed along the street. When she let them go, Clara shooed them back towards their father and set off for the Metro. Her previous thoughts wormed their way back in; her mother's cajoling; her father's concerns. "But why can't you live here and go to your college classes? It will save you money. The war will be over soon. Until then you will be safer at home. At least wait until the army has defeated the Germans. Then, maybe it would be a better time to leave home." So ran the argument from her parents, over and over again. She was sick of repeating that she needed to be amongst her fellow students. She needed to become independent. The whole war thing had become a non-event. There was nothing France or Britain could do about Poland. The Germans had finished Poland off with the help of Russia. Any day a negotiated settlement was expected and things could get back to normal. The arguments would soon be over. She was moving into a room in Montparnasse at the weekend. For the last few months she had been spending more and more time in the bistros and bars of Montparnasse and she had built up a circle of friends. They all encouraged her to move into the area and they had helped her find the room. She had also met Marc. He was almost seven years older than her but in maturity it seemed much more. He was a post-graduate student at the Sorbonne and, on top of that he was a tremendous trumpet player and vocalist. His band, Les Libres was becoming well-known all over Paris. As well as being a philosophy graduate Marc had an encyclopaedic knowledge of American jazz and blues music. His record collection was the envy of all jazz/blues afficionados and his band was renowned for being right up to date with the best tunes and songs. Given his status amongst his peers, Clara was at first shocked and then delighted to be so much the focus of his attentions.

The breach with her parents had come on this, her eighteenth birthday. It was to be the year in which she started at the Sorbonne to study biology. She didn't know then that the German invasion would put paid to any plans of university for many years and that her life would undertake a radical change of direction. That night her parents had prepared a celebration for her with a small group of family friends. But Marc had invited her out to dinner that same night and she had chosen to go with him.

He met her beside Notre Dame Cathedral and they walked together to the 4th Arrondissement where he had booked a table for two at an intimate restaurant on Rue des Barres.

"You look unhappy," he ventured when they were seated at a window table. "Has something happened?"

"It's my parents. They are angry that I have come tonight. They wanted me to stay at home with some friends they have invited. It's my eighteenth birthday today."

"You could have said. Why didn't you tell me? We could have done this another evening. I haven't even bought you a present."

Clara blushed. She looked down at her hands in her lap. "I preferred to spend this evening with you."

Marc smiled. "Well, soon you will be in your own place here in Montparnasse where we all hang out. We will be able see much more of each other."

Clara often attended band rehearsals along with other girlfriends of band members. Marc had heard her singing along with records he played in his apartment.

"You have a very good voice. I'm going to audition you for the band."

Clara could not believe what she was hearing. This was too good to be true. Marc selected three paper-sleeved 78s and handed the records preciously to her. "Learn these songs.

25

You must be word and scan perfect. No reading from word sheets if you want to perform the song as opposed to just reciting it. Tell me when you are confident to sing them with the band and I'll audition you."

Clara was so overcome at the opportunity he was offering her that she was completely defenceless when he lifted her into his arms and carried her to his bed. It was the first time they made love. She was a virgin. It had been painful at first, but Marc knew exactly what to do and very soon Clara was enjoying every moment of their lovemaking. Clara had expected that Marc would invite her to move in with him. But the conversation never came up. He obviously valued his independence too much. So, when the time came around to move out of her parents' home she moved into a small, one-roomed bed-sitter on Rue de Cels, just a block away from the Montparnasse cemetery. She found work as a chamber maid in the nearby Hotel Mistral and so was able to prepare for her life as a Sorbonne student amongst fellow students. This was in February. In May the Germans attacked. By June they were in Paris.

Marc became obsessed with how patriotic French men and women should behave under the occupation. To remain under Nazi rule and continue life as normal seemed to him to be too much like collaboration. At first, he considered moving to the Vichy region, where he thought French life might continue independently. It soon became clear to everyone however, that Vichy was a Nazi state under a different name. When talk of a Resistance Movement became current, Marc became galvanised. Clara and he would spend hours and hours talking about how to resist, how to obstruct, how to frustrate the Nazi machine.

Five

Paris 1941

Patrick Lavelle, a dark-skinned, balding, middle-aged married man, who worked in the local government offices, came forward with a position for Clara as a filing clerk in his department. It was not what Clara had hoped for when she had left home expecting to go to university but it was a steady wage. Patrick was a non-combatant supporter of the Resistance who provided any information that he could to help them plan their activities. Clara liked the work situation. It was a tedious occupation but the other females in the department, the secretaries and filing clerks, got on well together. The department led by Patrick dealt with Paris real estate and so, useful information about Nazi occupation of residences could be passed to Gagné. Many assassinations of German officers resulted from Clara's access to those files.

Angelique was the clerk who worked closest with Clara. They spent many hours kneeling beside cabinets together or passing files from one to the other up a sliding ladder for the colleague above to place a file on a shelf close to the ceiling. Angelique was a couple of years older than Clara. She was extremely thin and had had a mild attack of polio as a child which she had recovered from, apart from a slight turning in of her left foot, which caused her to almost drag it forward as she walked. An orthopaedic surgeon would spot that she walked with the slightest of limps, but it was hardly discernible to the layman. She had a pretty face with sharp, intelligent features. Her wavy blonde hair nestled attractively on her shoulders. The two women quickly struck up a close friendship and often went for a coffee together after work.

"We must go out together one night," Angelique said one lunchtime as they shared a cheese baguette in the café they frequented close to work.

"That would be lovely," Clara responded. "But I am often busy with the band." Angelique was intrigued to hear about Clara's role within Les Libres and promised to attend one of their forthcoming performances.

Clara remained vague about when their next show might be because her nights were often taken up with Resistance activities. But eventually she had to agree to letting Angelique know about their next club booking.

"I'm really looking forward to hearing the band tonight," Angelique said as she passed files up the ladder to Clara.

"Don't get your hopes up too high," Clara replied. "I would hate for you to be disappointed."

"Go away with you, I bet you are a wonderful singer."

"Stop now, Angelique," Clara laughed. "You'll make me blush. Do you want me to call for you and go with you to the club?"

"No, I'll be fine. I know where it is. I'm going to spend a long time getting ready and I wouldn't want to make you late."

"It's probably best. I do have to be there very early, to set up and join the sound check. You would be bored hanging around."

Les Libres were actually into their third number when Angelique arrived. Marc turned to Clara, disbelief in his eyes when he saw her wave at the girl who had just walked in on the arm of a Wermacht Feldwebel.

While Jean-Paul took a trombone solo Marc sidled across to Clara and asked, "Is that your friend with the Nazi Staff Sergeant?"

Looking glum, Clara replied, "I'm afraid so."

"Ah well," Marc replied, "Every cloud….."

Clara glared at him knowing the grim meaning of that innocuous comment. During the first half, Angelique sat entranced by Clara singing. Marc watched Angelique's boyfriend to gauge his reaction to the songs they played. So much American music was banned by the Nazi authorities that they had to be careful not to be reported for sedition. Apparently, the soldier boy either did not recognise the tunes or he was not interested in enforcing ridiculous rules.

"Clara, you are marvellous," Angelique enthused as Clara joined her and her boyfriend during the interval. "This is Jurgen," she went on. "Jurgen, this is Clara. She and I work together. She is my best friend."

Jurgen stood up and bowed his head. He held his hand out to shake Clara's and said, politely and in schoolboy French, "It is my esteemed pleasure to meet you."

He reddened when Clara and Angelique laughed at his clumsy pronunciation, but he took it in good spirit.

In the noise of the cellar bar Clara and Angelique were able to swap a few comments without Jurgen hearing.

"He is very good looking," Clara said. "Where did you meet him? And why didn't you tell me?"

"Some people are funny about French girls dating German boys. I wasn't sure how you would react."

"You are silly, Angelique. We are friends. I would support you against those bigots." It was five days later when Marc and Jean-Paul waited for Jurgen as he left Angelique's apartment. They each put a bullet in his head.

Clara approached their supervisor, Madame Babin. "Where is Angelique? She wasn't in yesterday and she isn't here today."

"She has reported in sick. She hopes to be back at work next week." That evening Clara called at Angelique's on her way home. She felt a complete hypocrite. She was going to comfort her friend whilst knowing about, and even aiding in, the assassination of her boyfriend. "Oh Clara, you shouldn't have come. I'm not fit to receive a guest."
"Don't be silly. I'm not a guest. What is the matter? Madame Babin says you are ill." Angelique's face was a picture of despair. "Thay have killed him."

"Who?"

"Jurgen." On uttering his name her face contorted into an expression of agony and she let out a low desperate moan of grief. "Those bastards! Murderers! I hope they all die at the hands of the Gestapo. He wasn't even a Nazi. He hated them. He was sent to the front for what they call asocial behaviour. He had even refused to join the Party."

Angelique dissolved in tears again. Clara embraced her and muttered soothing words. "Oh Clara, I loved him. I know he loved me too."

"Are you sure?" Clara ventured. "There are a lot of wartime romances going on that might not lead to anything."

"Jurgen was different." Angelique paused. She looked hard into Clara's face. Clara felt she was being critically assessed. Angelique made a decision. "I know he was genuine," she said. "I'm having his baby and he knew it. He was happy when I told him," she sobbed. "Now what can I do?"

Clara felt her face must give her away. She knew that she had betrayed a good friend. At the same time, she tried telling herself that it was a necessary evil. The Germans had to be defeated.

"I don't know what to say," Clara whispered. "What do you think you will do?"

"I will have to get rid of it. Oh, it breaks my heart to think of that. If not for this damned war I could imagine Jurgen and I having this baby and many more. Now the little angel inside me will have to go. What else can I do? I can't bring a baby into this war-torn world without its father. There will be no future for it or me. Oh this damned war! I hate it!" "Whatever you decide to do, I will help you," Clara promised.

Angelique, overcome with gratitude fell into Clara's arms and sobbed, "Clara, what would I do without such a loving and loyal friend as you?"

Marc snubbed Clara's first approach about helping Angelique. "She can go to the devil. Les poules à Boches like her will be shot when the war is won."

"Marc, don't be so callous. She is a young woman with a fatherless child inside her. She can't have the child. It will destroy her life."

"She chose it. She chose a German Nazi. She can live with the consequences. Anyway, what you are asking me to do is illegal."

"Ha! Illegal? As if that matters to you. The man who executes people at will."

"That's different. We are at war. Okay. Immoral then. It's immoral."

"Ha! again is all I say to you. Don't you of all people preach morality."

Marc brushed Clara aside as he moved from the chair he occupied in the living room to his bed which earlier they had shared. He took his newspaper with him and told Clara to leave him alone.

It took Clara almost two weeks of daily cajoling to get Marc to agree to help. Her suggestion that Angelique could be more useful as a source of information from inside the department was one of the determining arguments in her favour. Eventually Marc conceded defeat and set about finding a solution to Angelique's problem.

"Okay," he said one evening when he turned up at her apartment. "I've found someone. Apparently, your Angelique isn't the only one in search of someone to solve this problem. Most of the girls seeking help are rape victims, which is a bit more excusable in my book."

"Don't start that again, Marc. We know where you stand on the sanctity of life. If you ask me, it's very shaky ground."

"We have to find a way of getting her to Cherbourg. There is a woman there who knows what she is doing. Does Angelique know that there is risk attached? Not just from the illegality of abortion but from the fact that some women die after the procedure."

"She knows. Is there anything today that isn't life-threatening?"

"I am collecting documents from our source tomorrow. It involves crossing into Vichy where they are probably even stricter than in the occupied territories. If they discovered the real reason why you are travelling, you will both be in mortal danger."

"Both?"

"Of course. You will have to travel with her. The documents will say you are sisters. Your reason for travelling is to care for a seriously ill mother."

"Why do I have to go? Isn't that an unnecessary risk?"

"It is safer. It's a better cover. You will only stay two nights. Angelique will probably be weakened by the procedure and you will have to assist her on the return journey."

Clara got up from her seat and moved towards the kitchen. "When do we go?"

"The day after tomorrow. You need to pack. Tell Angelique when you see her at work tomorrow that you leave from Paris St-Lazare on the 9.48 train."

Clara came through from the kitchen with two bowls of soup and handed one to Marc. "I suppose I should thank you," she said.

"You most certainly should. If word of this gets out amongst the Resistance comrades we will be ostracised."

Despite an unending nervousness experienced by both young women throughout the trip, everything went off exactly as planned. Madam Marie-Louise Giraud was as efficient as her reputation boasted. Angelique suffered cramps and some bleeding but nothing life-threatening.

Back at work the following week, Clara looked forward to seeing Angelique. She felt the shared danger of the adventure had forged a bond between them. It soon became apparent that Angelique felt the opposite. For her, Clara was a constant reminder of a deeply unpleasant experience. Gradually she put a distance between herself and Clara. It was hurtful to Clara to be pushed aside but part of her understood how Angelique must feel.

"I wouldn't feel too bad about it," Marc consoled her. He had arrived at Clara's apartment to find her in a melancholy mood.

"Angelique knew that the girls were getting together for coffee during lunch and she didn't tell me. She wasn't even embarrassed when I walked past and saw them all together through the café window."

"It's better if you keep your distance from her. Let's face it, you are the one mainly responsible for the double loss of her lover and child. What would she think of you if she ever found out.?"

"I had nothing to do with the assassination of her German boyfriend."

"Oh yes you did. If you hadn't befriended her, she would never have come onto our radar. That's how she would see things, I'm sure."

"I want you to leave, Marc."

"What?"

"You heard me. I want you to go. I'm in no mood for you tonight. Please leave."

"I will not. I've come to spend the evening with you."

"I don't want you here. Now get out."

Marc studied her. Knowing him as she did, Clara could tell that he was weighing up his chances of enjoying the evening with her or not. He made a sudden decision. "Okay. As you please." He picked up his hat and left without further comment.

Six

Clara Bisset gazed unseeingly at the magazine in her hand. The early evening was cooling fast and the chill wind gusting up from the river caused a shiver to run down her spine. She stood in front of the newspaper kiosk, which was on the corner opposite 93, rue Lauriston in the 16th arrondissement. The building she was watching housed the Carlingue or the French Gestapo. At last week's resistance meeting in the church Michel Gagné had outlined the policy that the leadership had decided on. Their strategy was going to concentrate on those French men and women who had prostituted themselves to work for the Nazis.

"We must send a signal to our compatriots that treason and collaboration will not go unpunished. Those who have become French auxiliaries working for the Gestapo will be our prime targets."

And so today Clara was initiating the first stage of their next mission. They would assassinate a senior member of the Carlingue. Clara kept the brim of her hat pulled down low as she scanned the entrance to the building opposite. She was not aware of the kiosk holder staring at her. He interrupted her thoughts.

"Are you intending to buy that magazine, Madame, or are you just going to stand there reading it from cover to cover?" The kiosk owner was waiting to lock up but hoping for a final sale of the day.

"I am so sorry," she said. "I got carried away. It is so good. Here let me pay you for it."

She handed over a few francs as a group of French Gestapo men walked up. Clara bent down provocatively to fix the buckle on her shoe strap. One of the men made a lewd comment making the others laugh. Carla straightened up and

35

turned to smile at the men. She tossed her hair back and said, "You are very cheeky, monsieur."

The men laughed some more and gathered around her. She felt a hand on her back and another on her bottom. "What's your name, beautiful?" the one she knew to be the leader asked.

"Maria," she replied. "And what is yours?"

"My name is Jacques and I would love to see you tonight."

"Well, I'm afraid that won't be possible but maybe another night. I will see you here again no doubt."

"Of course. And soon, I hope."

The men walked away glancing back at her as she smiled provocatively. When she turned to move on the kiosk owner leaned across his counter and spat in her face. "Poule a Boches," he hissed. Clara didn't mind. She preferred that attitude amongst her countrymen than that of the Carlingue. She wiped his saliva from her face as she crossed the square.

Marc was waiting on the opposite side. He had watched the encounter carefully. He had discreetly taken photographs of all the men, although he knew some faces would be obscured in the movement of the group as they had circled Clara.

"What did that kiosk seller do?" he asked angrily.

"Nothing. Forget it."

That night, the developed photographs were pored over by members of their cell at the home of Michel Gagné. Michel's wife, Martine fed them onion soup and bread while they discussed their plan. Patrick Lavelle presented the pictures and gave them all the information he had been able to gather about the collaborators.

"Their leader is Jacques Moreau. He is originally from Carnac in Brittany. He has a wife and four children – three girls and a boy. He is forty-three years old. He has three previous convictions: two for burglary and one for assault."

"Merde!" muttered Marc. These bastards are just crooks and gangsters."

"That's truer than you might imagine," responded Patrick. "The Gestapo have deliberately recruited from the prisons. I've read the policy paper. It refers admiringly to the British policy of recruitment of the Black and Tans in Ireland, which was identical."

"With friends like the British……" Marc let his sentence fall away.

"Hey," Jean-Paul retorted. "They're the only friends we've got. And thank God for them."

The members of the group laughed mildly, ironically. The six of them – Marc, Clara, Michel, Martine, Patrick and Jean-Paul knew each other from before the war because of their mutual love of music. All of them, except Patrick were musicians. Patrick ran the department which Clara worked in. It oversaw building regulations and Patrick had used his knowledge to develop a healthy side-line as a booking agent for suitable venues. His affection for Les Libres and the music they played had led to a lasting friendship developing between him and the members of the band. Although never having played professionally, Michel and Martine both played competently on piano and were afficionados of the American music genre that Les Libres played.

"Moreau lives at 47 Rue Cauchy in the 15th Arrondisement. The Rue runs alongside parc Andre-Citroen. If you decide to take him at home the parc could provide a functional escape route. Across the parc to the south-west is the Gare du Pont du Garigliano. You could use ...."

"Enough Patrick," Michel interrupted. "The less you know about what we actually plan, the better. For now, do you have any information about his route home or his after work habits?"

"He has a driver. His usual route is from Rue Lauriston, through Trocadero, alongside the Seine all the way to Avenue de Versailles until they cross at Pont Mirabeau. Then they take Rue Balard as far as Rue Cauchy where his wife and children wait at home for him. As for afterwork habits, there are several brothels in and around the streets close to Lauriston, which he often visits. But he and his driver and several of their colleagues regularly call for drinks at a bar called Les Magots. They also frequent Cabaret Du Barry."

"I might have known it," Michel said. "Du Barry is a favourite haunt of the Germans and their willing French whores. Patrick, you have done well. You can leave now. Keep safe."

Patrick collected his brief case and overcoat. He bid them farewell and bonne chance. Once he had left Michel continued. "This is a job for you, Clara." Michel looked at her, quizzically, testing her reaction.

"Very good," she commented. Do you have a plan for me? Or should I just get on and do it myself?"

"Just a minute," Marc interjected. "Why have you selected Clara alone to carry out this mission? Why can't we work together?"

"Because there is no need to risk more lives. Clara is quite capable of executing this task. Right, Clara?"

"Of course."

"What about her escape from the scene?" Mark

insisted.

"We'll use Patrick's idea. Across the park to the Metro."

"But that's unnecessarily risky," Marc argued angrily. "I could be waiting for her nearby with a car."

Michel was containing his annoyance with Marc's interference. He calmed himself and reacted in a conciliatory manner. "All right, Marc. You can have a car. But you must be on the far side of the park. If something goes wrong and the area is quickly sealed off, we can't afford to lose both you and Clara."

Marc slammed his fist onto the table and pushed his chair back so that it toppled over behind him. "Merde! What is the matter with you?"

Michel was on his feet by now and the men were shouting across the table at each other. They stopped when Clara stood and demanded their attention.

"It's all right, Marc," she said calmly. "I am a soldier in this war, just like you. I can take my orders and follow them. From tomorrow evening, around the time of Moreau's expected arrival home, I will wait at the corner of Rue Cauchy. When he climbs out of his car I will kill him."

"What about his driver?" Marc insisted.

"I will decide what to do at the time. If the driver moves off quickly, I'll take Moreau as he approaches his door. If not, I may have to take the driver as well."

"But, mon dieu!" moaned Marc. "It's too risky."

"Which part of our work is not risky?" Michel countered. "Are you suggesting that Clara is not capable because she is a woman? Or do you have another reason?"

Marc looked ready to come to blows with Michel. Clara approached hm and put her hand on his arm. "Marc," she said. "Come on. It's time to go." She turned to Martine and thanked her for the food and hospitality. Martine smiled, grateful to her for easing the tension.

"You're more than welcome," she answered.

"God go with you." The women embraced and Clara did the same with Michel. "I will do my best," she said.

"I know you will," Michel replied. "I have every faith in you." Clara took Marc's arm and led him away.

It wasn't her feet that ached, it was her legs. Wearing stout flat-heeled shoes saved her feet but her calves protested at all the standing around she had been doing over the last four nights. In a dark duffel coat and men's trousers, she was unrecognisable as the attractive young singer from Les Libres. But, with the nights drawing in, she went barely noticed by the busy, preoccupied Parisians as they hurried home to beat the curfew. It was on the fifth night that all the waiting seemed to have been worth it. Moreau must have come home directly from finishing work. It was still light and Clara had not long been in her surveillance position. As soon as Moreau climbed out of the car it sped away. Clara began to walk rapidly towards him. He stretched his back, uncurling from the cares of the day and headed towards his front gate. She was level with his next-door neighbour's house and within perfect firing range. She began to withdraw her pistol from her pocket. With his back to her Moreau was a sitting duck. She slipped off the safety catch and raised the pistol. An instant before she fired a young girl's voice called out.

"Papa."

Moreau stopped in his progress through the gate and looked along the street. A long-haired girl, maybe thirteen or fourteen years old was running towards him. He turned to face her and held out his arms. The girl ran into his embrace and they hugged and laughed. Clara kept walking. She drew level with the oblivious couple. Her hand was on the butt of her pistol which was back in her pocket. The safety catch was now on. She kept her hood up and walked on to the end of the street. At the corner she glanced back to see Moreau and his daughter walk up their path and into their family home.

"You failed," Michel shouted directly into Clara's face.

"Michel!" exclaimed Martine. "I will not have Clara spoken to like that in my house."

"Shut up, Martine. This is war business."

"I will not shut up. You need to respect your soldiers. I think Clara made the right decision. We are going to have to mend France when this disgusting war is over and the less trauma our children experience the easier that mending will be."

Quite calmly Clara spoke up. "I will not shoot a parent in front of his or her child. That is my line that I will not cross. If you can't accept that I will have to step back from active duties. There was a better way to take him anyway. He has already cast his eye over me at the magazine kiosk. I could easily get him on his own."

Marc stared at Michel, daring him to suspend one of his best agents from duty. Michel took a deep breath. He shook his head. He sat down and emptied his glass of red wine. "I don't like it," he said. "That man is responsible for multiple murders of Resistance fighters as well as many more innocent Frenchmen and women. And he is still alive."

"We'll get him," Marc said with urgency and determination.

"You were right Marc. I should have sent you on this mission."

Marc said nothing. He gave a guilty look at Clara and turned away. He agrees with Michel, Clara thought. The knowledge was hurtful, but she decided to ignore it.

"No. You were right to send Clara," hissed Martine angrily. "She has taught us something. We have to temper our brutality with what's left of our humanity. Don't you see?"

"Okay, here's the plan. Jean-Paul and Marc will have drinks in Le Petit, the café opposite Les Magots. Take as long as you need to get to know Moreau's routine. Then Clara, it will be up to you. Taking him near to his home was a bad idea." Michel shrugged, expressing humility as far as he was able to. "You will get close to Moreau and persuade him to take you alone into the Trocadero gardens. Make sure you go to the area around the fountains. Marc and Jean-Paul will be waiting. It will be well after curfew time so the area should be clear. All you need to do, Clara, is to keep him occupied until Marc and Jean-Paul put the dog out of his misery. Good luck."

Clara had been reprieved by Michel for her previous failure. She was neither resentful of his previous attack upon her nor grateful that he had relented. She was confident that she had made the right decision for her and convinced she would do the same again if the situation arose.

For the next three days Marc and Jean-Paul met after work and sat at a pavement table drinking coffee watching the comings and goings at Les Magots. They carried their guns with them. This was a dangerous habit. If Germans or French security stopped them for identification papers, which they often did, they might decide to search them. If the guns were found, they would be arrested and almost certainly shot.

Moreau usually arrived at Les Magots around 8 p.m. His driver sat with him while they sank the best part of two bottles of vin rouge. Moreau certainly had an eye for the ladies. His position as a secret service officer leant him a status which was not natural to him but which he revelled in. On the fourth night, Clara was brought into the operation. Marc had met her at her residence and watched as she got ready. She applied thick powder and lipstick to her face.

"You're really going to town on this, aren't you?" Marc commented.

She stopped in her preparations and smiled at him. "If I am to die tonight, at least I shall be beautiful."

"Don't talk that way," Marc complained. "It's bad luck."

"I don't believe in luck," Clara grinned. "I believe in fate."

"It's an unlucky man whose fate it is to be with you tonight when Jean-Paul and I arrive on the scene."

"You'd better not be late Monsieur Durand. I don't want to have to kill him myself."

"You won't be armed so I don't know how you think you would kill him. If something went wrong and they discovered a loaded pistol on you it would be goodbye, Clara." Marc paused in thoughtful contemplation. "Would you do it, if it came to it?" he asked. "You know what happened last time."

"Of course," snapped Clara impatiently. "Why do you ask? You know I had my reasons last time. Do you think women can't fight in war?"

Marc shrugged by way of reply. "Come on," he said, "time to go."

Clara walked through the pavement tables towards the door of the busy café. Moreau recognised her at once and called her over. "Maria, come here. Come and join us."

He was with five others tonight, all members of the Carlingue. She tossed him a pert smile but with a turn of her hip she ignored his request and walked into the bar. He winked at his comrades as he got up and followed her in. He joined her at the bar and immediately put his arm around her waist. She sank into his embrace and looked up at him with a provocative smile. The presence in the crowded café of a German sympathiser – a paid up employee of the occupying Nazis – did not ruffle the feathers of the clientele. Clara recognised their type. Collaborators, chancers, black-marketeers, anti-Semites, fascists – all celebrating their opportunity to climb to the top of the pile, propped up by France's enemy. In other words, traitors. Sitting alone at a window seat was a neighbour of hers from the apartment block. His name was Philip Caron. He had a wife and a fifteen-year-old daughter. He was often on the stairs when Clara came and went. He always said 'bonjour' and 'au revoir' and was politely pleasant. But Clara felt his eyes upon her, and it made her uncomfortable. He was a squat, powerful looking man with a square head and a flat nose. She wondered what he was doing amongst this crowd. Maybe it had always been his bar of choice and he was loath to be driven out by the new crowd. Maybe he was sympathetic to the Nazis. He was staring at her now in his usual manner.

Despite her distaste for these opportunistic apologists and collaborators, she smiled cheerfully as she looked around at them.

"You're looking especially lovely tonight, Maria," Moreau whispered in her ear. "Look. I've got something for you."

He pulled a package out of his coat and handed it to her. She opened it to find a pair of stockings and a pack of cigarettes. "You're very good to me," she beamed.

"Now you need to be good to me," he responded.

"Of course," she said. "Let's go. It's going to be a bright moon tonight. Wouldn't you like to be with me under that moon? Nothing but moon and stars above us and the dark night and the open air for our blanket?"

As they walked out of the café Moreau's buddies hooted. Passers-by stared at the commotion. Many of them gave contemptuous looks at Clara. They guessed what was going on. They saw her as une poule à Boches. Well, that's what she wanted them to think. She linked her arm with Moreau and said, "Come on, I know a quiet place where we can be alone. There I can show you how grateful I can be." Philip Caron ducked his head into his glass, his eyes peering over the rim at Clara.

Clara avoided glancing across the street to where Marc and Jean-Paul were finishing their coffees and settling their tab. She guided Moreau towards the Trocadero gardens which would be empty by this hour. Marc and Jean-Paul were used to breaking curfew. They were unknown to the Germans so far and, like Clara, had excellently forged papers. Keeping off the main boulevards they followed Clara and Moreau on parallel lanes. Nearing the site Clara had chosen, they hurried ahead to get in position.

From behind sculptures beside the fountain, they saw Clara and Moreau approach the gardens. They each wrapped their palms around the handles of their revolvers and extracted them from their coat pockets. Across the silence, the scrape of Clara's shoes on concrete carried to them. They held their breath.

The sound of a police van screeching up burst the atmosphere and the shouts of men calling to Moreau alerted Marc and Jean-Paul to danger. They crouched lower in their hiding places and waited. As they watched, the van pulled up beside Moreau and he fell into conversation with the driver and two passengers. The driver was urging Moreau and Clara to get in the van and go with them. At first Moreau was reluctant. He turned and said something to Clara. Moreau and Clara seemed to be in disagreement. She was shaking her head and beckoning him to go with her into the gardens. But Moreau made up his mind. He seized Clara by the arm and pulled her into the back of the van. A mighty cheer went up and the van sped away. Marc and Jean-Paul came from behind their sculptures and made their way to Michel Gagné's home as quickly as they could.

As soon as she was thrown into the van Clara's worst fears became reality. Perhaps not her worst fear; that would be to be identified and arrested as a Resistance fighter. But this was a singular nightmare. Two other men were in the back. With the three up front there were six men in all. As the van took off, the two in the rear pushed Clara to the floor and pulled her coat from her. Her only relief came from the fact that she had not brought a gun with her. Next, they pulled her blouse off and removed her bra. While this was happening, Moreau was stepping out of his trousers and removing his underpants. Clara struggled violently but it was useless. Moreau reached up her skirt and tugged her stockings from her suspenders. His fat hand grasped her knickers and pulled them down to her ankles. With her arms held tight by the two others she could not move. Moreau's weight settled onto her and he forcibly entered her. His breath filled her nose and mouth making her nauseous. As she lost the energy to fight, the two men holding her let go of her arms and began to unbutton their own trousers. By the time they had finished with her the driver had parked beneath a bridge beside the Seine. The three up-front came back to take their turn. When they had finished Moreau decided that he needed another turn.

When it was over the atmosphere changed. The men's near hysterical behaviour had calmed. They talked quietly and Moreau helped Clara to dress. He handed her clothes to her and gave her a cigarette.

He pulled her to him and sat her on his knee. He began to feign affection for her. He stroked her face and kissed her temple. "You were very good," he said. "Next time there will be more gifts for you. You must tell me the things your family needs. We will take care of them. You are one of us now. One of the victors."

Clara was bleeding. She pulled away from Moreau saying she didn't want to stain his clothes. He found a blanket and tossed it to her. She pushed it between her legs. The pain was excruciating but she was determined not to show weakness in front of these men. To her surprise she found her angry thoughts aimed at Marc and Jean-Paul as much as at her rapists. Where had they been? Why hadn't they come to her aid?

"I want to go home," Clara said to Moreau.

"No," he cajoled. "I want you to come with us."

Clara felt fear well up and her eyes moisten. "Where are you going?"

"Cabaret Du Barry. You'll like it there. Good people. Good fun."

Just as Michel had said this club was well known to all Parisians. It was the haunt of German Wermacht, SS and Gestapo, as well as the French police collaborators and the Carlingue. The club was crawling with French whores too, who had latched onto the victors and prostituted themselves for black market goods and similar privileges. For some it was the only way to feed their hungry children and stave off starvation. Moreau soon lost interest in Clara as he consumed more and more wine. She slipped away to the rest room as soon as she could. She sat in a cubicle and let the tears come. She scrubbed herself, desperate to remove the stains they had left inside her. She came close to passing out. Eventually, she gathered herself and emerged slowly from the cubicle. There were two other women at the basins. She stood beside them washing her hands. "I need a cigarette and some air," she said. "Is there an exit to the alley?"

"You look all washed out, my love," one of them replied. She was in her thirties, plump and quite attractive. With a bubble of black hair, she wore thick make-up and red lipstick. Her bosom was unnaturally large, Clara suspected padding. The woman smiled in a kindly way and said, "Out of here, go to the left along the corridor. There are a few steps at the end and a door leading to the back lane."

Clara thanked her and was gone. Every step along the corridor she imagined a dread hand on her shoulder. She crashed out of the door into the lane and ran. It was now late and she was in danger of being stopped by the police or security service to explain her presence on the street. She took her high heels off and walked silently, clinging to walls and hiding in doorways when she heard footsteps approaching. Eventually she made it back to her apartment.

There was a crack of light from Philip Caron's doorway as she passed it. She knew he was watching. She sat at her bidet for over an hour. Tears flowed in a torrent. Her anger was inconsolable. Betrayed by Moreau. But worse, abandoned by Marc and Jean-Paul.

When Marc arrived at Clara's apartment the following afternoon she was not there. Panic set in. He went to a phone box and called Michel Gagné. "She's not in her apartment. What can we do?"

"I'll speak to a contact and find out if she's been arrested," Gagné replied. "Call me back this evening."

When evening came Marc called three times before he caught Gagné at home.

"She's not been arrested. My contact overheard some lewd banter between Moreau and his crew about her and the fun they had had with her. I think she's alive and safe but I'm worried that she's been damaged. We need to find her."

If he had thought about it clearly, Marc would have found Clara quickly. But it didn't occur to him that she would have gone back to her parents' house. She had fought so stubbornly to leave that it was furthest from his mind. In a constant panic he hurried from safe house to safe house in a vain attempt to find her. It was an old school friend of Clara's that he bumped into one afternoon who mentioned in passing that she was back at home. Clara's father opened the door.

"What do you want?" he growled.

"Is Clara here?"

"That's none of your business."

"Let me speak to her, please."

"No. You've got a nerve. After what my daughter has

been through because of you. Go away. She wants nothing more to do with you."

A gentle voice from behind him said, "Papa, it's all right."

He turned. "No, please Clara. Go back in. I'll send him away. You can stay here now."

"Please, Papa. I want to see him."

Papa turned back to Marc. "Can't you leave her alone? You know what you've done. She can't live that life anymore. You will kill her!"

Clara squeezed past her father and ushered him inside. She stood facing Marc on the doorstep. He attempted to embrace her but she stepped back. She looked thin and pale. Her hair was tangled and unkempt.

"What do you want?" she said.

"I want to see you. I have been going mad with worry. I thought you were dead." His eyes filled with tears. He reached out and this time she didn't have the energy to repel him. She began to sob. They stood like that for several minutes. Clara shivered. "You need to get back into the warmth. But tell me, what are you going to do?"

"Papa has me under house arrest. I haven't objected. I am overcome with lethargy. I was angry and confused." She stood back and looked angrily into his face. "Why did you leave me with those men? You deserted me." He pulled her to him once more.

"I will never forgive myself," he whispered. "Jean-Paul has been stood down from action he is so distraught. Michel thinks we are both too damaged to continue. He is seeking reassurance that we can continue without letting our emotions jeopardise our safety or the safety of others."

He leaned away to fully take in her face. "I'm so relieved you are alive and safe in your parents' care. I'm going. You don't need to feel guilty. You have played your part in the fight against our enemy. I love you. I will miss you, but it is better if you follow your father's wishes. When the war is over all will be different. We can be together again then."

"Hello, Clara." The greeting came from just outside her gate where the Beck girls, Michelle and Jolie were walking past with their mother. Clara smiled and waved and the girls giggled as they went. Marc pulled Clara to him and kissed her lips. Then he was gone.

Seven

Paris, May 1941.

Angelique carried a bundle of files out of her section and walked along the tiled corridor towards the Buildings Department where she and Clara had once worked together. Since her abortion she had been transferred to the Roads and Transport department. She had resented the move that Patrick Lavelle had forced upon her but was now happy in her new role with new colleagues and friends. It allowed her to put behind her the events that had led up to her double bereavement. If ever she saw Clara in the building, she walked the other way or stepped into an alcove to let her pass. She could not help associating Clara with her double disaster.

After delivering her files she called into the rest room on her walk back. As she sat in a cubicle, she realised someone else was occupying another. The sound of clothes being adjusted was quickly followed by retching and a subsequent moaning. She waited in silence until she heard the other person emerge from her cubicle.

"Oh, it's you." Angelique stared at Clara who was washing her hands and face at the basins. She looked Clara up and down, her expression turning to distaste. Realisation seemed to seep into her. "You're pregnant," she said accusingly.

Clara turned to face Angelique. "I've heard of your reputation. They say you throw yourself at them. How can you?"

"Who are you to judge me?" Clara retorted.

"Mine was a love affair," Angelique hissed.

"I don't want to argue with you, Angelique. We used to be friends."

"I wish we'd never met."

Reluctantly Clara had to turn to Marc for help.

"You can't be," he objected. Clara couldn't help noticing the look on his face. It echoed Angelique's.

"I'm sorry to disappoint you, Marc. But I am pregnant and there's no getting away from it."

"Is it.........?"

"No, it's not yours. I know when I had my periods. It's the result of......" Clara couldn't go on for the welling up of tears and the choking in her throat.

"Those bastards. I will kill every one of them."

As if it was an afterthought Marc moved to sit next to Clara and placed an arm loosely around her shoulder.

"I need you to help me," Clara whispered. "Please don't judge me."

"How can I help?"

"The way we helped Angelique."

"Oh no! Not again!, Marc groaned, as if the problem was all his. "You know how I felt about that."

"It's the only way. I can't give birth to it." Clara stood up. She was getting angry. "There were six of them Marc," she shouted. "I won't ever know which one of them is the father. I can't live with that."

Marc stood up and took her in his arms. "Okay," he said. "Calm down. I'll make the arrangements."

"You won't tell anyone, will you."

"No, of course I won't."

"You have to promise."

"I promise."

Angelique's encounter with Clara in the rest room proved fateful. The knowledge that Clara was pregnant

53

became an obsession with her. It was an obsession that grew exponentially. Her mind revolved faster and faster around the thought that Clara was connected to the death of her lover. She began to suspect that Clara was linked to the Resistance. Why else would Jurgen be targeted so soon after meeting her. When she wasn't thinking that, she wallowed in loathing for Clara at the thought that she was prostituting herself to the Germans and the collaborators. Clara's debauchery was nothing like the purity of her love for Jurgen.

One night Patrick Lavelle turned up at Michel Gagné's apartment.

"What are you doing here, Patrick? We have no meeting scheduled."

"I'm sorry, Michel. It may not be important, but I cannot put my mind at rest. I had to come and speak to you."

"Take a seat. What's on your mind?"

"There is a woman at work. She is no longer in my department but she has been to see me twice. She says if I don't do something she will go to the Carlingue."

"Get to the point man."

"She has a grudge against Clara. She wants me to fire her. She claims she is involved with the Resistance and that it's my duty to do something about her."

"Oh. I see. That's serious."

"At the same time, she accuses Clara of being a poule a Boche and that she should not be allowed to continue working for the administration. She's a very contradictory woman but I think she is unstable and she could cause real trouble."

Michel got up and went to the window. He stood there in thought for a few seconds. He seemed to make a decision and turned back to Patrick.

"Okay. Leave it with me. I'll see to it."

Patrick looked worried. "I hope I haven't made something out of nothing. I couldn't get any peace until I'd mentioned this."

"No Patrick, you've done the right thing. You should go home now. Think no more about it. It's my problem now. And thank you. You have been very vigilant."

It proved too difficult to arrange for Clara to travel into Vichy to get to Cherbourg. Under threat of exposure Madame Giraud was persuaded to travel to Paris to conduct the procedure. She was smuggled in by a contact of Marc's who insisted on rich reimbursement for the use of his truck on such a dangerous and, to him, distasteful errand, Madame Giraud's occupation being an open secret for anyone familiar with Cherbourg. Once again, the lady carried out a successful termination and Clara was left for a time to recuperate at her parents' home where they were told she had suffered a severe urinary infection.

On her return to work, Clara made a point of seeking out Angelique. She was sure that she could repair the rift that had happened between them. She was going to ask her to her apartment for a meal and maybe a stroll together beside the river. She waited for her near the entrance to the canteen. Along came her group of girlfriends but there was no Angelique. Clara stopped one of the girls and asked about her. "Angelique?" the girl responded. "We haven't seen her for a few weeks now. She hasn't been into work and she hasn't reported sick. No-one knows where she's gone. In fact, her position has been taken by a new girl."

Eight

Alabama 1942.

Huey stepped off the sidewalk to allow three white men to pass. One of them nodded at him. They recognised each other from when the guy had been a regular at the club where Huey played guitar in the house band.

"You know that nigger?" one of the other guys asked him, as if Huey wasn't there.

"Sure. Plays a mean guitar at the Starburst."

"They don't let niggers in there."

"They do, through the back, if they're in the band."

The three men laughed as they walked on.

Huey clutched his guitar case and hopped back onto the sidewalk. Two white women were approaching, holding parasols to protect their skin and looking at him as they whispered something. He checked the traffic and hurried across the street. The sun beat down on him as he walked out past the depot and onward to the shacks.

"What's with the mean face?" his Mama asked as he walked into the two-roomed cabin he called home.

"Nothing that a world war cain't cure."

"Don't you be making no fun of that war. Plenty good American men gonna die there before it's over."

Huey stood his guitar case in a corner behind the bed he shared with his brother. The one bedroom behind the living area was shared by his Mama and three sisters. Since his Papa had been killed by the Klan in a lynching fury following the alleged rape of a white girl in '29, his Mama had managed to raise Huey, his brother Clarence and his three sisters, Ceceline, Danika and Mary, by working as a help up in the Heights. Clarence helped out now with his job at the corn canning factory. He crawled out of bed at five in the morning in time to board the ancient, rust-bucket company bus that drove them nearly thirty miles to the factory. With twenty stops for pick-ups and drop-offs the thirty sweat-drenched miles stretched over nearly two hours each way. Knocking off at six meant he didn't get home till nearly eight each night. Six days a week he worked and handed his wages over to Mama every Saturday night.

"You got no work today?"

"I told you, Mama, I had to get Louie to look at my guitar. The machine-heads was coming loose. I don't want Leroy to fire me for messing up the band's sound, do I?"

"Beats me why you stick with that no-good Leroy. How much he pay you? A few lousy dollars a show. What good is that? You should join Clarence out at the factory. Get some regular work and reliable pay."

"Oh Mama, don't start on that old tune again. I get work when I can. I'll be on the corner tomorrow first thing. I promise you. I'll take anything I can get. Even old farmer Irish, that son-of-a…….."

"Don't go cussin' in my house. You not too big for a slap."

"Sorry Mama."

Mama had left for work upon the Heights the next day when Clarence walked in the cabin. Huey was at the table eating grits before setting off for the corner.

"What you doin' back home? You left at five this mornin'. No bus or what?"

"I ain't going to that factory no more. Had enough. Ridin' that bus best part of a day and cannin' corn the rest of it. I'm done."

"Mama's gonna skin you."

"No she ain't 'cos I'll tell you what I'm gonna do. I'm signing up. I've always wanted to go to Europe and that's what I'm gonna do."

"Oh boy, is Mama gonna skin you?"

"She can do what she like. It'll be too late. I'm gonna be first in the line when the office opens."

"You could get yourself killed over there. Have you thought about that?"

"I can get myself killed right here every day of the week if I just look at a white man the wrong way. If I don't step off the sidewalk he gonna lynch me. If I talk to his wife I'm dead. Hell Huey, it's much safer bein' shot at by Nazis than it is takin' a stroll round here."

Huey shook his head in a way that acknowledged the truth his brother spoke. "She still gonna skin you."

It was late that evening when Huey got back from a day's labour out on Irish's farm. Clarence was already home. Mama was out front preparing corn for supper.

"She skin ya?"

"She skinned me."

"And?"

"Ain't nothing she can do about it. I done signed up and I take off for training week Friday."

Huey looked closely at Clarence's face. "She give you that whopper?" he asked.

"Nah. Couple o' whiteys didn't like me lining up behind them. One of 'em popped me. A guy inside heard the commotion and came out. He gave them a talking to and then sent me round back to the coloured line."

Nine

Clara and Marc hurried along Avenue Denfert-Rochereau, dodging puddles that were forming under the deluge that had fallen from a summer thundery shower. They skipped up the steps to the Assomptionnistes Entraide Catholic church and walked the echoing aisle to the sacristy. The look-outs posted along their route to the church noted their passing and the guard who had admitted them at the gigantic doors nodded almost imperceptibly. As they approached the sacristy the rising rumble of excited conversation urged them to even greater haste.

Inside, the room was heavy with smoke and voices were clashing with one another in urgent tones.

"What's going on?" Marc asked the first comrade whose attention he could attract.

"Haven't you heard. There's to be a round-up of Jews."

Clara grabbed the man by the arm. "What did you say?" she ejaculated in disbelief. But the man didn't answer. Michel Gagné was banging the table with an ashtray and calling for order.

"Comrades," he called when some semblance of calm had settled on the room. "Comrades, settle down, pay attention. We have urgent business to conclude. There is no time to waste. The Nazis and their collaborators have planned a round-up of Jews. They intend to imprison them and deport them. God knows what their ultimate fate will be, but we know from past experience what sort of conditions they will be kept in. No food, no medical assistance no sanitary facilities."

A voice at the back of the room called out, "Good riddance to them!"

Immediately he was set upon. The man nearest to him landed a direct punch bursting his nose. Three more men leapt in and began to beat him to a pulp. Gagné had to rush to the back of the room and, with the assistance of his lieutenants, break up the fracas before the man was killed. When order was restored the anti-semite lay unconscious on the floor, his blood pooling on the varnished timber around him. Gagné was furious. "What the fuck are you doing?." he screamed at the assailants.

"What the fuck are you doing," one of them yelled back at him, "allowing someone like that in here?"

Gagné calmed down. He signalled two of his lieutenants to remove the prone figure. "Take him somewhere safe where he cannot do any damage."

With the situation settled and Gagné back in position he called upon a member of the Paris police officer, a comrade, to brief the meeting on the round-up plan. The   police officer was a young sallow-skinned man. He wore a beret and a scarf covered his mouth and nose, preserving his anonymity. He was playing a dangerous game. Earlier, double agents working inside the police force for the Resistance had suffered terrible fates upon discovery. His nervousness came through to his audience as he delivered his address. "We have received precise expectations from
Director Hennequin," he began.

"Emile Hennequin is a bastard," someone shouted from the back to a chorus of agreement. "We should have shot him years ago."

"Silence," yelled Gagné. "Hear the man out."

The young man continued. "The plan was originally set by the Nazis to run from the thirteenth to fifteenth of July. They obviously have never heard of Bastille Day."

A few loud guffaws punctuated this statement and the assembled crowd warmed to the speaker.

"When someone reminded them of it, they moved the dates. Although they banned Bastille celebrations, they worried that there might be spontaneous rioting if they were rounding up French men, women and children on our sacred day. So, the operation will run through the sixteenth and seventeenth. In other words. It starts tomorrow. Dawn raids will take place at the home of every known foreign or stateless Jewish family. However, we have been told not to be too particular. If they are Jewish take them whether they are foreign, stateless or not. So, many true French men, women and children who happen to be Jewish are destined to disappear tomorrow. The only exceptions we are told to look out for and leave alone are those who have proof of either American or British citizenship. These are described as sensitive cases. Hitler does not want to provoke America and he is hoping to appease Britain into giving up on the war.

"We've been ordered by the Germans to round-up twenty-eight thousand Jews. As I said, our prime targets are foreign or stateless but it's going to be a broad sweep and many of our compatriots will be caught up in it. After discussions the Germans were persuaded that it might prove antagonistic if children were also arrested. They had agreed to exempt them until our wonderful Prime Minister Laval opened his big mouth and argued that it would be inhumane to separate children from their parents. So, the Nazis are taking the children too."

Exclamations of "Merde," and "Putain" rang out and the mood in the room was beyond furious. Gagné thanked the young officer for his contribution and took over.

"Okay," Gagné said, "We've now got the details of the districts the raids are planned for, right down to the streets and addresses. These will be handed out to each district commander. There are two spikes to our response. First, tonight, with the utmost urgency, we will call on as many homes as we can and warn the people of the danger they are in. We will assist, in any way we can, those who want to disappear, leave Paris and go into hiding. Secondly, in your districts and under your district leaders you will plan and carry out your own defensive actions. This will include assassination operations against any raiding parties that can be organised in the time left to you. Go back to your districts now and bonne chance to you all."

The sacristy rapidly emptied apart from the members of Gagné's group. As his team members took up the vacated chairs Gagné walked around handing out papers. Marc and Clara, along with Jean-Paul looked at theirs. They were identical and they identified a list of addresses in their area which they had to visit before tonight was over. On the rear of the sheet were three suggested positions they might take up with a view to attacking the expected raiding party in an attempt to drive them away from their intended victims. After a brief discussion, on the most efficient route to take to cover the addresses, they hurried away.

Ten

With her hair tightly packed into her beret, Clara knelt by the window of the tabac. It was 5.30 in the morning and she had been walking all night, going from house to house, warning families to get out, go into hiding, do anything to make sure they weren't at home the next morning. Several families had thanked her gratefully and profusely. Some others had cursed her and told her to 'fuck off'!

Now she rested her head on the windowsill and waited. The rifle across her forearm gave her a feeling of security. Her tired eyes struggled to stay open, but sleep was something she was learning to live without. Diagonally across the street, she could see the window in the boucherie, where she knew Jean-Paul waited with his rifle resting in his arms. Further down on her side, diagonally opposite Jean-Paul, she knew Marc was similarly positioned at the window of a boulangerie; the three of them forming a deadly triangle. Just before 6 am the sounds of police horns broke the silence of the dawn. Clara lifted her rifle into position and rested the nose of its barrel inside the tiny crack she had opened in the window. Now she was wide awake, adrenaline tumbling through her veins. She did not know how many families had taken their advice and disappeared. Their joint endeavour was to shoot and kill any policemen who emerged from buildings with captives. The plan was fraught with danger and she had argued with Marc about it.   "If we open fire when they emerge with captives, we are very likely to hit the innocent victims. We should kill them as they arrive. We know what they are planning to do. So why not kill them first?"

"If the families have heeded our advice and gone into hiding, we will have no need to expose ourselves. If there is a danger that you will hit a family member, don't fire. As soon as you see captives shoot any gendarme in the vicinity away from the parents or children. Best of all shoot the drivers."

So here they were. Dozens of police and Nazi SS, pouring out of the vans and breaking into houses and apartments along the street. Clara knew the apartment above her French-owned shop was empty. They would not be interested in it. She had her escape route planned; out of the rear through the yard, across the alley, into the house behind and out of its front door, two hundred yards from the Metro station, which she would enter and run through the southbound tunnel to the next station. Trains were running so infrequently since the invasion that she was happy to take her chances down there.

She heard the thunder of boots running into houses and along the street. In her field of vision so far, she had seen no victims being dragged out of their homes. Happily, these families had taken their advice. But then she saw a flash from the boucherie and it was instantly followed by the crash of gunfire. Jean-Paul had begun the attack. As a panic engulfed the Germans and their police allies, they wheeled away from the boucherie and backed off in the direction of Clara. A half-dozen of them clambered for shelter behind one of the vans, leaving their backs fully exposed to Clara. She opened fire. Three lay dead before the remainder realised that there was lethal fire coming from behind them. The other three were dead before they could react. That was all Clara could do. Now she had to escape. Gunfire still ricocheted along the street where Marc and Jean-Paul were continuing to engage. Children's screams competed with the rapid gunfire as Clara slipped away from the scene. Emerging from the Metro twenty minutes later, minus her rifle which she had left in a secret Resistance hiding place inside the tunnel, she was just in time to cross the boulevard and enter the church of St Thérèse and take communion at the seven o'clock morning Mass.

Mingling with the exiting congregation as its members wandered down the steps of the church, she picked up the excited tones as news spread amongst them of the gun battle that had been taking place across town. Several voices strongly rebuked the actions of those 'fanatics' in the Resistance. "The Germans will exact retribution," one woman complained bitterly. "Who knows how many French citizens will be murdered all for the sake of a few Jews who shouldn't be here anyway."

Clara caught sight of Marc at the edge of the pavement. His infinitesimal nod told her to follow him. They kept several metres apart as they headed for his apartment block. The ever-growing throng of workers emerging from their homes heading to the office, shop or café cocooned them from too close observation by the patrolling police and army vehicles. Unexpectedly, Marc turned into a café just a couple of blocks from home. When she went in, he had placed a coffee upon an empty table. He gestured her to sit down and take it. "Give me five minutes," he whispered and hurried out.

Clara took a couple of sips from the coffee and then left. She walked slowly towards Marc's apartment building and slipped inside the lobby. Standing below the stairs she could see onto the first landing and Marc's front door. He was standing there with his arms around a young girl. She was around her own age, Clara thought, but maybe slightly younger. They were kissing. Marc held her at arm's length and said, "You'd better hurry. You'll be late for work."
The girl swept her hair back and tied a scarf around her head. She skipped down the stairs to the front door.

"Be careful," Marc called down. "The Nazis are on the prowl."
She turned her pretty face up towards him. With an attractive smile she blew him a kiss and left.

Clara heard Marc's door close. She struggled with her emotions. Marc knew that she would be returning to his apartment after the morning's action. It had been agreed. So why did he have one of his lovers stay over the night before? He wasn't even going to be there. He didn't care that Clara knew. So why bother to deflect her with a coffee in order to shoo her away before Clara arrived? Perhaps he thought he was being considerate. The aftermath of the bloody battle raged through her veins. A rising anger against Marc crashed together with those feelings and made a turmoil of her mind. She thought about getting out of there and leaving Marc to stew. But then the memory of the gendarmes falling dead under her hail of bullets came back and she wondered if anything ever mattered. Thinking, 'what the hell,' she mounted the stairs.

The moment he opened the door, Marc took her in his arms and lifted her to his bed. Clara suspected there was something unhealthy in the overpowering lust they both succumbed to following the bloody action they had taken part in. She knew that one was a direct consequence of the other. It was always the same. Marc was rough and selfish in his lovemaking. The feeling of excitement was sweetly unbearable.

"You were magnificent today," Marc moaned, glorying in the success of their action. "Magnificent," he repeated constantly as they reached for their climax.

The subsequent feeling of disgust that affected her was not unexpected. They lay apart staring at the ceiling, not speaking. Clara was the first to rouse herself. She washed and dressed in silence and left.

The news of the German reprisals reached Clara in her safe house hideout. She had been transported by the Resistance Underground. Moving only by night, she was driven by several different guides from safe house to safe house, until she arrived at a remote farm in Brittany. The farmhouse was located eight miles from the nearest village and four miles from its nearest neighbour. Clara had paperwork identifying her as a niece of the elderly farmer and his wife and she recuperated by working the farm alongside them. The city girl, as her pretend uncle called her, was given the task of feeding the pigs, hens and horses each day. She also took care of the vegetable garden and shared the cooking and cleaning with her 'aunty'.

In later life this period would be looked back upon as one of the happiest episodes in her wartime experience. She was half reluctant to end it when summoned by her superiors to return to Paris and continue her service in the Resistance. Her return was to be managed by placing her back with her parents for a settling in period. Once they could be sure she was not high on the Nazi wanted list she would be brought back into operations. "I'll clear the dishes, maman," Clara said. The dullness of life with her parents was more of the soothing medicine she needed, if not as therapeutic as life on the Brittany farm. Her father took up his chair beside the radio and lit his pipe. Mother sat sewing under a picture of the Sacred Heart of Jesus in the faint glow of a flickering red light emanating from that very heart. The clatter of the plates prevented Clara from hearing her mother who had just spoken.

"What was that, maman? I couldn't hear you."

"I was just thinking of the Becks."

"What do you mean?"

Her mother paused in her sewing and looked up at Clara. Her eyes were glistening. "It's too sad. It breaks my heart to think of it."

Clara drew nearer to her mother, wiping her hands on her apron. "What is so sad, maman? Tell me."

"Lovely little Michelle and her sister Jolie. And their parents. Monsieur and Madame Beck. So kind and considerate."

"Maman," Clara interrupted sternly. "Please tell me."

"It was just before you went away. The police raided the Beck's home. They were taken away. All of them. I saw it myself. Two vans turned up with six Carlingue. That Inspector Brodeur was in charge. He ordered their detention. They were pushed into separate vans and driven away. We've not seen them since."

Clara felt her heart explode. "Why? What had they done?"

Clara's father, who had been pretending not to listen, said, "They are Jews."

"What? I didn't know they were Jews. But they are French. I remember Madame Beck being pregnant. Both times."

"We remember Monsieur Beck's parents. They were Beckrowich then. When Beck came back from the trenches he had changed his name to Beck. We thought nothing of it. Anyway, Brodeur must have known about them. It didn't matter to him that they were as French as anyone else. He had them seized and taken away. I doubt we'll see them again." Clara ripped her apron from her and stormed out of the front door. She dashed along the street to the Beck's home and hammered on the door. A confused-looking woman in her thirties opened it. "Can I help you?" she asked.

"I have called to see Monsieur Beck. I have something for his daughters."

"I am sorry there is nobody called Beck here,"

"And who are you?" Clara demanded."

"I am Madame Henri. But I don't know who you are, and I don't like your tone. Why are you speaking to me in this manner?"

"Who is it, my love?" It was a man's voice and his footsteps could be heard approaching along the hallway. He appeared beside his wife and looked down at Clara. He wore spectacles and sported a moustache. His dark hair was closely cropped. "This woman has come asking about... what name did you say?" she said turning back to Clara.

"Beck. Monsieur and Madame Beck and their daughters Michelle and Jolie. Where are they? This is their family home and it has been all my life and more."

"And what is your name, may I ask?" enquired the husband. Sensing Clara's hostility he pushed in front of his wife.

"I am Clara Bisset. I live along there. The Becks are my neighbours and I want to know where they are."

"Well Mlle Bisset, you are asking the wrong person. I work for the new city administration and they have allocated this house to me. If you want to know where the Becks are you must ask the police what they have done with them."

From this man's accent she could tell he was from north-west France. He worked for the new administration. That was code for Nazi collaborator to Clara. He also knew that the Becks had been seized, hence his comment about asking the police for their whereabouts. She locked eyes with the man and held them until he flinched. Without another word she turned and strode back to her own home. The clatter from her dishwashing was exponentially louder than any other time. Her parents, sensing her fury, said nothing to her. When she had finished in the kitchen, she muttered goodnight and went to her bedroom. Instead of sleeping she fumed and plotted, plotted and fumed in equal measure all night long.

Eleven

Paris, August 1942

To his credit, Marc had listened respectfully to Clara's tirade about the Becks. Once she had vented her outrage, she went on to outline her plan.

"It's pointless approaching Gagné," she argued. "He will refuse permission. He's too focused on disrupting communications and transport now that the deportations of Jews are happening. He's obsessed with explosives."

"What do you want to do?" Marc asked patiently.

"Brodeur," she hissed. "Brodeur has to be eliminated. He has carried out the Nazi's odious policy for them."

"Is that it?"

"No it's not."

"Well?"

"Monsieur and Madame Henri. I have to get them out of the Beck's home. I can't live with myself if they play happy families inside that lovely house when the Becks have been dragged away like criminals."

"I thought you were against killing collaborators in front of their children. They have a son and a baby daughter, don't they?"

"I'm not going to kill them. I'm going to burn the house down. If the Becks can't have it, I'm going to make sure nobody can."

Marc moved closer to Clara and slid his hand along her thigh, inside her skirt. "I really like you when you're plotting to kill Nazis."

"Marc, that is awful." She put her hand on top of his and stopped his uninvited progress. "Will you help me?"

He raised his wine glass and, as if proposing a toast, he said, "To the destruction of a Nazi house and the removal of a despicable chief inspector – vive la France!" They drained their glasses and fell together towards Marc's bed.

Twelve

Paris, November 1942

Parisians were no longer surprised or outwardly bothered by the ubiquitous German tanks or trucks that patrolled the streets. Whatever their inward thoughts, they paid as much or as little attention to them as to a local tram or bus. If they encountered an incident say, where a vehicle suddenly disgorged a group of Wermacht soldiers to pounce upon some unsuspecting pedestrians and scuffle them into custody, they scarcely paused in their progress towards their planned destinations.

The young red-head in the belted white raincoat drew no more attention than would be expected. The first of the winter winds racing up from the river whipped the hem of her coat about her knees and sucked the dry leaves from the gutters into the air. Most men passing her on the pavement could not resist a glance at her, given her youth and attractiveness. But any man who didn't steal a look would be considered unusual. Madame Valette, a retired teacher from Calais was in Paris for the christening of her nephew's first child. Her sister and brother-in-law had accompanied her along with their two sons Philippe and Marcel. They had breakfasted early and planned a visit to the Eiffel Tower before the christening, which was to take place at 2pm that afternoon. They hoped the wind would not be the cause of preventing trips up to the tower's platforms.

Pierre and Jacques Christel were brothers who had fought against the invading Germans but were now discharged and spent their days outside of their lodgings scraping a living around the city's churches selling pendants they made from scrap tins. Travelling in opposite directions, they came together at the bottom of steps outside a police station. To avoid bumping into each other they had to pause and separate on the pavement. Neither party could have guessed what the timing of their passing would expose them to. Inspector Brodeur and two uniformed officers hurried out of a doorway and almost collided with them. The witnesses failed to agree on how many assailants took part in the attack. However, all of them gave vivid descriptions of the young redhead. Her long hair flowed down around her shoulders from beneath a bright blue beret. Her fierce expression was something several declared would haunt them for the rest of their lives. And the delight she seemed to take as she poured bullets into the head and torso of Inspector Brodeur was something they described as evil personified. The traumatised witnesses could only watch in horror as her accomplices ripped apart the uniformed officers with their machine guns. From the prostrate position to which she had flung herself, Madame Valette craned her neck to watch the assassins flee. With her red mane flowing behind her from beneath her beret, the female killer sped across the street into the warren of alleyways opposite. Her male companions had disappeared in different directions, and all were out of sight before anyone emerged from the station building in reaction to the atrocity.

"Clara, you are being insane. You have to get out of Paris. There are posters of you all over the city. There's a tenthousand-franc reward offered for your capture and twelve young Parisians have been seized as hostages. They will be shot if you are not captured within three days. Most Parisians want you found and shot."

"Marc, I don't care. The posters look nothing like me anyway. I have burned the red wig and the beret. No more bright blue berets for me. I know Gagné has sent you here with his orders. But you know I've still got something to do before I get out of Paris. And, if you remember, you promised to help me do it."

"The Henris. What is so important about them? There are hundreds of administrators who have been moved into houses seized from the Jews. What's so important about this family?"

Clara looked at Marc with a mixture of indifference and disappointment. He felt as if she was dismissing him. He didn't like to be snubbed.

"You are being ridiculous you know," he added.

"I know. But everything we do is ridiculous. Our whole lives are ridiculous. And while this war goes on we'll carry on being ridiculous. This matters to me and I'm going to do it with or without you."

"Okay. Have it your way. How do you want to do it?"

"They must not know that I'm involved. I can't put my parents in danger. I'm going to do it when they take their Sunday, after-mass stroll. Their house is the same as my parents'. I know how to break in. I need you to get me a container of fuel and I need Jean Paul to tail them to make sure they don't return earlier than expected."

"Okay. The day after tomorrow. I'll prime Jean-Paul and I'll be with you at 11a.m. But now you listen to me. As soon as their house is ablaze we get out of Paris. If Gagné finds out we haven't left he'll likely court-martial us."

"Thank you, Marc. I appreciate your help."

Marc looked at her and sighed. "Are you absolutely sure you want to do this? The Germans will only find them someone else's house to live in."

"It matters to me, Marc. I can't let them walk all over the Becks' memory without doing something."

"Okay."

It was twelve-thirty on Sunday when the residents of a quiet Saint Denis street poured out of their homes in response to cries of "Au feu! Au feu!" Men and women banged on the doors of neighbours calling them to evacuate their properties in case the fire spread. By the time the Henris returned from their stroll, the house they had come to call home was irreparably damaged. Flames danced in the midday sun and black smoke swept in gusts along the street. Heading north out of Paris, an unremarkable coal truck contained one passenger in a compartment carved out of the space within which the coal was carried.

Thirteen

Burtonwood, Lancashire, England. July 1943

Huey wiped grease from his hands. He was standing inside an enormous hangar looking up at a B-17 Flying Fortress, the lethal monster Uncle Sam was unleashing against the Nazis day after day. He heard the pilots complaining regularly that the Limey crews got the easy ride flying night-time raids only. He was tired and hungry after a long day with his head inside one of its four gigantic engines. He had a faint sense of pride. He had made good progress and he was sure he'd have this baby ready for action again by the end of tomorrow.

It was Clarence's arrival back home in Alabama that had decided Huey to sign up. Three days after Clarence's funeral he lined up at the back entrance to the draft office and signed his papers. It came as a surprise to Huey himself that he had reacted to Clarence's death this way. Perhaps he felt some guilt. If he had done more to bring some dollars into the house maybe Clarence wouldn't have resented the canning job so much. How could he tell? Even so, when news came that Clarence had been killed, they were stunned. It was an open secret that blacks weren't allowed into combat units. They were segregated into support units; some skilled, some menial. Clarence had been killed landing in Oran, North Africa, in support of U.S. combat troops. Nobody shot him, nobody bombed him. He had drowned under the weight of his kit when his landing craft was overturned.

Huey had filled up with anger at this news. He struggled to decide where to aim his anger. The buddies who had let his brother drown; Uncle Sam for sending him there; the fascist Vichy French who were running Algeria for Hitler - or the Nazis. Whoever it was, he decided he could only work

77

through it by doing all he could to knock the hell out of Germany.

No-one had been more surprised than Huey himself when he discovered he could fathom an engine like he was born to it. He figured it was to do with the music in the machinery. When he was assigned to a Mechanics Division he shot to the top of his training class. His tutor told him that 'engines and Huey Tate fit like a glove'.

"Hey Hue! What's up? Come on. Time to knock off. Let's get washed up and get out for a drink."

It was Marvin, his best buddy since arriving in England. Marvin was from Chicago and had taken Huey under his wing when he'd turned up in Burtonwood.

"Nothing we can do tonight," Huey replied, reluctant to walk away from the bomber that had consumed his interest all day. "It's whitey night in town tonight. It's more than our lives are worth to set foot in there."

"No problem. This is Uncle Marvin you talking to. Don't I always sort things out right for you?"

"What you been scheming now?" Huey grinned.

"I fixed it up with Maggie. Last time we met 'em. Maggie and Betty are getting the bus out here to the village. We're meetin' them off the bus at eight."

"You old devil. Where we gonna go with them?"

"That little old English pub by the cross. A little bit of 'oldee-worldee' romance is just what's needed for two hard working soldier boys"

"You think that's ok?"

"Why not. You ain't in Jim Crow land now Hue. You got to shake off your oppressor and widen your horizons."

"No Jim Crow? Is that why we're not allowed guns like the whitey?"

78

"Hey, be thankful for small mercies. I ain't begging to be on the front line." The two men stepped out of the shade of the hangar and walked across the endless runway to the washroom and locker area. After showering they headed to the canteen and filled up on beef stew and mashed potatoes. Finally, they booked out a jeep to drive to the accommodation blocks a couple of miles on the other side of the once sleepy village. Huey headed down between the double row of beds and fell onto his. Within seconds he was asleep. Fifteen minutes later he opened his eyes and for moments had no idea where he was. He expected to hear Mama working by the kerosene stove. Instead, he heard Marvin.

"Hey, sleepy time is over. Come on. Time to beautify yourself for the night ahead."

The conversation stopped dead when Marvin and Huey, Maggie and Betty walked into the pub lounge. Glasses froze halfway to mouths and all eyes fell upon them. The landlady broke the atmosphere.

"Good evening folks," she called out across the room. "Come into the warmth and tell me what's your poison."

Relieved chatter broke out, but curious glances continued to shoot towards them. Marvin paid for the drinks and carried them across to the table the other three had occupied. He looked around the room, returning the stares that came his way. He switched on his biggest smile and called out, "Hi folks. Uncle Sam says, hello and thank you for welcoming his sons to your beautiful country."

A moment of uncertain tension was broken when a woman chuckled and a tiny old man with a pint glass bigger than his head shouted, "Sit down son, you're amongst friends here."

Maggie and Betty were unlike any girls Huey had encountered before. They had no understanding of the boundaries he had spent his whole life assimilating. Where he could sit; who he could speak to; places he could enter; who he might desire. Their innocence was almost intoxicating. As he sipped his third drink of the flat, warm beer he was developing a taste for, he felt more relaxed than he had ever been in his life. He knew Betty liked him. He knew in the way that a man or a woman always knows about the feelings of someone interested. He had experienced it back home from different white women, but he knew that to follow up on the signals would have been fatal. Betty's hand had slipped into his not long after they had been seated. Unlike any girl back home she hadn't slapped him when he'd reached out and snaked his arm around her waist. Along with Maggie, she worked in an underground munitions factory on the north-east edge of Warrington. That's all she would say, conscious of having signed the Official Secrets Act. He was wondering how to finish the evening. He had spent a long time in male company since entering training and being shipped overseas. He was subject to strong urges. But he liked Betty. He liked her more than he would have expected to, and he didn't want to be what his Mama would call 'cheap'. His dilemma was solved for him when five of their white, so-called comrades walked in. They had arrived back a few minutes early from their trip into town and had called in for a nightcap. A guy he recognised caught sight of them and nudged his buddies.

"Well lookee what we got here," he exclaimed in his broad Texan drawl. "A couple o' niggers wi' their white whores."

One of the five G.I.s groaned and immediately turned back to the door. "Come on, Pete," he said to the man next to him. "I'm not getting into this Texan crap."

The two of them walked out followed by catcalls of abuse from the Texan. Marvin got to his feet but Huey reached out and grabbed his arm. He pulled him back.

"Leave it, Marv," he whispered. "Let's just go."

"What?" Marvin said, plenty loud enough for everyone to hear. "You take this down in Alabama from these Klan whiteys? We don't take this shit in Chicago."

"Who you calling a Klan whitey?" the Texan yelled, approaching Marvin. The whole scene was going to kick off until a thin voice called out, "And who you calling whores, Yankee?"

It was the tiny guy in the corner. He was struggling to his feet and coming round his table. He was less than half the size of the Texan but he was fearless. The three G.I.s turned to look at him as he came towards them. The Texan guffawed.

"Whoa! Now I'm scared. Here comes the pride of the British Empire."

His two buddies stepped between the Texan and his tiny opponent. "Jake," one of them said, "let's cool it shall we. It ain't nothin' to do with us."

Jake sneered. "You Yankees ain't got no standards. How can you ignore these niggers takin' white women?"

At this point the landlady intervened. She came out from behind the bar and barged her way into the middle of the bunch. She spoke directly to the Texan. "I don't know what's upsetting you Mister, but everything here was fine until you came in. Now your friends can stay but if you don't leave right now, I will be reporting your behaviour to your company commander."

The little guy was still annoyed and chimed in. "You're in England now, sonny-Jim. We don't have any of your race laws here. When in England you follow English rules."

The Texan looked at him with incredulity. He wanted to laugh at the absurdity of the situation. His buddies were tugging him to leave with them. He finally succumbed to their pressure but not without turning and pointing at Huey and Marvin. "You ain't heard the last o' this. Watch your step, niggers."

As they headed for the door the tiny guy clapped slowly and the rest of the crowd joined in. Huey and Marvin and the girls finished their drinks and left soon after. The little guy shouted, "TTFN. That's English. It means make sure you come back soon." Huey said "Sure we will. And thanks." The guy dismissed his thanks with a wave.

Betty and Maggie waved from their bus as it set off to carry them back to town. Huey and Marvin hunched their shoulders against the northern England night chill and headed back to the base.

Fourteen

Paris, July 1943

Philippe Caron pulled his flimsy curtain aside and peered down into the street below. He recognised the woman walking away from the entrance to the apartment block as his neighbour, Mlle Bisset. Telling his wife that he was going out for some cigarettes he hurriedly slipped his jacket on and disappeared. He carefully looked both ways as he pulled the street door closed behind him. You couldn't be too careful these days. German soldiers were everywhere, even though many were off-duty tourists fulfilling Hitler's promise to allow every combat soldier one trip to the French capital. Any one of them could turn nasty for no reason. Worse than that were the French police. Curfew was just over an hour away and if he was caught out after that he could be tossed in gaol and God knows what might happen to him after that.

Clinging close to the walls of the apartment blocks he shadowed Clara from a distance. When she made a left into Rue Boulangerie he guessed where she was heading. The narrow, cobbled street ran across a small square which contained three café bars and was a popular area with the invaders and their French collaborators. Les Boches was how Caron thought of them. He had no love for them.

He waited for Clara to enter the square but when a woman appeared at the exact time, he expected her to arrive he was confused. This woman did not carry the shopping bag that Clara had had and she had long blonde hair beneath a narrow brimmed hat. But he quickly recognised the figure that he admired so ardently, the light jacket and the blouse and skirt as Clara's. 'She's disguised herself,' he thought, arousing himself with the prospect of something exciting to spy on.

Clara passed provocatively in front of the young, headstrong Boches spread around the tables. They were emboldened by the drink they had taken and immediately began staring at Clara and discussing her. One of them, a dark-eyed, handsome boy of around eighteen or nineteen must have decided that if he didn't act fast someone would get to Clara first. He gulped down his beer, grabbed his jacket, skipped away from the bar and landed himself at Clara's side.

Caron was torn between distaste and envy when Clara smiled at the young German and linked her arm in his. They walked out of the square. Caron was unsure about crossing the square between so many invaders and collaborators. He ducked back along Rue Marceau and zig-zagged the tiny warren of streets to come out approximately where he guessed the couple would have walked to. Although strong, he was unused to moving swiftly and so he arrived sweaty and dishevelled at a corner, around which he could see Clara and her beau disappearing into an alley way. He was about to follow when a movement caught his eye. A block away a man was sitting astride a stationary bicycle, smoking a cigarette. He looked around him constantly. His nervousness infected Caron. What convinced Caron of the need for extreme care was the presence of two unmanned cycles propped against the wall beside the stranger. He pinned himself close to the wall and waited.

When the pistol shot rang out, followed by one more, he was not surprised. He was terrified. Seconds later, Clara and that lover of hers who was always calling at her apartment, came running past his hiding place. They bolted to the man with the cycles, leapt astride them and were gone. Now here he was, in the vicinity of an assassination and would be sure to be rounded up. Curse that Clara!

But Philippe Caron congratulated himself on his resourcefulness. As an employee of the city authority with responsibility for water management he had an unrivalled knowledge of the city's sewer system. He needed to be quick because the nearest entrance to the underground tunnels was about one hundred metres away. He was strong but he carried several kilos too many about his girth. He ran for all he was worth and made it in minutes to the manhole cover he wanted. The effort needed to lift the circular iron disc was not inconsiderable but it was something he was used to. The sound of the approaching Paris gendarmerie was blaring across the rooftops as he slipped down the ladder into the underworld and worked the cover back into place.

He uttered a curse, directed at Clara, every time he sloshed his feet through something obscene or when the stench-ridden liquid soaked his trouser cuffs and socks. He arrived home in a foul mood.

"Oh, Philip," Madame Caron complained. "You can't bring that smell in here." She backed away from him as he entered the living room. He vented his anger upon her. Cornering her against the table he punched her as hard as he could in her stomach. As she doubled over, he slapped her face.

"Don't tell me what I can or can't do in my own home," he growled.

As he moved across the apartment towards the bathroom, his daughter emerged from her bedroom. Before she could ask what was happening, he slapped her too and ordered her back into her room.

When he finally re-appeared his wife and daughter were sitting together on a sofa. "Here," he exclaimed, flinging his filthy clothes at his wife. "Get these cleaned and dried. I will need them for work in the morning." His wife gathered up the malodorous bundle and scurried off into the kitchen area to do his bidding.

Later, as they sat in silence, the mother sewing, the daughter reading, neither had the courage to ask him why he sat beside the door listening carefully to any movement on the stairway.

After dumping their cycles, Clara split from Marc and Jean-Paul. She half-ran, half walked the rest of the way back to her apartment block. Hurriedly letting herself into the lobby she leaned back with relief against the mail-boxes and wiped sweat from her forehead and top lip. She swallowed bile and worked to control her breathing. She was suffering from a mixture of over-excitement and disgust; guilt and elation. The adrenaline she had produced during the assassination was now receding. She felt her legs trembling as she climbed the stairs to her first-floor apartment. Sliding her key into the lock and pushing open the door there rose a tremendous feeling of relief racing through her.

"Bonsoir, Mlle Bissett. I thought I heard you coming in."

Clara turned to find her neighbour, Monsieur Caron, very close behind her. Her anxiety rose again as her hopes of hiding away in the sanctuary of her rooms were dashed.

"Hello, Monsieur Caron. Is anything the matter?"

"Nothing is the matter at all," Caron replied. "Things couldn't be better."

"What are you doing?" Clara demanded of him as he pushed past her and walked right into her apartment.

Caron did not reply. Instead, when she had reached him in her living-room, he pulled her to him and began to kiss her.

"I see you are no longer wearing the blonde wig I saw you in earlier. Have you thrown it away with the red one you used to wear?"

The threat he implied shocked Clara. "What do you want?" she demanded.

"I know what you do for these Nazi Boches," he breathed. "If you can do it for them, you can do it for a loyal Frenchman."

His hands had reached up inside her skirt and he was pushing them into her knickers, kneading her buttocks, all the while pushing his wet mouth against hers. She could feel his erection rubbing against her stomach, but she did not have the strength to push him away. Although she had not even had time to get out of her jacket, she knew where this was going. Memories of her night in the hands of Moreau and his gang came flooding back. She felt an angry, steely resolve invade her whole being.

"Stop it!" she demanded. Caron paid no attention. Still holding himself tight against her and molesting her from her breasts to her vagina, he walked her backwards towards her sofa. He pushed her down onto it and began to unbutton his trousers. For Caron, this was where he made his mistake. Although her skirt was around her waist and her knickers halfway down to her knees, her hand in her jacket pocket was on the butt of her pistol. Momentarily released from his grip, Clara was able to pull out her gun and point it at Caron who now stood with his trousers and pants around his ankles and his genitals exposed. Clara sat up and placed the barrel of the gun against his erect penis.

"Bastard," she called him. "You will pay for this."

Now, suddenly and pathetically flaccid, Caron attempted to assert himself. "I know what you do," he cried. "I know what you have done tonight."

"Do you? That could be an even bigger pity for you tonight, Monsieur Caron." Clara stood and, in doing so, pushed Caron so that, with his feet trapped in his dropped pants, he fell backwards. She re-arranged her clothing and picked up the telephone.

Twenty minutes later two men Clara had never seen before arrived at her door.

"Who are you?" she asked, whilst looking at them through the spyhole.

"Calais," came the reply.

Recognising the codeword Marc had told her when she'd called him, Clara opened the door. Caron was lying on his back, naked from waist to ankles where his trousers and pants still lay.

"Leave him to us," one of the men said. "Your contact wants to know if you are all right. What shall we tell him?"

"Tell him I'm fine. But this traitor has threatened me. He thinks he knows what I do. I believe he is an informant."

"No, no," sobbed Caron. "It's not true. I don't know anything. I am a loyal Frenchman."

"We'll deal with him. He won't trouble you anymore."

The two men reached down, each one grabbing an arm and lifting him to his feet. When Caron attempted to reach down to raise his pants one of the men elbowed him in the face. It was a brutal blow, splitting Caron's left eyebrow wide open. Blood poured from it, half blinding him. They walked him out of the apartment, his feet making rapid tiny steps inside his lowered trousers, his white bottom, shining jarringly, his shrunken penis illustrating his fear. This was the figure he cut when his wife opened their apartment door. The men shoved him in, so that he fell at her feet. They picked him up again and walked him through to the living area. His daughter shrieked at the vulgar picture of her father as he stood trembling in front of her.

One of the men took out a gun and pointed it at the daughter. "Shut up," he hissed, "Or you will die. And so will your parents."

Both men then took out small coshes and began to beat Caron's legs. They battered his shins, his calves and his thighs. They did not take particular care to avoid his genitals. Caron screeched in agony. When they had finished, they picked him up and threw him into a chair. His legs now looked more like the trunks of a tree; black and purple and brown. One of his kneecaps was cracked, both shins splintered.

"Your man is under sentence of death. He is a rapist. I hope he makes you proud. He is suspected of treason. If we prove his guilt we will be back and he will be executed. France will not tolerate collaborators or traitors."

The spokesman then turned to Caron, who was a broken snivelling wreck. "If we come back for you, we will be forced to eliminate your wife and daughter too." He paused and looked pointedly at the females. Looking back at Caron he added, "Don't make us do that."

Fifteen

Burtonwood, Lancashire, England.

August 1943

It was time for Huey to go looking for Marvin. He smothered his hands in a rich lather and worked it into his knuckles and fingernails until the engine grease began to lift and merge with the soap. He reached his arms right up to his elbows into the barrel of water that stood just inside the door of the hangar, where he had been working all day. Swilling away the grease and the soap, he wiped his limbs dry on the threadbare towel that drooped sadly from a nail in the wall. He straddled the Harley motorbike he had been allowed use of and revved it across the concrete runway towards the exit into the village. The bike was a Harley XA just like most of the other bike riders used. But Huey was the only black mechanic to get the use of one. The bike was his pride and joy but it had caused some jealousy amongst white G.I.s stationed on the base. His superior officer in the maintenance department hadn't made things much better by threatening to put Huey's tormentors on a charge. Captain Bill Hancock had demanded a bike for Huey when he realised just how talented he was when it came to engines. There had been opposition to it from the higherups but when Hancock explained the necessity for Huey to be able to get to the hangars at any time of the day or night they had relented.

Huey always rode with a serious expression on his face. It was the only way he could stop himself looking smug when he rode past a gang of white G.I.s trudging back to the accommodation site. They were pretty much used to seeing him now and paid him scant attention.

Huey swept the bike into position outside Marvin's billet. He peeled off his leather helmet and locked the engine.

The hut Huey and Marvin shared with twelve other black soldiers was empty when he walked in. He guessed the guys would be over in the black social area where they could get a Bud and play a game of pool. But Marvin should have been there. They had plans to meet Betty and Maggie.

After showering and putting on his smart uniform, Huey walked across to the social area and asked around for Marvin. Eventually a corporal told Huey that Marvin had been called for an interview with the camp commander.

"What the heck? What he do now?"

"Nothing as far as I know. It seems the father of the English girl he's been seeing has filed a complaint."

"Complaint about what? That girl Maggie, she's crazy about Marvin."

"Yours too, so I hear." The corporal laughed and Huey blushed.

Huey thanked the corporal and headed back for his bike. It was the tail-end of a glorious English summer day. The days were not as long as they had been in June. Huey had never known daylight lasting until ten at night before arriving in England. Now the sun went down earlier but it was still light until around eight-thirty. Huey revelled in the sense of freedom he experienced from his bike and the English country road that wound its way towards Warrington. Instead of turning south towards the town centre, Huey swung north and then east towards his destination. The sun, now falling lower but still sparkling bright, dappled through the alder and willow trees, turning the road ahead into a kaleidoscope of flickering shapes.

It was white night again in the town but Huey and Marvin had planned to meet Betty and Maggie on the outskirts in Culcheth village.

Maggie was already waiting by the three poplar trees in the middle of the green. Huey looked around as he left his bike and walked across to meet her. His sweep of the green was to check if he could see Betty approaching. His heart was in his mouth, as it always was when he knew he was about to be with her.

Their relationship had moved at a rapid pace. It was happening to a lot of folks. People said it was the war. It changed things, knowing you might be dead the next minute, the next day, the next week. The locals around here called it 'living for today'.

Two weeks earlier.

It was now more than a week since he and Marvin had met the girls for that night out in the village when the Texan had caused trouble. He'd thought about her every day. Six weeks they had been going together. Longer than any girl he had ever been with. Huey could hardly believe it. She was special to him and he knew it. It was Saturday lunchtime. His all-night shift had kept him busy until six this morning and he had slept until twelve. Marvin's immaculately made bunk was empty. Marvin and Maggie were meeting separately. She had planned a picnic on the south side of town in the grounds of Walton Hall. Betty had other plans. She was a keen sports fan. She had done some cross-country running as a schoolgirl and had not lost her taste for the sporting life.

He alighted the bus in the centre of town — a circle called Market Gate. She was waiting on the busy pavement against a store window. Her face lit up when she saw him and he was thrilled to see it. She dodged straight across the pavement and linked her arm through his. Huey became very self-conscious when she did this and more so when she stood on tip-toes to kiss his cheek. He scanned the faces of the passers-by. In their woollen jackets and their flat caps or their fitted jackets and headscarves, for the most part they paid no attention. Just one or two looked askance and a few more looked with disdain. Betty was oblivious to it all. His crisp uniform gave him a status he would not have owned back home. It balanced his insecurity.

"Come on then," Betty urged. "we don't want to miss the kick-off."

She guided him down Bridge Street towards the silently, sliding River Mersey which dissected the town. It blew his mind when she told him that the Romans had settled around here. Nobody back home could talk of history going that far back. Crossing the river, they began to become part of a human trickle that eventually swelled into a river itself. Betty was taking him to a thing called a rugby match.

"It's a bit like your football," she'd said. "Only better."

Summer was not the season for rugby but the war had brought an end to all conventional sporting fixtures. Excuses had to be found for staging matches whenever they could be found. The British RAF, which also had a base on the edge of Warrington, had put together a team of top players; players who had played at the highest level before being called-up. A nearby army base in Bolton had done the same. The two services were meeting this afternoon to test their skills against each other in a game of Rugby League.

Swept along in the human current, the air of expectation was infectious. A blue sky overhead, dotted with the occasional pure white cloud drifting on the intermittent stiff breeze, had lifted all spirits. Several strangers said, "Howdy Yank," or "Howdy partner," to which Huey always replied with a beaming, "Howdy to you."

"Hey up, Lass, thar fella's got 'ell of a tan, ain't 'e!" or words to that effect came a few times, but none of it was too aggressive. Some children pointed at Huey in disbelief. He always smiled back at them.

Huey struggled to follow the game, but Betty took great delight in explaining the intricacies to him. The crowd bellowed in support of any brute collision or a speedy break out. The one fight that broke out involving all twenty-six players excited the greatest response of all. Throughout, Betty held on to Huey's hand. He was very conscious of her fingers moving gently, and slowly across his own. He tried hard to keep the smile from his face that seemed to have a life of its own. Betty, who had been a bundle of joy, tensed slightly as she looked along the row to the seats where her father and his friends were sitting. She waved at her dad and he nodded a return acknowledgement.

At half time they went below the stand to get two cups of tea that were tasteless and hotter than volcanic lava. Betty's father was called Alfred and he was reservedly polite to Huey. They shook hands and Alfred thanked Huey for his courage in coming to fight in Europe on the side of England.

"Will you be home for tea, madam?" he said to Betty as they parted to return to their seats.

"Maybe a bit later, dad," she replied.

"Seven o'clock, not a minute later," he insisted.

Betty reached out and hugged her dad. Alfred gave his daughter a loud, wet kiss on the cheek, the way a parent would kiss an infant. Huey sensed there was a strong and loving bond between father and daughter.

"Goodbye, son," he said to Huey. "and God go with you."

"Thank you, sir," Huey replied and saluted. Alfred liked that. He smiled behind the fat cigar he was puffing and headed upstairs with his friends.

"So, what was the final score again?" Huey asked as they strolled slowly over the white stone bridge crossing the Mersey.

"Fifteen to ten."

"And who won?"

Betty shoved Huey. "Come on," she laughed, "Stop teasing."

"No. I'm serious. Who won? Was it the team in blue and yellow or the red stripes?"

"The RAF, in blue and yellow. It wasn't fair really. They had three top Wiganers playing for them. The army only had one international and a couple of second teamers. They did well to hold the RAF to fifteen."

The shops lining the slope up to Market Gate were still busy; the pavements full with window shoppers. Halfway up, three scruffy waifs began to follow behind them. Huey had experienced this before. Children who had never seen a black man before took to following him, like he was the Pied Piper. Betty turned and shooed them away and they scattered like magpies. Betty held his hand and led him through a warren of narrow streets until they entered a market. It was getting towards closing and most of the stalls were winding down but a tea-room, set against a far wall, was open and many rugby fans had made their way there. Their waitress was very attentive and spoke respectfully to Huey.

"I hope you don't mind me saying, love," she whispered shyly to him. "But I'm so proud to have you here and it's a privilege to wait on you. You men, fighting alongside

95

our boys - it's fantastic. My Bert's in North Africa, we think. I can't tell you how relieved we are to have you on our side."

"It's our privilege to be here," Huey replied. "You're most kind to welcome me that way."

"Can we get some service over 'ere?" a gruff voice yelled. "It's not niggers only today, is it?" The waitress turned and a firebrand voice shot out of her. "Shut up Jack or you'll get nowt in 'ere today." Jack laughed and winked at Huey, "No offence, pal. You got to keep these females on their toes."

Two weeks later.

Huey was going to ask about Betty when he realised what had made him think there was something different about Maggie. It was her sunglasses. It didn't take him long to work out why she was wearing them. As she turned sideways, glancing across the green, he could see the purple bruise bulging from her left eye. A southpaw blow if ever he saw one.

"What's happened?" he asked.

She wasn't sure what he meant until she saw where he was looking.

"Oh that. That's nothing. He's got a sore shin for his troubles."

"Who?"

"My bastard father."

"What's it all about?"

"What do you think?"

Huey nodded his head acknowledging the stupidity of his question.

"Your dad knows about Marvin?"

"Exactly. What's more he didn't like the news I gave him."

"News?"

96

Maggie's expression went from despair to mischievous glee back to bewilderment.

"I'm pregnant."

"Oh my!" Huey gasped. "Marvin?"

"Yes!" Maggie insisted adamantly. "Who else? What do you think I am?"

"I'm sorry Maggie. I didn't mean anything by it. It was thoughtless." He reached an arm around her shoulder and hugged her to him. A door opened at the far end of the green as two couples came out of the pub. A burst of laughter fell out of there and flew like a rag across the green.

"What are you going to do?"

"Do? I'm not going to do anything. I'm going to have Marvin's baby. I love him and I think he loves me. I'll wait for him and if he asks me, I'll marry him."

Huey was moved by this and he squeezed Maggie's shoulder tighter to him. "Where is Marvin?" asked Maggie.

"Your Pa has got him in trouble with his commanding officer. He's reported him for pestering you."

"Oh my God! I told you he was a bastard. I'll kill him when I get home. I'm moving out of his house as soon as I can."

"There's not a lot the officer can do to Marvin. If he did, he'd have to take some kind of action against almost every US soldier in England."

"I'll go and see that officer if I have to. I'll give him a piece of my mind."

"Maybe, maybe not. Let's wait and see. Marvin's a wily fox. He'll take care of himself."

The void that had been nagging Huey all this time surfaced. He looked around the green again. Before he could ask, Maggie knew what he was going to say. She handed him a letter. "It's not just me who's been stood up tonight," she whispered.

Huey recognised the handwriting on the envelope. He opened the flap. It was from Betty. Some of the writing was smudged but it was all decipherable. Maggie stepped away from him and leaned against the trunk of a tree, giving him the privacy she considered appropriate.

My Dearest Huey,
I'm sorry I've let you down tonight. Please don't hate me. If things weren't the way they are I'd be with you tonight and every night. But I can't see you again. Life is too difficult at the moment and you'll be going overseas soon. My parents are very unhappy with me and life has become intolerable at home. I need time to get things back to normal.
I will always be thinking of you and praying for you. Life will be so dull without you. Please don't forget me – I'll never forget you.
Your Betty.

He shook the sheet in his hands, looked at Maggie. Then he lifted it and read it again. He began to screw it up but stopped himself. He passed it to Maggie.
"Read it," he said. "It's okay."
She read it and handed it back to him. He folded it neatly and replaced it in the envelope. He looked again at Maggie.
"Why? What's happened?" he asked, perplexed.
"When she says parents, she means her father."
"But I met her Pa. He seemed fine."
"Oh, he can seem fine alright. He's a two-faced bastard. He's not a bastard like my old man but he's a bastard

just the same. Betty's different with her dad. With mine it's just pure mutual dislike. We'll be glad to see the back of one another. But Betty is the apple of her daddy's eye. She's been the precious daughter all her life. The rugby together, the ponies, the holidays, they've been like best friends. Look Huey, I know Betty and I know she loves you. She loves you as much as I love Marvin. But her dad is going to come between her and a lot of fellas. If Betty's not careful she'll be in a marriage of three not two. Her dad has made life very unpleasant for her since he found out about you. He's kept her at a distance. They were so close that it's a kind of cruelty. She's been torn in two. She basically can't take it anymore. She couldn't take the step to break completely with him. If you ask me, she'll regret it for the rest of her life. But at this moment, she can't do it."

Huey hung his head. Speechless. Maggie reached out and wiped a fat tear that was rumbling down his face. "Ah, don't cry. Love is hard. Rejection is worse."

"I thought this was it. She was perfect. I don't want anyone else."

Maggie took on a tough guise and said, "It's a hard lesson. We all learn it sometime. You'll get over it. I'm not sure Betty will."

She took Huey's arm and pulled him after her. "Come on." she said. "We've both been stood up. You can buy me a drink in that pub and we'll both drown our sorrows before it's blackout time."

Sixteen

Normandy, July 1944.

Three jeeps bounced along a pitted road. Huey and Marvin had pitched up in Normandy ten days after the initial D-Day landings, part of almost nine hundred thousand Allied troops. Now, after almost two weeks of bitter fighting over often unmanageable terrain, Huey and Marvin found themselves east of Caen. After weeks surrounded by the high hedgerows and deep embankments of Normandy, which the Germans had turned into a blood-soaked killing field, they were glad to be crossing open country. Marvin was driving the third jeep in the tiny convoy. With him were Huey and three other black support troops who had been rounded up by Captain O'Kane of the 82nd Airborne Division. The other two vehicles contained O'Kane's white troops. Huey and his companions had been separated from their 4th Infantry Division during fierce fighting around Bayeux. The only other Allied troops they had encountered had been British. Caen was an objective for the British but the dogged resistance by the Germans had scattered and split many of the troops and the armies had often found themselves off course and on someone else's patch.

"Come on, Marv," one of the guys in the back shouted after a particularly severe pothole had launched all of them a foot out of their seats. "Take it easy with the roller coaster, will ya?"

Marvin laughed his big guffaw. "That's nothin'. Wait till you see what's coming up." Huey rubbed his neck with one hand whilst holding onto the door sill for dear life with the other.

"Keep up with the others," he called out to Marvin. His concern came from the knowledge that all of the early objectives of the invasion had failed. German troops were still very much a threat and an ambush could happen at any time.

Marvin slowed the jeep down in response to a raised arm by O'Kane in the lead jeep. Up ahead they saw a small hamlet cresting a gentle slope that rose to the middle of the village and fell away afterwards. The road they were on led straight through the middle of the clump of about thirty houses. Apart from the drivers, the men in the other two jeeps dismounted from their vehicles and O'Kane signalled for Marvin's crew to follow suit. Eisenhower's lifting of the ban on black divisions carrying arms couldn't have been more timely. Huey was now used to the warmth of a rifle butt in his hands. He climbed out of the jeep and walked alongside it as Marvin slowly guided the vehicle forward.   Three jeeps and twelve soldiers formed a careful procession into the hamlet, between the rows of houses either side. O'Kane again raised his arm and the men halted. There was an absence of life in the street. The gentle engine-ticking of the idling jeeps and the crunch of boots punctuated a brittle silence. O'Kane's arm came down and the troop proceeded. Glancing left and right at the house windows, Huey felt eyes on him. A twitching net curtain made him jump. O'Kane's arm was raised again. The men halted. The street ahead rose and curved into the village square. A patch of grass and a chestnut tree stood in the middle. A scattering of deserted tables and chairs evidenced the presence of a café or bar on one side. O'Kane had halted the men because a young woman was standing in the middle of the square. She held a white handkerchief aloft and waved at the men. "Bonjour messieurs," she called. "Bienvenue."

O'Kane turned to his men. "Vigilance!" he commanded. "First and last! Vigilance!" He waved them on and the men walked slowly forward. Huey's eyes kept flying back to the woman. He scanned the street either side but always his gaze was back on her. She was slender, about five-two with dark hair. Something conflicting in her face gave her an appearance of intense vulnerability. For Huey, in that moment, she was Marianne, the symbol of liberty and the spirit of France; young and determined.

O'Kane was about fifty yards from her, the men in train behind, when she suddenly screamed, "Attention au danger! Mettez-vous à couvert! Embuscade!"

No man needed French fluency to understand what was happening. The woman began to run towards the men. A shot rang out and she fell.

"Back up, back up!" yelled O'Kane. "Take cover!"

The jeeps screeched in reverse to form an impromptu barricade about twenty yards further back. The men crouched behind them. O'Kane swept the square with his binoculars. "Upstairs," he declared. "The middle house of three opposite the café. Return fire." Rifle fire rang out. Bullets poured into the window O'Kane had identified. Shattering glass fell to the cobbled street. Fire came back. Bullets pinged off the bodies of the jeeps. They were pinned down. O'Kane spotted three other sources of incoming fire – all from first storey windows around the square. Lying at the edge of the square, in the middle of the street, the young woman, writhing in pain, was clutching a shattered thigh which was losing a torrent of blood. Marvin shuffled along to O'Kane.

"Sir," he pleaded. "We can't leave her there. She saved us from being massacred."

"What are you suggesting, soldier?"

"You know where the fire is coming from. Give me cover. I'll get her."

"You know what you're risking?"

"Yessir."

O'Kane looked at Marvin as if seeing him for the first time. "Okay," he whispered thoughtfully. "Give me a minute."

O'Kane moved up and down the barricade and gave clear instructions to the men. Huey's task was to pour non-stop fire into a window on the far side of the square just to the left of the chestnut tree. He swallowed bile and felt a surge of fear. He watched Marvin creep to his jeep and slip inside the driver's seat. "You ready, soldier?" O'Kane asked.

"You bet," Marvin replied.

O'Kane turned to his men. "Ready? On my order, continuous fire. FIRE!"

The fusillade crashed into Huey's ears like the gates of hell opening. Marvin gunned his engine and screeched up to the square. Huey was only vaguely aware of Marvin's progress. He could not take his eyes off the window into which he poured an endless river of bullets. His comrades were busy doing the same into their targets. At the edge of his vision he saw a flickering of movement as Marvin slammed his brakes next to the woman, jumped out, lifted her into his arms and put her in the jeep. Jumping in beside her he slammed the accelerator to the floor, screamed around in a tight circle and was heading back to the troop when a rocket-propelled grenade fizzed through the air ripping the world in two. Marvin and the woman were just yards from the troop when the rocket struck the back end of their jeep. It jumped into the air, like a startled rabbit, made a half spin and fell to the cobblestones on the driver's side. The woman was thrown clear. Two of the men ran out and carried her back to the cover of the remaining jeeps. Marvin could just be seen trapped under the burning jeep.

Without hesitation, O'Kane leapt up, yelling, "Cover me," and ran to Marvin. With an immense, almost inhuman effort of strength he put his shoulder to the jeep and heaved it upright. A limp, lifeless Marvin was thrown over O'Kane's shoulder and carried back behind the line.

After ordering up support and medical assistance, O'Kane turned to his men and said, "Right, men. Here's what I intend to do. We're going to mount an assault and we won't be taking any prisoners. Does anyone have any objections to my proposal?" The men didn't speak. They just looked at him with steely-eyed assent.

The attack was planned in minutes. Six men would move with O'Kane towards the square in a frontal approach. The other five men, including Huey, would skirt around the back of the buildings and attack from there. Carefully pinpointing the three buildings they were to attack, O'Kane gave the order to move out. With two of their own shoulder-held rocket-grenade launchers, O'Kane's party let loose a terrible bombardment upon the targets. By the time Huey's party had reached their positions behind the buildings the Germans were attempting to escape. They ran straight into the mouths of the American guns. It was the first time Huey had killed. His fury could not be sated. He was ravenous for revenge. He poured round after round into each hapless Nazi. When he finished with one, he searched for another to riddle.

An ungodly silence fell over the hamlet. O'Kane could be heard yelling, "Cease firing!" It was only then that Huey noticed he was trembling like a leaf. His ribs rattled and his limbs twitched. His breathing came fast and hoarse.

Huey and a white soldier called Flynn were ordered back to Marvin and the French woman. O'Kane took the rest of the men to mop up any wounded Germans or to see if there were any left unharmed and hiding. The French woman was sitting upright, leaning against a house wall. A white-haired woman in a knee-length black dress and a head scarf was binding a tourniquet around her thigh. Marvin was lying, spread-eagled on his back, mouth and eyes open, under a cloudy French sky. Huey thought of Maggie and her baby. His trembling turned into sobbing and convulsive retching.

Intermittently, they could hear a single gunshot. Then another. O'Kane was keeping to his promise. No prisoners. Support and medical assistance were five minutes away. The last Huey saw of Marvin was when his body was lifted into a truck and driven away. The woman was treated in a field ambulance before being taken away too. O'Kane gathered his men around him. Huey looked at his high-cheek-boned, Boston Irish face with a kind of awe and admiration. "Well done men. You fought bravely today." Looking at Huey he added, "We lost a brave comrade today. I will be recommending him for a posthumous honour."

Seventeen

Three exhausting days without sleep followed the village square battle where Marvin had lost his life. They had fought their way towards Vimoutiers. Every time Huey picked up his rifle he blessed Eisenhower under his breath. The D-Day landings had succeeded and the bridgehead had been established, but almost everything else had gone wrong. The Germans had fought back and smashed most of the first objectives of the invasion. Huey's platoon had been involved in firefights for three long days.

"Okay, men, we'll rest up here."

There were thirty-seven of them now and although but a small band of infantrymen they almost doubled the adult population of the small hamlet. Many of the buildings that had not been destroyed were badly damaged. The villagers had welcomed the G.I.s into their cottages, despite the devastation the fighting had caused. With French stoicism they accepted that the pain had to be gone through if liberation was to arrive. "Tate, Miller, take the first watch. Everyone else, heads down, sleep!"

"Sir," Miller spoke up.

"Yes soldier. What can I do for you?"

"It's just, well, I mean you've paired me with Tate."

"And...?"

Miller looked carefully at the Captain's expression which was beginning to redden.

"Ah nuthin' sir."

"Excellent. Carry on!"

Like every other village they had passed through, the church dominated the centre. Huey and Miller took up their position at the top of the church tower. From there they had a commanding view of all approaches to the village. It was a cloudless, July night, a shining half-moon and a billion stars if you looked long enough. They crouched at diagonally opposite corners of the square tower which, between them gave a complete panoramic view of the approaches to the village. "Where you from, Tate?"

Huey hesitated in replying. He knew his answer would stake him out in Miller's mind. Not that he wouldn't have already formed an opinion based on Huey's accent. "I'm from the good ole USA," he finally replied. But his reluctance to offer up the information Miller's question was clearly hoping to uncover made him laugh at himself. "Alabama," he added. "Dixieland."

"I ain't never been south," Miller said. "What's it like for you niggers down there? We hear lots of stories from the liberals and bleeding hearts in New York but, heck, we never know who to believe."

"You from New York? I knew you was a Yankee, like, but I couldn't have said from whereabouts."

"Rochester, New York State. Yeh, most of what we hear comes from New York City. Lots o' liberals and such there."

"Well I don't know what they tell you, but if it sounds bad it's probably only half true."

"So they making things up?"

"Nope. If they ain't lived it they only giving you a sample. It's twice as bad as what they say."
"Really? You free ain't you?"

"We're free all right. Free to do nothing. Free not to go to school, go to a bar, stay in a hotel, get a decent job. Free to do none of them things."

Miller did not respond he turned and sat with his back against the low wall. He looked across at Huey. Huey felt

Miller's eyes on his back. "Hey man, shouldn't you be watching the approach?"

Miller sat in thought. "It don't seem like you have a great affection for your homeland. Yet here you are fighting for it, thousands of miles away on a goddam foreign continent. How come?"

"Huey laughed. "Beats me, Miller. I guess I'm soft in the head." Miller chuckled at that and then they fell into silently scrutinising the village streets and the land around. "You ain't a bad guy Tate. I'm sorry for what I said back there to the Captain. I'll partner you anytime."

The blanket of night enveloped them for a time. The blacked-out village lay below them like an ink blot on a black sheet. A dog barked. Both men crouched and peered apprehensively into the surrounding country.

"Nothing, I guess," Miller said.

He sat back down with his back to the wall and looked at Huey. "I think I go along with them liberals to a degree. Things ain't fair. That's a fact. Schools, houses, jobs. Something should be done about it all. But, you know, up in New York City, there's lots o' blacks and there's Italians and Irish and Hispanics. But you know what? The blacks and the whites they still don't mix. Don't you think people prefer their own? Maybe separation, or segregation is it? Maybe that's the best way. I mean — it should be fair and all that. But mixing don't work. Marriage between a white man and a black woman — well that would never happen. But some white women do marry black men. But you know what, them marriages never last. Too much difference between the races. Always turns out bad."

"You know how many kids been fathered by white men with black women?"

"Yeah, yeah, we all know about that. But we know what that's all about, don't we? It ain't about love and marriage and happily ever after, that's for sure." A gust of wind caused the leaves in the trees to rustle like a waterfall. Huey scoured his viewpoint. Nothing.

"Hey," Miller said. "I hope I didn't offend you. Here, have one of my cigarettes. It's gonna be a long night." He stood up and walked across towards Huey.

Huey could never decide which came first: the blood that spurted from Miller and splashed onto his uniform or the crack of a rifle shot. Miller collapsed onto him groaning in agony. Huey fired three rifle shots into the air, sending the signal to his platoon captain and the rest of the men. He rolled Miller onto his back as bullets ricocheted off the walls of the tower. Miller was wounded in his neck. He was losing a lot of blood. Huey plugged the hole with his fingers as he tried to decide if Miller was fatally wounded. Right then the sound of American voices barking orders filled the night and rapid gunfire followed. A firefight was in full flow. Huey wound up his radio and connected to the captain.

"Man down, Sir, over."

"How bad? Over."

"Pretty bad. He needs immediate medical aid. Over."

"No way I can send a medic up to you. We're pinned down. Do what you can. Report back in five minutes. Over."

Huey knew he had to stem the flow of blood if Miller was going to have a chance. With a neck wound a tourniquet was out of the question. It would stem the blood-flow but just as likely strangle the patient.

Huey stripped off his jacket and protective vest. He pulled his T-shirt over his head and packed it as tightly as he could into the wound. Miller was unconscious by now. He took off Miller's belt and, looping it around the T-shirt, under Miller's chin and over the top of Miller's head, he managed to slow the bleeding. He now got back to his lookout point and scurried around the whole perimeter of the tower. His buddies were pinned down inside the houses whilst the Germans were hidden in the trees and fields that surrounded them. He studied the incoming gunfire for a couple of minutes. He wound up his radio again. "I can see the encirclement, Sir. I think I can pinpoint one area where there doesn't seem to be any fire coming from. It's south-south-east – from the centre of the square. Approximately where the pond lies. Over."

"What are you thinking, soldier? Over"

"If you could get a group of men to cross the pond maybe they could get behind the Germans and begin to pick them off, sir. Over."

"Interesting. Status report on Miller? Over."

"Not good. He's lost a lot of blood and is unconscious. I'm bringing him down. Over." "Negative on that, Tate. I'll call you back." A few minutes later the Captain was back on the radio.

"You won't make it with Miller. You are to give us cover fire. Your suggestion is the only working proposition we have so I'm acting on it. From the moment I say 'over', at the end of this transmission, you commence firing into the areas either side of the pond. We estimate four minutes for twelve men to wade across. Four minutes constant firing from all of us will cover the noise they will make crossing the pond. Over."

Huey checked Miller. He was still breathing. Adjusting the T-shirt to a slightly tighter position he scrambled to his position and began firing. The barrage of noise that broke out as all guns blazed enveloped the village. Huey ceased firing when the barrage stopped. Now he decided he had to disobey his captain's order. Hanging his rifle from his right shoulder he hoisted Miller onto his left. The guy was a good one hundred and eighty pounds plus the weight of his uniform and kit. Steadily down the spiral stone steps, pausing for breath and balance, he gradually conveyed Miller towards the medical support he needed. The lull in firing was shattered as the Germans found themselves under attack from in front and behind. Huey pulled open the door of the church and crouched as he scrambled down the steps to the edge of the square. The velocity of gunfire rose to a crescendo and he realised his buddies had seen him and were giving covering fire. Their sole medic was holed up in a cottage about fifty metres around to the left side of the square. Huey was unable to run with the load he carried. He walked as directly and steadily as he could. Bullets hit the stone walls of the houses beside him and into the pillars of the short colonnade that gave him some shelter. The doctor was waiting for him, had prepared his instruments and cleared a treatment table. Huey staggered in and lowered Miller carefully to the table. "Well done, son," the doctor said. "Sit down there. I'm going to give you a shot to take your heart rate down."

Eighteen

Paris, August 1944

O'Kane called the men together. They had been resting up behind the front lines after twelve solid days of action flushing out resisting cohorts of Germans. Now that the Germans were retreating eastwards, Allied Command had allowed forward troops to rest up whilst newly landed troops went forward.

The men gathered in the large salon of the chateau they had occupied. They numbered fifty, having been replenished with new blood following later Normandy landings. Just over half of the GIs were black. The rest were men from the north-eastern and midwestern states. Any racial friction had been worn away to nothing by the fire-fights the men had shared.

For the first time in weeks, they were refreshed and well-fed, and good humour had returned to those naturally inclined that way.

O'Kane stood in front of a blackboard. He stood with his hands on his hips and his legs astride, watching his men as they entered and settled into the rows of seats spread out before him. His men thought his military pose a bit of a joke but they loved and respected him for bringing them this far and for looking out for each and everyone of them in their push across France. A natural silence fell on the room as the men craned their necks to get a full sight of their boss. Virtually, to a man, a cigarette was lit, and a smoke cloud began to fill the room from the ceiling downwards.

"Okay men," O'Kane began, "holiday time is nearly over."

A few half-hearted groans ran around the room accompanied by random laughter. "Now men, there's no need for that," O'Kane continued with a sarcastic grin. "I can see from here you're all putting on weight with the amount of food you're getting here and the lack of exercise you're doing. Well, don't worry. We're going to put that right, TOOT SWEET!"

He turned and drew on the blackboard. His inexperience in this activity showed when the chalk stick snapped in half and he cursed out loud. He drew an extremely rough map showing their position in Alençon and the route from there to Paris.

"As you can see men, we're going to approach the capital through this wooded, rural parkland. As far as we know the Germans are in retreat, probably running to fortify Paris. And guess where we're headed?"

Groans again, but light-hearted and half-jokingly. A hand went up from the back and O'Kane pointed at the soldier.

"Yes Private?"

"We were told that Paris wasn't on the target list. We were supposed to be bypassing the capital and chasing the Nazis over the frontier."

"Correct, soldier. But things have changed. Allied Command have got wind of the fact that the Resistance intend to start an uprising. Seems they don't want to leave all the fighting to us. Stands to reason. Where you from son?"

"Dayton, Ohio, sir."

"Well suppose the Nazis had been trampling all over Dayton for the last four, five years and they was on the run. What would you do?"

"I'd start shooting the bastards, sir."

"You hit the nail on the head there, son. And that's what the Frenchies are gonna do."

"So why we going there? It's their fight."

"Well, That ain't exactly the full story, soldier. See, we didn't exactly ask to come into this war but after the Japs attacked Pearl Harbour this Hitler fella declared war on us. So any fight against them is our fight. Plus the fact, Eisenhower and the rest of the Allied Command don't want to be breezing by Paris whilst a massacre is going on. And that's what could happen to the Frenchies if things go wrong."

"Anymore questions?"

"No sir."

"Good. We head out at six-thirty sharp tomorrow morning.

The approach to Paris had been plain sailing. Huey and Ernie, along with most of their buddies, had bounced along hoovering up the sights and sounds of the beautiful French countryside, mesmerised by the sheer peace and tranquility. The Germans had withdrawn fully to within the Paris precincts. From thirty miles west of the capital the smoke rising from the burning flour mills could be seen. Street battles had raged for four days now and Huey's platoon had been involved since arriving two days ago. The Resistance had organised barricades and had surrounded the German fortified positions. They had implemented a good strategic plan but had been running short of fire power until the Americans arrived.

O'Kane began liaising with the first Resistance fighter they encountered who held officer rank. His name was Michel Gagné and he led a troop numbering around twenty-five. They were besieging a building on Rue Lauriston which had housed the French Gestapo for the last four years. O'Kane's men had reinforced the Resistance fighters manning the barricade and were returning fire towards the Gestapo headquarters. A man leaned himself against the barricade next to Huey. He looked agitated. More than the others.

114

"They have prisoners in there," he said, half to himself.
"What's that?" Huey asked.

"Prisoners. They have prisoners still. Some of our best
men. We have to get them out safely. There's no telling what
those bastards will do."

Huey weighed up this man. Ernie crept along the
barricade to join them. "What's happenin'?" he asked.

"Not much," Huey said. "Keep your head down.
They've got sharpshooters in there." He turned to the French
man. "Hey, buddy. Our Captain is a good man. Your boss will
be explaining to him about the prisoners, right."

The French man looked at Huey. "Of course."

"Well Captain O'Kane will be very mindful of the
situation."

"Look, Monsieur, I don't know your name, but I take in
good faith what you say about your Captain. All I can say is I'm
not sure I have as much faith in my superior. He can be very
cautious. I want you to come with me."

"Where to?"

"To speak with them."

Huey looked at Ernie. Ernie shrugged. "Not much
doing here. You might as well."

So Huey crouched low as he followed the French man
across the street into the lobby of the bank that the
Resistance had occupied from which to orchestrate its assault
upon the Gestapo building.

O'Kane and Gagné were in deep discussion when
Huey's French comrade burst into the room. Gagné turned
and looked angrily towards the disruption caused. "Marc,
what is it? Can't you see we are busy?"

"Michel, I have come to plead the urgency of the
situation. The Carlingue have prisoners. We need to get them

out before those bastards wipe them out. They won't want to leave any living witnesses to the atrocities they have committed in there."

"Excuse me, Captain," Gagné said to O'Kane. "Monsieur Durand is not the most patient of men, nor the most strategic of thinkers."

"For heaven's sake," Marc exploded. "They are our comrades. We can't let them be killed so close to our liberation."

Gagné was about to respond when the door burst open again and in came Ernie. He was accompanying, what Huey at first thought was a boy because of the workingman's attire and bandana. But it turned out to be a young woman.

"Clara!" Marc exclaimed.

But Ernie took charge. He drew himself up to attention in front of O'Kane. "What is it soldier?"

"Sir, this young woman has approached us from behind the building. She claims that executions have begun inside. It's true as far as we can ascertain, Sir. We can hear gunfire coming from inside the building's precincts."

Marc rounded on Gagné and both men exploded into a fusillade of French which the Americans could only stand back and witness. They continued until O'Kane stepped between them and demanded to know what Marc was proposing.

"We have to get inside the building. We cannot wait until our comrades have been murdered."
O'Kane turned to Gagné. "What is the problem?"

"It has very little chance of success. We could lose as many men attempting a frontal assault as we would save."

O'Kane took less than a few seconds to make a decision. He addressed Huey and Ernie. "We're going in. Get

back to the barricade and tell the men I want ten volunteers."
Huey and Ernie looked at each other. "Make that eight, Sir,"
Ernie said.

"Excellent. Eight volunteers."

O'Kane passed rapid instructions to Huey. Turning to
Marc, he added, "Your Resistance fighters can join us, but you
will be under my command." He turned to Clara.
"You have come from behind the building. Have you assessed
the defences?"

"Yes, Captain. The bulk of the defence is positioned at
the front of the building facing the barricade. We have a small
group at the rear preventing any attempts by the occupants
to escape."

On a sheet of paper O'Kane sketched out the plan.
"We're going to throw a fake frontal attack at them while my
volunteers," he hesitated, "and your men," he added glancing
at Gagné, "circle to the rear and force an entry there."

The action unfolded as O'Kane had planned. Nine
Resistance fighters joined the G.I. volunteers and, splitting
into two groups, crept around both sides of the building to
meet at the rear. In the meantime, from the barricade the
remainder threw a battery of weaponry at the front, drawing
a furious response from the Carlingue. The Germans had
overrun Europe with their vast military resources – resources
that no other country had been able to match. But the
Americans were on a whole other level. Here was another
dimension in wealth and weaponry that they had to face. This
was how a truly rich man went to war. The French
collaborators were about feel the wrath of the liberators.
Four rocket launchers punched massive holes in the rear wall
where, sure enough, recently executed corpses lay in the
yard. Huey found himself running over broken masonry, firing

as he went, alongside, not only Ernie, but also the young woman who had brought the news of the executions to O'Kane and Gagné. Almost overwhelmed by the assault from in front, the French Gestapo were surprised by the invaders picking them off from behind. More than once Huey witnessed both Clara and Marc put bullets into individuals who were raising their hands. They were fighting in anger and retribution. When the battle subsided and the building was secured, Marc approached the rounded-up captives. He asked the same question repeatedly.

" Où est Moreau? Où est Moreau?"

Moreau was nowhere to be found. In the meantime, Clara had led Huey into the basement area to the cells. She raced through them, looking at the prisoners there. Some were in a desperate condition. Most were malnourished and many were suffering the results of vicious beatings. Moving rapidly from cell to cell, Clara finally exclaimed in sheer relief.

"Jean-Paul. Mon dieu!"

She threw herself at a flimsy shadow in the corner of the cell and wrapped her arms around him. He looked as if he would break in two if she squeezed any harder.
The released prisoners were led away to ambulances
that had been called up. The French Nazis were lined up in front of the Carlingue building – prisoners of war. Clara and Marc went along the line inspecting every face. Carla pulled out four men and before O'Kane could intervene, she and Marc had despatched them with a bullet each to the head. O'Kane was not happy. "What the fuck is going on here?" he screamed and ordered his men to restrain Marc and Clara. They were dragged before O'Kane who demanded an explanation.

"This is French justice, Captain," Clara spat out defiantly. "Those men have been declared war criminals by the Resistance Command. They have already been condemned to death in their absence."

O'Kane remained furious that this had happened under his command until Gagné met with him and explained that according to the rules of engagement decreed by the Resistance these men were indeed war criminals to be hunted down and executed. Only later, in the aftermath of the battle, following extended communications between O'Kane and the Resistance leadership in Paris did O'Kane agree to forget his charges against Marc and Clara. The next few days saw the Germans entirely driven out of Paris.

Nineteen

Paris, 25th August 1944

Bois de Bolougne

The camp numbered around one hundred bivouacs, each accommodating four men. The battle for Paris is over and today is the liberation parade.

"Easy day for you and me today."

The voice came from outside Huey's bivouac. It was Ernie. Huey missed Marvin, but Ernie had attached himself to Huey across the French hinterland towards Paris. And Huey was glad of his companionship.

"How come?"

"Big parade. The day of liberation. They don't want no black faces on show today. You and me gonna laze around here smokin' and drinkin' and eatin' while French whitey struts his stuff. Hell, they ain't even letting them dusky North Africans who done all the fighting get a look in. Champs-Élysées gonna be all white today."

"Suits me," Huey muttered.

"What's that?"

"Nuthin'."

"Anyway," Ernie continued, "Seeing as how you ain't getting out o' your sack I brung you some breakfast. You decent?"

"I'm decent. You may enter."

Ernie pushed through the flaps and ducked into the tent. He handed Huey a tin plate full of sausages.

"Oh man!" he complained. "You cremated them again. Why d'you have to fry them till they black as soot everytime."

"Only way to eat them. Gives them taste and flavour. Nothing like these Frenchies, eating raw meat."

120

Nibbling his way past the blackened exterior, Huey ate the spicy interior. Washed down with strong coffee it tasted good. Huey knew it was a free pass day and he had no intention of going near the parade.

The Resistance fighters he had met during the attack on the Carlingue had invited O'Kane and his men to share their rations when the siege had ended. They had been taken back to Gagnés headquarters to be fed. The GIs had provided as much in the way of rations as their hosts had. Nobody minded. Huey and Ernie had been seated at a table with Marc and Clara, the two ferocious fighters they had fought their way into the Carlingue building with. The action behind them, they reverted to everyday topics of trivial conversation. As the large canteen they occupied rang with the relieved chatter of battle-weary men and women, it emerged that Huey shared a love for the same kind of music as Marc and Clara. When Ernie boasted of his friend's proficiency on the guitar Huey was invited to join them at their club whenever he was allowed free time.

The previous day, the woman called Clara had found Huey and Ernie at a café beside their camp site and informed them that they were keeping away from De Gaulle's Liberation Day Parade. She described it disparagingly.

"What? You not taking part in the parade?"

"We are not wanted. We are not invited. De Gaulle wants the country to believe that he won the battle for France. He wants us erased from the records. It wouldn't do for our countrymen to think we had kept up the fight while he warmed his feet in a London bed."

"So, what are you going to be doing?"

"I'm meeting the band. We're playing at a club. Marc has asked if you want to come along and sit in with us."

"You bet," Huey answered.

She gave Huey the directions to the club and away she went on her bicycle.

Le Sous-Sol was a cavernous basement running under three shops that fronted the main street. Arched pillars supported a blue brick ceiling. Most nights, even during the occupation, the walls had rung to the jazzy swing sounds of Les Libres, the resident five piece band. At the beginning of the occupation, they had entertained members of the Wermacht, the Gestapo and the SS. Their choice of repertoire had been restricted but they had managed to slip in some Louis Armstrong or Duke Ellington without the Germans realising. Playing Negro music was a crime of subversion in Nazi Europe and likely to land you in a concentration camp.

Over the next few weeks, while the liberation of Paris was secured and planning was progressing for the advancement against the Wermacht into Germany itself, Huey found himself in Le Sous-Sol whenever he had downtime.

Huey was enjoying not being totally sure if it was the music that drew him back or Clara, the beautiful Resistance warrior. She fronted the band when female vocals were required. It didn't matter. He didn't just feel good, he felt doubly good just thinking about the day ahead.

Showered and shaved and in his best dress uniform, he made his way out to Nanterre. On his back the guitar he had managed to keep safe with him all the way from Burtonwood, Lancashire. Its case had taken two bullets, but the guitar had survived intact. Marc Durand, firebrand Resistance fighter and trumpet player/band leader had welcomed him to sit in on guitar whenever he could, and Huey was looking forward to an afternoon's practice and an evening of sublime music to become immersed in.

The streets of Nanterre were quiet. Down inside Le Sous-Sol, Clara and Marc were nowhere to be seen. The band was just messing around, improvising on a Billy Eckstine tune. Huey unpacked his guitar and took a seat. He checked his tuning and then let his fingers slide into position as they coaxed the chords alive. Twenty minutes later the music faltered and faded. The lack of a leader and a purpose took its effect. Some guys put down their instruments and shuffled around smoking. Others stretched and walked off into the depths of the club, muttering about Marc not turning up. The club was due to open in thirty minutes. He needed to show his face soon.

The door to the street opened and footsteps sounded on the stairs. At last. This must be Marc. But it wasn't Marc. Who's this old guy? Huey thought. He wore a working man's beret and jacket and he was flushed with exertion. Close to, Huey realised that he wasn't as old as he had first appeared.

"Hey Jean-Paul," the trombonist said. "What's the big rush?"

Huey recognised him now. Jean-Paul, the man Clara had been desperate to rescue from the Carlingue cells. Jean-Paul sat down and gathered his breath. "It's Clara," he croaked. "She's been arrested. Her neighbour denounced her as a collaborator. He's accused her of sleeping with the Nazis. She's in real trouble."

Clara finished her lipstick and gently tapped powder on her cheek. She stood and ran her hands down her dress to smooth it. The day was hot and she decided against a cardigan. Marc would be arriving soon to travel with her to the club. She took one last look into the mirror before leaving for their meeting place on the corner.

The streets were empty apart from the occasional passer-by. It was as she saw Marc approaching from two blocks away that Pierre Caron appeared. He was not alone. There were two women with him. They were his wife and daughter. The daughter carried a pair of scissors. From his distant viewpoint Marc saw Caron grab Clara, pinning her arms to her sides. His wife clutched a handful of Clara's hair and her daughter began cutting chunks from it. Clara screamed and, from nowhere people began to emerge from nearby shops and bars. Marc raced towards the scene. By the time he got there he had to fight his way through the bunch who had gathered to watch. He burst through and swung a punch at Caron, catching him a blow on his temple. Caron staggered and let slip his grip on Clara. Marc caught hold of the hand wielding the scissors and twisted it until the young woman screamed in pain and dropped them. As he turned to attack the mother holding Clara's hair, he was himself seized by two police officers and dragged away.

Huey was stunned by this news. The woman he had fought beside during the siege of the Carlingue was a committed anti-Nazi. What was going on here? Did her accusers know of some other activities she had been involved in? Had she played both sides of the fence? Maybe she had jumped to the winning side at the last moment? If Clara had spent part of the war as a collaborator, no better than a fascist whore, sleeping with Nazis, how would his feelings about her be affected? But it wasn't making sense. Surely, Marc and Jean-Paul, and Gagné would know all about her war record and they had never suggested anything of the kind. She had definitely been relentless in hunting down collaborators in the Carlingue. But, he couldn't help thinking, what if her motives for destroying the Carlingue, especially the individuals she and Marc had assassinated, had been to do with covering up the truth of her wartime behaviour? He grabbed his guitar and ran through the streets to Nanterre Police Headquarters. Caron, his wife and daughter had given full statements and been released. Clara was in isolation. Telling himself that the French were not conditioned to racist Jim Crow attitudes and that he could assert himself in his uniform. He marched into the station and requested to see Clara. His request was politely refused. But he was permitted to see Marc.

"The opposite is true, Huey, believe me," Marc said. "Clara was no collaborator."

Twenty

"You have no idea what it was like living under the Nazis," Marc was saying.

"Are you sure about that?" mumbled Huey.

Marc ignored the barely heard comment and continued. "It was survival at all costs. We all did things we're not proud of."

They were sitting on a wooden bunk in a tiny, twelve by ten-foot cell.

"Why are you here?" Huey asked.

"That bastard Caron. He accused me of assault. Don't worry. I'll soon be out of here. But you need to get busy now. These women Clara has been mixed up with can suffer some horrendous treatment. Get to a telephone. Call Hôtel de Matignon. Ask for Captain Michel Gagné. They are setting up a provisional government there. You met Gagné at the Carlingue siege. He led us and planned our actions in the Resistance. He will know what to do. But it is very important. You must be quick. Collaborators can come to serious harm before any process of law is enacted. Clara is in immediate danger."

At the Hôtel de Matignon Michel Gagné was at the centre of a chaotic scene. On every floor of the building men and women scurried around like ants. They were each absorbed in their own task. Accumulatively, that would result in the creation of a basis for the new French government which was at that moment being set-up in negotiations between the Allies and the Free French. On every floor the walls echoed to the name de Gaulle. A telephone rang out amidst the chaos. An arm in gartered shirt sleeves reached out to lift the receiver. A rugged face nodded as the message was listened to. The listener placed the receiver on the table and vacated his seat. He began to worm his way through the crowds and mounted the stairs with Huey right behind him. Each person he asked about the whereabouts of Michel Gagné waved him deeper into the building. Eventually he reached the end of a teeming corridor and passed through an open doorway into a grand, high-ceilinged room furnished with an elaborate oak desk and Louis XVI style seating. Taking the captain by the elbow the messenger whispered into his ear. Gagné dropped the papers he had been holding onto a desk, turning caught sight of Huey. "My American friend. We meet again. How can I help you?"

"You know the name Clara Bisset? The woman who fought with us at the Carlingue."

"But of course"

"She's been arrested as a collaborator."

"Ah, putain! Where is she?"

"Nanterre police headquarters."

"I need to get there quickly. Some of these women will be shot. Don't get me wrong – plenty of them will deserve it. I would pull the trigger myself. But not Clara. She did everything for our cause. Sacrificed more than anyone. She was braver than most."

When Gagné's driver skidded to a halt outside Nanterre police headquarters, Huey was already there. Gagné took the lead at the desk. He slammed his official papers down and demanded to see the senior officer on duty. The gendarme on desk duty looked at the group in front of him and at Gagné's papers. He hurried away. Within minutes he returned and led them through into the back of the station.

Huey saw immediately that there was hostility between Gagné and the Chief Inspector. He rose from behind his desk when they entered but he did not offer to shake hands. He wore a sweat-stained white shirt which was only partially tucked inside his pants. His nicotine-stained moustache glistened with the sweat which ran down his overweight face onto it. He extinguished a cigarette by dropping it into the dregs of a black coffee. Addressing Gagné in French he asked, "What do you want?"

As they spoke, Huey speculated on the reasons for the brittle nature of their exchanges. The Inspector was possibly the only overweight Parisian he had seen since arriving. Also, he held a high position in the Nazi sponsored force, which the French police service had been. He had done well out of the occupation. Here was a probable collaborator standing face to face with a leader of the Resistance. Their voices rose and fell, sometimes becoming extremely angry, especially Gagné's. Gagné punctuated his remarks with gestures towards Huey. If the Inspector had acquired his Nazi sponsors' attitudes to race, he did his best to hide them. Eventually, after an explosive exchange Gagné turned to Huey.

"Okay, this slug has finally succumbed to my threats. We are going down into the cells to get Clara."

"How have you pulled it off?"

"I've told him you've been sent to take her into protective custody because the Americans know of her heroic service in the Resistance. Anyway, he's scared. His days are numbered. He'll soon be occupying the cell Clara is about to leave."

Huey postponed his relief. He would not believe Clara was safe until he had her away from here and back in her apartment. They followed the Inspector back out to the lobby. He snapped at the desk for the keys and led them down into the cell area. The keys proved redundant. When they reached Clara's cell it was open and empty.

The Inspector yelled and a uniformed constable came running. Before the Inspector could move, Gagne had grabbed the startled man by the throat and was screaming repeatedly, "Ou est-elle?"

The Inspector, scared out of his skin, intervened and dragged some sense out of him. He explained the situation to Gagné. Gagné, out of nowhere, delivered an almighty slap across the Inspector's face. The sound echoed along the bare-tiled corridor. The Inspector looked almost about to cry like a child.

Huey stepped forward and pulled Gagné by the shoulder. "Hey, forget this. We need to find Clara. Where is she? What's happening?"

"Clara has been taken to be paraded through the streets along with any French woman who slept or associated with Nazis. She is in danger."

"Okay. Let's go," Huey snapped. "Inspector," he added, "You're coming with us."

"Huey!" A voice was calling from behind a cell door further along the corridor. It was Marc. Huey grabbed the Inspector and pushed him to Marc's cell. The Inspector unlocked the door and Marc came out.

With the Inspector struggling to keep up, the four men ran out of the station in the direction of the main square. As they approached, they could hear a baying crowd. The previously quiet streets were now full of outraged citizens. They battered their way through the crowd, knocking incensed men and women flying. Walking slowly across the square between the rows of indignant citizens were twelve women. Their hair had been shorn from their scalps and they were splattered with phlegm and rotten fruit. Two had been badly injured by over-enthusiastic onlookers choosing to throw glass bottles or rocks. Blood ran down their faces from the tops of their heads.

In the middle of the group Huey saw Clara. "Okay, let's go," he yelled. Pushing the Inspector ahead of them, they rushed into the group of women and surrounded Clara.

The crowd fell silent. They struggled to understand what was happening. When the Inspector started barking orders at the constables who had been managing the parade the crowd grew angry. The men who had previously facilitated the humiliation of these women now struggled to form a protective guard around them. The crowd became uglier and the volley of rotten fruit recommenced.

As the women were guided back to the station, Clara was safely removed from the mêlée and within minutes she and Marc and Gagné were in Gagné's car and speeding away.

Twenty-one

Paris, September 1944

Le Sous-Sol was bursting at the seams. The liberation celebrations seemed destined to continue right up to Christmas at this rate. Money in pockets was at a premium but the desire to drink in the freedom of movement and association that had returned after the Germans had been driven out was insatiable. Huey was taking a three-song break from playing. Clara was in his arms as they swayed to the strains of Les Libres' version of 'Night and Day'. It was a magnificent feeling to hold her close but there was discomfort too. The warmth of her embrace cooled in his mind when he thought of Marc. No matter how close they held each other Huey knew that Clara would be leaving with Marc.

Since Liberation Day in June Clara had relinquished her own bed-sitter and moved in with Marc. It made her happy and sad. She had always believed that she and Marc were destined to be together, but the sadness came from knowing of his other lovers, of whom there were at least two, maybe more. Since becoming publicly known as a resistance hero, his attraction for the opposite sex had risen. His love for Clara notwithstanding, the temptation laid before him was irresistible. Clara felt cheapened but she believed it was a phase that would pass. He might stray but he would always come back to her.

It was only gradually, as weeks went by, that she found herself looking forward to Huey's presence whenever the band was together. He couldn't be with them all of the time because of his army commitments. If Clara turned up and spotted that his seat was vacant, she was surprised at the disappointment she experienced. When he was with them, she found herself gravitating towards him. Her attachment to

Marc was passionate but she realised she was rarely happy when with him. On the other hand, Huey made her laugh, feel relaxed and able to be completely herself.

Ironically, it was a Texan that Huey thought he had seen the last of back in Burtonwood, England, who made Clara suddenly realise that she loved Huey. It was after one of Huey's last appearances with the band before his company was due to move north to support troops driving into southern Germany. Marc had quickly disappeared with a dark girl from Brittany, with whom he had been dancing earlier in the evening, while Clara sang 'Anything Goes' and watched him from the stage. As he packed his guitar into its case Huey felt a hand gently touch his elbow.

"Night Huey. Please be careful. Don't let those Nazis get you. We'll be waiting for you to come back once the war is over. We just don't sound the same without your guitar."

Huey affectionately squeezed her forearm. "Don't you worry about me, Clara. I've got a charmed life. I hope you mean what you say about me coming back. Paris suits me. I've never been able to be myself before. As soon as I'm de-mobbed I'm coming back. If France will have me, I'm going to become a Frenchman."

They both laughed. Huey offered to walk Clara back to the flat she shared with Marc. "I don't think I can go back there yet," she said, thinking of the Breton girl. I might be unwelcome." Huey shook his head. "I don't know why you put up with him. He treats you very badly."

"I know," she whispered. "But what else can I do?"

Huey recognised a rhetorical question and just suggested that they take a walk down to the Seine where they could stroll until it was safe for her to get back to her apartment.

And that's where they met the Texan. He was with a

buddy coming towards them. "Don't I know you, nigger?"

Clara stepped forward. "How dare you? Who do you think you are? Bringing your disgusting attitudes over here."

"Get out of my way whore. This nigger makes a habit of taking white women. Sadly, there are always some dirty whores who's happy to go with him." He pushed her and she stumbled to her knees. Huey lunged forward, took the Texan by his collar and delivered a blow to his stomach. The Texan doubled over and heaved. It would have been all over but his buddy swung a punch at Huey's temple and floored him. Pushing Clara back to the ground the two G.I.s started kicking Huey until he lay unconscious. Clara's screams brought passers-by and a gendarme to the scene just in time to stop them throwing the unconscious Huey into the Seine. The two soldiers ignored the attempts of the gendarme to detain them. They just pushed him aside and walked off. Their laughter echoed on the surface of the water. It was the sound of that laughter that tipped Clara over. She could have no idea, when she took off after the laughing G.I.s, that what she was about to do would come back to haunt her years from now.

Her blood was up but she was in her Resistance fighter mode. She picked up a large rock from the crumbling towpath and quickly gained on Huey's assailants. Coming close behind them she brought the rock around in a large speeding arc and slammed it into the head of the man who had first attacked Huey. He crumpled to the floor, blood beginning to pour from his scalp. His comrade turned, saw his battered friend at his feet and took in the sight of Clara. She stood facing him, rock in hand, ready to take him on. Before he could attack her, she hurled the rock at his head. As he ducked and turned, she ran up behind him and pushed him into the river.

Huey was unconscious when he was stretchered into the ambulance that had been called. Clara brushed aside the attentions of one of the medics who wanted to wash her cuts and check her bruises. She shouted at him that she was fine and he needed to look to Huey. As she looked at him, lying there unconscious, she knew what she had only suspected until then. She loved him.

The American hospital in Neuilly-sur-Seine was experiencing overcrowding. Huey's ambulance was turned away and re-directed to the nearby Hospital Du Perray. It was soon discovered that Huey's spleen had been ruptured and that he was suffering severe internal bleeding. A splenectomy was to be immediately performed and blood transfusions commenced. Clara sat all alone in the hospital corridor, biting her nails whilst the doctors and nurses rushed Huey through to theatre. As she waited her tears ran freely down her face and splashed onto her coat. Her mind roamed blindly. Her impulsive act of revenge did nothing to calm her anger. She worried herself sick about Huey. Would he survive? What would she do if he didn't? She would be insane with grief and regret. Her thoughts were interrupted when a group of armed gendarmes arrived at the hospital to arrest her for the assault on the G.I.s.

Huey didn't know whether to feel lucky or cursed. The pain was excruciating but his splenectomy determined that he would be laid up in this hospital bed for at least four weeks. While Ernie and the rest of his comrades headed north towards the Ardennes, he was lying back on clean white cotton sheets. Clara's conviction for assault seemed trivial in the light of Huey's experience. Although the guilty verdict pleased the American prosecutors, her paltry sentence of three months house arrest, mitigated by the acceptance of self-defence, infuriated the US military and confirmed their stereotype of the French as untrustworthy.

Twenty-two

Alabama, April 1945

Honourably discharged, unfit for service, Huey had arrived back at the family home just in time for Christmas, 1944. When the joy of being re-united with his Mama and sisters had receded, he began to see his hometown in its old light. The comparison with Paris was stark. Even thinking of Burtonwood in Lancashire filled him with nostalgia for a happier place to be. A happier place to be a black adult male.

Despite his Mama's obvious regrets, she encouraged him to follow his dream of returning to France. The ending of the war in Europe made his mind up for him. There was no work for him that suited his army acquired skills. His obsession with engines now rivalled his love for his guitar. The canning factory was not for him. The Alabama heat of August had weighed down on him, making him restless to be away. Once he had settled his affairs and handed most of his de-mob pay to his Mama, he packed a shoulder bag and set off for Halifax in Nova Scotia. With his veteran's pass he could travel the railroad for an affordable amount. Once in Halifax he signed up on a cargo ship taking Canadian livestock to Le Havre. Six weeks on the stormy Atlantic did two things for him. First, it filled him with admiration for the men of the merchant fleet who had braved the U-Boats during the war. Second, it filled his pockets with unspent pay. Immediately upon disembarkation he headed for the railroad station and bought a one-way ticket to Paris.

Since his departure from France, he and Clara had kept in touch via letters. Hers had become more and more affectionate as the time had gone by. She asked him constantly about life in Alabama, especially about the segregation laws and practices. She reacted with outrage to almost everything he had to say. She was appalled by the Ku Klux Klan and its leaders in Alabama. Stories of the brutalities suffered by blacks enraged and confused her. Were these stories from the same country that had sacrificed so much to defeat Nazism? How could this form of racial Nazism carry on there?

Clara carefully tied her growing pile of Huey's letters in a blue ribbon and hid them in a shoebox inside her wardrobe. She did not hide them explicitly from Marc. There was no need. Huey's epistles disappointed her in that he never matched the affection she expressed to him in hers. So, there was nothing in them to keep from Marc. Also, Marc showed little interest in Clara's day-to-day business. If it wasn't about her singing or making love, he was always busily engaged in the business of becoming a lawyer.

Twenty-three

France, June 1946

After eight weeks at sea, the train ride from Le Havre to Paris was heavenly comfort to Huey's body. The few weeks back home had softened up his war-hardened muscles but the hard graft of a merchant seaman had re-cast them as iron. He was newly invigorated and set to begin his new life. The exhilaration of the freedom he was anticipating was enhanced by every rock and sway and rattle of the train as it sped him on his way.

"Take off that trilby." It was Marc who gave the command to Huey.

"What you say?" Huey grinned.

"Take it off."

"I can't go out without my hat."

"Yeh you can. Just do it."

"Okay," Huey conceded reluctantly.

As he placed his trilby on the chair beside him, an object span across the room towards him. He reacted in time to snatch it out of mid-air. As soon as it landed in his hands, he knew what it was – a beret.

"Put that on. You're a Frenchman now."

Hesitantly, Huey fitted the beret to his scalp. It fitted perfectly. He shuffled across the room to his mirror and stood turning his head this way and that. When he turned back to Marc, he was wearing a big grin. He spread his arms as if to ask, 'what do you think?' Both men burst out laughing.

"You see," Marc exclaimed. "It is perfect. I knew it would be." They grappled with each other in a manly hug. Marc broke away, looked at his watch and said, "Let's get going. We don't want to be late."

Le Sous-Sol was packed that night. Three numbers in Huey reluctantly removed his beret from his sweat stained brow.

Clara took over the vocals from Marc when they slipped into I Get A Kick Out Of You. Marc placed his trumpet on its stand and went to the bar. It was a song Huey particularly liked for its 6ths, major 7ths and especially the A7b9. He always told himself that this was what was meant by the phrase seventh heaven. Without Marc's trumpet he took the instrumental lead break and nodded his thanks to the crowd when they burst into applause at its conclusion. He was not disappointed to see Marc slip down the corridor towards the dressing room area with the young woman he had been chatting to, at the bar, in tow. Now he would get to lead on several more songs until Marc returned. He felt a bit of a heel when he dragged his eyes away from the neck of his guitar and saw the deflated look on Clara's face.

Marc returned after the short interval and for the second half he was brilliant. He had the crowd in the palm of his hand. His trumpet painted the ceiling of the club in glorious musical technicolour, and he roused the crowd to a frenzy of dancing and cheering. Alongside Clara, harmonising with her crystal-clear vocals, he won her over too and they ended the evening wrapped in each-others' arms as they blasted out the last chorus of When The Saints Go Marching In.

"Vive La France!" he shouted after the band had played La Marseillaise. "Et Vive La France Libre!"

The crowd bellowed their approval and reluctantly began heading to the door. Relative quiet settled on the room. Normal sounds became audible again. The scrape of shoes on the stage, the rattle of instrument cases, the dragging of chairs to be stacked.

139

The euphoria of the performance had momentarily struck the members of the band dumb. Only slowly did normality creep back in.

Huey watched Marc approach Clara at the bar where she was sipping a cognac. She had resurrected her annoyance with him. He was leaning in close and whispering in her ear. Half playfully, half seriously she pushed him away.

"I don't like you tonight," Clara pouted.

"Come on, Clara. It was nothing. You know that."

Huey became self-conscious about overhearing them. He snapped his guitar case shut, jumped down from the stage and called out to no-one in particular, "Good night, buddies. See you all tomorrow."

Marc slid from his bar stool and hurried over to Huey. He grabbed his arm before Huey could begin to mount the stairs. "Where do you think you're going?"

"It's home for me, Marc. Where else. I've got to get out early tomorrow. Job hunting."

"I wanted to talk to you about that and your residency permit. Don't go job-hunting tomorrow. Come to my office. I've cleared my diary for 10 am so don't be late. Now come on, Clara and I will share a taxi with you to your place and see you safely home."

"You don't need to do that, Marc."

"Hey, we know we don't need to. We want to. And – what are you forgetting?"

Huey was non-plussed. "I don't know. What am I forgetting?"

"Your beret! How can you be a Frenchman without it?"

Huey was relieved that Marc had reminded him. His beret lay where he had left it earlier and he would have been mortified to lose it.

Twenty-four

It was ten o'clock sharp when Marc popped his head out of his office and called along the corridor to Huey. Huey had waited patiently as advocates and secretaries hurried to and fro with bundles of files in their hands. There was a sense of well-ordered chaos about the place; everyone knew exactly what they were doing in a scene that appeared totally random to him.

"Come in, Huey," Marc said. He stood back and extended his right arm to guide and welcome Huey into his office.

"I'm sorry I kept you waiting."

"Not at all," Huey objected. "It is exactly ten o'clock."

Marc smiled. Huey knew that Marc took pride on his punctuality in his professional life and that he had known all along that it was precisely ten.

Marc's office was a corner room, not as grand as some of the other rooms that Huey had glimpsed as doors had opened and closed but it had a grand first floor view onto the Champs Élysées. Marc was a junior associate in the firm, but it was a highly prestigious firm and Marc knew he was in a privileged position.

"Come in, sit yourself down." Marc pushed a button on his desk. In seconds the door opened and in walked a young secretary with a tray of coffee and pastries. Looking at the secretary Huey immediately knew that she would become one of Marc's conquests, if she wasn't one already. As if Marc had guessed Huey's thoughts, he winked at him and smiled.

"Thank you, Jennifer, that will be all," he said.
"Help yourself, Huey," he added.

Huey was intrigued to find out why he was here, but he knew Marc was enjoying showing off his status and he did not begrudge him. "So, Huey," Marc began, "You'll be wondering why I asked you to come here this morning."

"Absolutely," Huey concurred. "Although, if it's just for the coffee and pastries, I'm not complaining."

"They're good, aren't they," Marc commented. "But, no, that's not why you are here." Marc paused and looked at his watch. "Fine," he mumbled to himself. Huey guessed that something had been timed.

"I've arranged for someone to come and meet you. He's due here at 10.30. So, we've just time to finish these and let Jennifer clear things away. There's one thing," he added, "that's bothering me."

"Oh?" Huey said. "What's that?"

"You're not wearing your beret."

Huey smiled and raised a finger signifying, "Hold on." He reached into his coat pocket and pulled out the beret. "I thought it only proper to take it off indoors."

Marc pushed his button for Jennifer and had the tray cleared away. At the stroke of ten-thirty he went to his office door, opened it. "Ah, Allan, please come in."

Huey stood as Marc followed his new guest in. He was a short squat man, about forty years old. He had a square face, which was topped with a riot of black curls. He looked immensely powerful from his barrel chest to his tree trunk legs. His expensive suit fought a battle to contain his physique and he walked in an upright stance with the confidence of a successful man. Without introduction he walked over to Huey with his hand offered in friendship.

"You must be Monsieur Tate," he said as he gripped Huey's hand in his and shook it vigorously.

"My pleasure, I'm sure," Huey responded.

"Huey," Marc interceded, "This is Allan Gachot. Allan and I go back a long way. He carried arms against the Nazis. Allan, Huey was with us when we stormed the Carlingue." Allan smiled at Huey and nodded his appreciation.

He raised his palm signalling to Marc. "We don't need to talk of those days. We had our fill of them at the time. I'm more interested in today and tomorrow." Marc nudged Huey. "You wouldn't know it to look at him but Allan is a student of philosophy."

"Now, now Marc, don't exaggerate. You will embarrass me."

"Anyway Huey," Marc continued, "Allan is here to talk to you about work. I'm going to leave you both to it, while I go and prepare for a meeting with a judge I am seeing this afternoon." He looked at his watch. "We said forty minutes, Allan. I'll be back in at 11.30." With that he left and Huey looked at Allan Gachot with absolutely no clue as to what was about to happen.

Twenty-five

Allan Gachot had offered Huey the chance of a career with the Renault motor company. Huey had been shocked. His best hope had been for something like street cleaning or tram driving to tide him over until he could discover something better. Here was a brilliant opportunity coming right at him first off. According to Allan, Marc had extolled Huey's prowess as a motor engineer.

"I know Marc well," Allan had said, "He has many faults, but I never considered exaggeration to be one of them. So, let's sit down and, for the next forty minutes, I'm going to listen to you telling me everything you know about engines."

Huey began tentatively to recount his wartime training and subsequent experiences in engineering. He warmed to Allan as he saw recognition of the many technical details he went into, reflected in his face. From aeroplanes to tanks, motor-bikes and jeeps, Huey catalogued his expertise and was encouraged as Allan nodded in agreement with much of what he said.

"We are developing new models and exciting engine innovations," Allan reported as Huey came to the end of his working history. "We foresee the day coming when mass car ownership will be the norm. We are planning to build a brand-new factory in Flins and moving to an automated assembly line production system. It's time we caught up with you Americans. You obviously have skills that we need. Of course, you will need re-training to apply your knowledge to the humble domestic motor car, but I cannot see any problem for you with that."

"I'm overwhelmed, Monsieur Gachot."

"Don't be. Marc was right. He sang your praises but did not stretch the truth. If you are interested in this offer of employment you will need to come to our head office tomorrow morning," he added as he handed Huey a business card. "The address is on there and that is my direct telephone number. Shall we say nine-fifteen?"

"For sure. I will be there. And thank you Monsieur. I can't tell you how much this means to me."

Gachot dismissed him with a self-deprecating wave of his hand. "I'm sure the benefits will be mutual. And you can forget the Monsieur Gachot. Call me Allan from now on."

It was the weekend following Huey's meeting at Renault head office. He had spent four hours in Gachot's company going through every detail of the role they wanted Huey to develop when the Flins factory opened. By the end of the day he had a signed contract, a secure pay deal, a starting date and an introductory four month training course to look forward to. Huey had immediately called Marc and invited him and Clara out to dinner as a thank you from him for the recommendation.

Despite the expense, Huey booked a table for three at a top restaurant halfway along the Champs Élysées. Huey arrived first and was led through to the table that had been prepared for them. He was surprised when Marc and Clara turned up to see that there was a third person with them. Marc immediately called a waiter over and instructed him to find a more suitable table to accommodate the four of them. Huey was aware that Marc had taken control of the situation away from him but, it was how Marc liked to operate and, to be fair, he was responsible for the reason they were celebrating. So, instead of Huey welcoming Marc and Clara to his table, Marc welcomed the others to his.
Marc then took further control of proceedings by doing the introductions.

"Huey," he said, "meet Dolores. She's your surprise guest." Putting Huey on the spot he asked, feigning genuine concern, "You don't mind, do you?"

"Of course not, I'm delighted to meet you," he said as they shook hands.

Dolores was an attractive woman of about twenty-five or twenty-eight years. She wore her jet-black hair long and had a habit of sweeping it back whenever it fell in front of her face, which it did at regular intervals. She had deep brown eyes and a pretty turn up to her nose. When she smiled, she exposed white teeth and her face came alive.

"I'm very pleased to meet you, Huey. Thank you for inviting me." She looked around the restaurant, wide-eyed and said, "I've never been in a restaurant as plush as this."

In the meantime, Marc was busily arranging the seating. He had Dolores sitting beside Huey who faced Marc. Clara, beside Marc, sat opposite Dolores. It became clear, as the evening progressed, that Clara had not met Dolores before. It never became totally clear how Marc knew her.

"I can see my office window from here," Marc said as they sat looking through the menu.

"Before we start," Huey said, "I want to make it quite clear that tonight is my treat."

"Not at all," interjected Marc. "This one is on me." Huey had not been prepared for Marc to say that, but he resolutely argued the point until, with Clara punching Marc's thigh and giving him a look of annoyance, Marc finally conceded. Apart from changing the wine that Huey had ordered for champagne, which he insisted he would pay for as an extra, Marc backed off and allowed Huey to relax. The sense of competition that Marc had engendered in him had irritated and frustrated Huey, but as the courses came and the conversation flowed, he put it out of his mind and began to enjoy himself. Clara wanted to know all about Huey's interview and the job he was taking up. "You must tell me what Allan was like in interview. I know him only as a bulldog resistance fighter."

"You underestimate Allan," Marc responded before Huey could speak. "He's been very successful since the war. He's a top man at Renault. They value him highly. Allan gets what he wants at Renault."

"I want to hear from Huey about how things went," Clara complained. "You don't have to answer for him."

"Come on now, Clara, we can't talk shop all night. Do you want to bore Dolores to sleep?" Marc leaned confidentially against Clara's shoulder and said, "Don't you think they make an attractive couple?"

Huey and Dolores looked at him and then at each other. They were both embarrassed. Clara felt more annoyed by this comment than she felt she had the right to. With no attempt to disguise her irritation with Marc she replied, "They are both very attractive people, so why wouldn't they make an attractive couple?" And then she added, "If they were a couple."

Marc laughed just a little too loud at this comment, seemingly unable to sense the discomfort around the table. "Well," he went on, "the night is young. Who knows what will transpire?"

The conversation wilted for a while as the main course plates were cleared away and they waited for desserts to arrive. When it resumed Marc talked about the work his firm was doing in tracking ex-collaborators and Dolores was given time to talk about her childhood in Basel, Switzerland, where her parents had fled to from Lens after the invasion, because her mother was Jewish. This initiated some recollections from the war including Clara's recounting of the fate that had befallen the Beck family. After Huey had spoken a little about life growing up in Alabama and how he worried for his family still living there, Marc became keen to hear about the Tate family and their Alabama existence. It wasn't long however, before the conversation inevitably turned to music. A little time was spent speculating on the theories surrounding the death of Glenn Miller and the disappearance of the plane. It was several years since the tragedy, but it still prompted public discussion, especially amongst musicians.

"It had to be the Luftwaffe," said Marc. "The Nazis despised American music and they would have been determined to prevent a morale boosting concert by Miller and his band in Paris and on the radio."

"I've heard a theory that the British did it so that they could blame the Germans for an atrocity," said Dolores.

"I can't believe the British would risk that. If it got out that they had assassinated America's favourite band leader it could have shattered the alliance."

"It was lost in the fog is probably the simple but true explanation," Clara said. Marc suddenly stopped the conversation by a sharp gesture with his hands across the table. They turned and followed his gaze across the restaurant to the entrance. A kerfuffle at the door announced the entrance of a small party of six. Entering first and leading the party across the room was Jacques Moreau, one-time senior officer of the Carlingue and now Deputy for Nantes in the Assemblée Nationale.

Clara turned a deep shade of red and, before Marc could do or say anything, she reached a restraining hand onto his forearm and pleaded, "Marc, please, don't!" Marc looked at her, in two minds about how to react.

"But why?" he asked.

"You know why. Please. Just don't." With great reluctance, Marc resumed his seat from the half-raised position he had assumed.

"These people need to know that they are living on borrowed time."

With a hint of exasperation Clara just said, "For me."

The foursome finished their desserts and, at Marc's suggestion, they decided to move onto a café where they knew there would be music and they could take coffee there. Huey knew that something unmentionable had crept into the atmosphere and decided to let Marc have his way, as he always did. He settled up with the waiter and followed the others out onto the boulevard. As they waited for a taxi Marc excused himself and ducked back inside the restaurant. He walked straight over to Moreau's table, picked up a glass of red wine and tipped it over Moreau's head. When Moreau tried to get up from his chair he shoved him back into it. Shouting across the restaurant he announced, "This man is a fascist supporter of Nazism. He is a murderer and a collaborator. We will bring him to justice." As he walked away, he deliberately barged his hip against the table so that most of the drinks were overturned.

"Where have you been?" Clara asked when he re-joined them on the street.

"Having fun," he replied.

His sardonic expression told her he had been provoking Moreau. "You are a fool, Marc. You know Moreau will resent being humiliated. He will look for some kind of revenge. This will only bring trouble."

"Stop being over dramatic, Clara. What happened to your sense of fun? Now where's that taxi?"

Twenty-six

Paris, December 1946

There were several more occasions when Marc, Clara and Huey arranged to meet up outside of band commitments. Each time Marc arranged for a different female to turn up and partner Huey. Clara always made her annoyance obvious. She had no intention of allowing Huey to form an attachment with someone else. Since the night of the attack on the riverside she had known her feelings and they had not changed. No matter how many times Huey or Clara told Marc that he didn't need a matchmaker, Marc persisted. In the end it was the woman they felt sorry for. Most of them were very nice and some of them were obviously interested in Huey. But unfortunately for them, Huey had no interest in forming a relationship. For Marc, it became a bit of a game. He seemed to think that the embarrassment it caused was all part of the fun.

Huey was due to play his last engagement with Les Libres at Le Sous Sol before going away for his four months training course with Renault. It was Friday night in the middle of December and the club was packed to the rafters. After a blistering set the band took a short break. As he always did, Marc used this time to mingle amongst the revellers and, as usual he lighted upon a beautiful young woman and began to charm her. Huey was sitting at the bar with Clara. He caught her stealing a look as Marc led the girl down towards the dressing rooms. He touched her elbow. "Why do you put up with him?" he asked.

She turned and faced him and said in a confrontational manner, "I don't know Huey. Why do you think I put up with him?"

Huey felt shocked and, implausibly, under attack.

He had no answer for her. Instead, he climbed off his bar stool and went straight to the dressing rooms. Clara raised her eyes to the heavens and smiled a faint, hapless smile to herself.

Huey pushed his way into the dressing room and stood above Marc and his conquest where they lay entangled on a couch.

"For Chrissakes, Marc. Don't you have any respect for anything or anyone?" With a complete absence of embarrassment, Marc disentangled himself, stood up and, taking Huey by the arm, walked him out of the room.

"Do yourself a favour, Huey. Go and tune your guitar and keep your nose out of my business." With that he went back inside and slammed the door.

As Huey approached Clara back at the bar, she got up and went back to her position on the stage ready for the second half.

Twenty-seven

Spring 1947

Four months seemed a lifetime as Huey stepped aboard a southbound train heading for his training and development course. It was close to Montpellier and linked to the university there. It would have been one of the happiest periods of his life if not for one thing – the absence of Clara.

Once he had settled into his accommodation on the university campus, he told himself to be sensible. Clara belonged to Marc. No matter how badly he treated her she seemed attached to him and unlikely to leave him. Their shared history was an unbreakable bond between them. In all other aspects of their life together Marc would be considered a good husband – except that he had never asked her to marry him. His personality was controlling but how many men were so different? His liaisons with other women were not an uncommon aspect of French life. The difference with Marc was that he was so blatant about it. He made no effort to save Clara the humiliation of seeing him pursuing other women. But maybe French women could put up with that. Clara certainly seemed to, even though Huey could tell it made her deeply unhappy.

Huey's time was divided between lectures on engineering at the university, where he sat alongside young, hope-filled students, and practical work with engines and assembly techniques alongside Allan at the Renault development centre nearby. His age and skin colour separated him out from his fellow students, all of whom were male except one. Hamia was a French citizen from Algeria and as such was an outsider, like Huey. She was one of the first students to take her lunch tray and sit beside Huey in the refectory. Hamia was obviously the top student in the year. As

153

a woman, she had to be. There was no other way she would have been accepted into the course. In tutorials, when the students were given problems to solve, Hamia would often partner Huey and he saw first-hand how lively and flexible her engineering intelligence was. He felt he learned as much from her as he did from the lecturers.

On off-weekends and off-days Huey would catch the local train, along with some other students and head south to the nearest beach. The springtime waters of the Mediterranean were a bit too chilly for Huey but he learned to get in quickly before his classmates dragged him under. As a Muslim woman Hamia would not join them. Huey thought that was a shame. With her knowledge of physics she could probably invent a world-beating swimming stroke.

Every other weekend Huey went back to his Paris apartment. He told friends it was to check that everything was fine there and to pay his rent. But he knew the main reason was in the hope of seeing Clara and getting to sit in with Les Libres.

One Friday in late April, Huey skipped his last lecture and caught the Paris train to get him into the capital before ten at night. Marc had sent him a telegram to ask if he could be back in time to sharpen up on several tunes because the band had been offered a booking at Le Ciel, a well established night club which had re-opened recently after the Nazis had shut it down during the occupation. It was a venue for dancers and musicians mainly and it would be a great opportunity for Les LIbres to spread their reputation. Huey had jumped at the chance. With a promise from Hamia to share her notes with him on his return, and a nod from his Renault supervisor, he boarded the train in high spirits. A rehearsal with the band, a top booking and a chance to see Clara. It was a recipe for a perfect weekend.

By the time he got to the rehearsal the band were already in full swing. They were working on Cruising Down the River, a new song from America that had swept into the Billboard Top Ten and become popular worldwide. Marc also wanted to adapt Burying Ground by Muddy Waters, for the band to make it more upbeat for dancing. It was a great number for Huey because the lead guitar was his to improvise on. It was after two in the morning when Marc called a halt to things.

"Okay, guys," he said. "Well done. We've got those new ones as good as they're going to get. Time to get home for some sleep. We'll meet up at Le Ciel at 7.30 tomorrow evening. Don't be late."

After an early start from Montpellier, a long train ride and an intense rehearsal, Huey was tired. However, he was looking forward most of all to catching a few minutes with Clara. He hurried to pack up his gear but by the time he was ready Marc and Clara had gone. She hadn't spoken one word to him. His disappointment was immense. Some of the other guys in the band came and chatted to him but he was hardly listening. People drifted away, home to their beds and Huey walked the three miles or so back to his apartment wondering why. Why had she not spoken to him the whole evening? He tried to remember if that had ever happened before. He was sure not. Most times he had been slightly embarrassed at the amount of time she wanted to spend with him. He could not fathom it and tried to put it down to the lateness of the hour. But it bothered him all night as he struggled to fall into a deep sleep.

It was a relief to get out of bed in the morning. The thoughts that had endlessly spun in his head all night long receded slightly and he could distract himself by getting ready for the concert that evening. In the cold light of day, it made more sense when he told himself that his affection for Clara was pure vanity. She and Marc were inseparable. He was a fool to harbour any thoughts of Clara. So what if she had paid him lots of attention in the past. She was a nice person, that's all.

"Get over yourself, Huey my boy," he muttered to himself. "Things are going well. Don't be greedy."

Just being in Paris on a Saturday morning was a mood lifter. He went out for breakfast as soon as he had readied himself. The streets around the apartment were beginning to bustle. The blossom was covering the cherry trees which lined the streets and Huey soaked up the scent of spring. He ate two fried eggs and toasted baguette in a nearby café and washed it down with three cups of coffee. Walking back under a faultlessly pastel blue sky he felt he had re-ordered his thinking into a more realistic frame.

At first, he didn't recognise the figure sitting halfway up the steps to his apartment was. But when he did it came as a shock.

"Clara? Is that you?"

Clara sat on the top step of the flight with her arms wrapped around her knees. The look she gave him suggested he was being deliberately dim. She stood up and went ahead of him up to the door of his apartment. He approached her and looked into her face.

"Are you going to invite me in?"

Huey unlocked the door and they went in. Clara slipped out of her mac as she walked along the hallway and went straight to the kitchen area, lit a ring and put the kettle on to boil. "I'm making coffee," she said. "Is that all right?"

"Of course it is," Huey responded, feeling a guest in his own home. "I'll do that if you want."

"No need. I can manage."

When the coffee was made and they were seated facing one another Clara looked at him and said, "When you were in Alabama did you get my letters?"

"You know I did. I wrote back to every single one."

"Did you read them?"

"Of course I did," Huey replied but he began to feel uncomfortable.

"What did you think of them?"

"I'm not sure what you mean."

"What was I saying to you?" Clara was looking fiercely at Huey and he was crumbling under the intensity. He gulped his coffee.

"What about Marc?" he muttered after an interminable silence.

"Never mind Marc. What did you think my letters meant?"

"Well..." Clara cracked a tiny smile as she watched Huey squirm.

"I guess I got the feeling you liked me."

"And what did you write in return?"

Huey's embarrassment was obvious.

"I'll tell you what you wrote – about the weather and the food and the creatures and walks you did and oh well anything you could think of to not respond to me."

Huey placed his mug on the table beside him. "But Clara, you're living with Marc. Marc has been a good friend to me. I couldn't. It wouldn't have been right."

Clara stood up, walked across to the large bay window and looked down on the street. She turned sharply and with finality said, "I'm leaving him."

She walked back to her seat and faced Huey. "Well?" she asked.

"I don't know what to say. Have you told him?"

"No. If I knew where he was I would. But he'll crawl back in later and I'll tell him then."

"And what will you do then? Will he move out?"

"Oh no. It's his apartment. I'll be the one moving out." She paused and gave Huey an inquisitive look which asked – 'are you being deliberately slow?' She then added, "That's up to you."

He stood up, all reticence vanished. He knew she was deadly serious. He reached down and pulled her upwards into his arms. They kissed. "I'll come with you," he whispered.

"No, I don't want you to," she insisted. "I'm not a child, I can do this myself." She pulled away from him and folded her arms. "When I have finished……..," she paused and walked over to the kitchen with the empty coffee mugs, "When I have finished, shall I come here?"

"Of course. You must. I can't believe this is happening. It's what I had dared not to dream. Clara, I love you."

They fell into each other's arms and kissed passionately. It was Clara who pulled away first. "I'm going back to pack my things. I will wait until he returns and tell him then. He will be back fairly soon because he will want a sleep before we go to the club tonight."

"How will he take it?"

"He will be furious, but I don't care. His philandering isn't the reason I'm leaving him. You are the reason I'm leaving him. I love you and I want to be with you for the rest of my life."

Clara picked up her mac from the hallway floor and left the apartment without looking back.

Twenty-eight

When Huey and Clara walked into Le Ciel together at 7.30 that evening, Marc was already there. He was sitting on the edge of the stage smoking a cigarette. He glared at Huey when he saw them, stood up and walked off behind the stage to the dressing room area.

"Take no notice of him," Clara said. "He's just in a big boy sulk."

Huey got himself set up on stage and tuned his guitar. The other guys wandered in and did likewise. They nodded at each other and said the occasional 'bonsoir' but for the most part they concentrated on their instruments and their placement on stage. Clara went backstage to change into her dress. Huey looked worryingly after her knowing that Marc was back there but he knew he couldn't start off their relationship by following her everywhere she went.

Clara pushed the stiff dressing room door open and went in. Marc was sitting in front of a mirror combing back his thick black hair. Clara began to take her stage dress out of its covers.

"You won't be needing that," Marc said.

"What do you mean?" Clara asked him.

"There's been a change to the song list."

"Oh, I see. You mean you've changed the song list."

Marc swung round in his seat to look at her directly. "That's right. I've changed the song list. You won't be needed tonight."

Clara slumped in exasperation. "Marc, you don't have to be so petty. What about all the rehearsing we did yesterday? The boys will want to know why we wasted our time."

"Well, you should be glad that's not your problem," he replied, getting up and pushing past her to leave. At the door he turned and put his face close to hers.

"I am an artist, Clara," he hissed through barely controlled fury. "How do you expect me to perform with you beside me when I know you have betrayed me?"

Clara laughed a dry humourless laugh. "I betrayed you? Marc, you are delusional." She studied his face. "You really do believe what you're saying, don't you? You are a very sad man, Marc. And do you know what? You have convinced me that I have made the right decision."

"I love you, Clara. I've loved you since we met. The dangers we shared only strengthened that love."

I'm sure you do, Marc. In your own way. There are lots of men like you. The trouble is, for you, love is not about 'how much', it's all about 'how many'. Huey is different. I've found a man who knows how to love properly."

"I'm happy for you," he replied sarcastically. "And now you can take yourself off to your new boyfriend's place because you are not needed here."

"I suppose you will be kicking Huey out as well. Be careful the band members don't turn on you. They might decide to kick you out."

Marc hesitated, as if contemplating his reply, but then he just flung the door open and disappeared.

On stage, Marc handed out sheets of paper to the band members. They contained the new set list. Huey scanned the sheet with dawning realisation. His best numbers had been omitted. So here was Marc's petty revenge. One or two of the others looked puzzled and approached Marc with a question or two. He shooed them away saying that he had agreed the list with the proprietor. Huey received a few sympathetic looks from the others, but nobody felt like challenging Marc.

Huey left the stage and went to look for Clara. He knocked on the dressing room door, expecting her to be getting into her stage dress. She opened it.

"You're not getting ready. What's the hold up?"

"He doesn't want me. He's changed the list. I won't be singing tonight."

Huey threw his head back in disbelief. "You are kidding. No-one is that petty."

Clara offered him a rueful smile. "You thought you knew Marc."

"I'll go and talk to him. He will see sense. He's not that vindictive."

Clara took his arm and pulled him back. "Leave it, she said. "I'm not concerned. I don't mind missing one night's singing."

"I'll pull out too. He can't be allowed to get away with this. For his own sake. He's going to look stupid in front of the other guys."

"No, you'll do no such thing. You play your guitar and enjoy the evening. I'm going to sit on the front row and watch every move he makes. I'll be watching you too. He thinks I'm going to slink off home. Well, let's see how he likes to be scrutinised. I'll be looking for every mistake he makes."

It was a low-key evening. Marc's mood spread to the band and the music was uninspired. It left the proprietor lukewarm about re-booking them, which made Marc's mood worsen. Huey was first to get his gear together and went over to Clara. As they headed for the door together, Louis the drummer joked, "Hey Marc, Huey is stealing your girl." The guys laughed, thinking it an innocent jibe. Marc lost his

162

temper. He rushed Louis and pushed him over his drum kit. Louis was a big man and didn't take kindly to Marc's attack. If the rest of the band hadn't come between them someone would have been badly hurt. Huey dashed back to help out and found himself grappling with Marc, helping to keep the two men apart. As the situation gradually calmed down and both men stopped trying to lunge at each other, the others loosened their grips on the combatants. Out of nowhere, Marc suddenly threw a punch at Huey. It caught him on the temple and made him stumble. The others rushed to grab Marc as he moved in to land another blow. Huey straightened himself and said, "Let him go."

The men stood back as Marc rushed at Huey. Huey took up a crouched stance and after dodging Marc's wild swing he threw a left uppercut to Marc's chin. Marc went down. He remained in a half-sitting position as Huey stood over him. Marc groaned and rubbed his chin. He poked around in his mouth with his tongue.

"You bastard," he hissed. "You've broken a tooth."

"You're lucky that's all he broke," Louis jeered. "If I'd got near you I'd have broken your arms."

Huey reached down a hand to help Marc to his feet. Marc rejected the help and pushed himself upright. He shoved his way through to the stage and began to tidy away his instrument and accessories. Clara walked to Huey's side and took his arm. He picked up his guitar case and they walked out.

After the adrenalin had diluted itself Huey and Clara found themselves laughing at the farcical nature of the scene in the club.

"It was lucky the crowd had gone home. If they'd stayed, they might have expected an encore like that every night."

"I felt sorry for Marc after I had hit him. He looked almost vulnerable squatting on the floor."

"Don't worry about Marc. His ego will absorb that blow. He'll have convinced himself that you caught him unfairly."

"I hope it doesn't end our friendship. He has been good to me since I arrived in France. And I am in his debt for the job with Renault. What about while I am back in Montpelier? Will you be all right? He won't come around taking it out on you, will he?"

"Huey, I'm a big girl. I can look after myself. Anyway, I know Marc. He's incapable of holding a grudge. It's a pleasant side to his nature, but it's also a flaw in his personality. I think it's because he can't take anything seriously. Life's a bit of a game to Marc. It's how he survived the war. Sometimes I almost believed he had no feelings. But then he was so loyal I couldn't quite get those two things to marry."

"He certainly is a complicated character. But I suppose the war messed with most of us."

"The war was good for Marc. It gave him a focus and a passion. He achieved a kind of star status after the war when pamphlets were published about the role of the Resistance. Many writers built him up as a major hero. He acquired a modicum of fame and women found that attractive. He was the least likely person to resist the approaches of women who found his celebrity exciting. I've no doubt that he would have stayed with me for life out of loyalty but he would never have been faithful. I wanted something better than that."

It wasn't immediately apparent to the band members but when they looked back on that night, they could see that it marked the beginning of the end for Les Libres. They played a few more gigs but the connection they had had was missing. Louis was the first to quit. He accepted an offer to play with another band. The membership dwindled until those remaining could see no point in continuing.

Twenty-nine

Clara proved to be a good judge of Marc's character. In the middle of the following week Huey was surprised to see Marc waiting for him as he walked out of the Renault training centre. Huey was feeling great after a day underneath a brand-new prototype car, marvelling at the latest developments in engine efficiency. He had spent a good twenty minutes massaging his hands in clumps of the new handwash product known as Swarfega. Marc approached him with his hand outstretched in greeting and a smile on his face. They shook and then Marc wrapped his arms around Huey in a warm embrace.

"No hard feelings, buddy?"

"Of course not," Huey replied. He was relieved and happy that any bad feeling between them was forgotten. Just as Clara had said, Marc seemed incapable of holding a grudge.

Marc seemed to know Montpelier as well as Huey did. He led them along Rue Foch until they emerged into Place Martyrs de la Résistance. He pointed to a restaurant.

"Here we are," he said. "I've booked a table for dinner at nine tonight. I'll let you get off to your digs and wash the working day off. I'll meet you back here at half past eight."

Over the remaining months of Huey's stay in Montpelier Marc made repeated visits. Their friendship seemed to be cemented. They usually ate and drank too much and Marc stayed over in Huey's rooms. He always brought news of Clara.

"I bumped into Clara last Thursday. She had been to visit Jean-Paul."

"I haven't seen Jean-Paul since the very early days. He used to hang around with the band but he seems to have slipped below the radar."

"He played with the band before the war. He was a very decent trombonist. The Carlingue tortured him you know. He was captured just before the Paris uprising. He held out, didn't tell them anything. But he suffered for it. They broke his fingers, amongst other physical injuries. But worse than that they broke his spirit. He probably could have put up with the discomfort and played again after his fingers were re-set, but his heart was never in it. He's been in and out of rehabilitation centres for years. Clara has a deep connection with him. I'm surprised she's never talked about him with you."

Marc accompanied this last comment with a curious look which Huey failed to understand the significance of. But it mentally tweaked his interest. He would ask Clara about it when he next saw her.

One Sunday evening, after a glorious day on the Espiguette beach, and a tiring bus and train journey back to Montpelier, Huey was ready to shower and fall into bed. The silky sand and the satin of the sea had put Huey in a mood of divine contentment. Thinking back to his Alabama days and the struggle to survive as a black man in a white man's world, he could never have contemplated then that his life could turn out as it had.

No sooner had he stepped out of the shower than a knock came on his apartment door. He opened it to find the block supervisor standing there. "How can I help you?" Huey asked.

"There's a telephone call for you. It's the phone in the lobby. I left it off the hook for you." The man turned and headed down the stairs whilst Huey hurriedly jumped into his pants and a T-shirt. He ran down after the supervisor, convinced in his own mind that it was Clara. He could hardly get down the stairs quickly enough in his haste to speak to her. "Hello Clara," he said a touch breathlessly.

"Huey, hello. How did you know it was me?"

"A lucky guess."

"Have you seen yesterday's Le Figaro?"

"No. Why?"

"You need to get hold of one. Your photograph is on the front page."

"What?"

"You and Marc."

"You're kidding."

"I wish I was. It looks like it was taken during Marc's last visit to see you. It's not flattering. You are coming out of a seedy looking club."

"But why? It doesn't make sense."

"When you see the paper you'll understand. I warned Marc not to provoke Moreau."

"Moreau? What's he got to do with this?"

"He's not the sort to let Marc get away with humiliating him."

"But Clara, you haven't explained."

"Moreau addressed a right-wing congress on Friday. He made a blistering attack on foreign workers. He used you as a prime example of the sort of foreigner coming into France and stealing jobs from French men. After Marc caused that scene in the restaurant, he must have had him followed. He acquired several photographs of you both going to and from work and college and getting drunk with Marc. Le Figaro has used some of them to illustrate their reproduction of his speech. They have added an editorial accusing the government of betraying French workers by letting people like you into France to steal jobs. Renault has received a bit of a savaging too."

Huey felt his stomach sinking lower and lower as Clara went on. "What will happen?" he asked.

"Lord knows. But whatever does happen it was all unnecessary. If only Marc could control himself."

"You can't be too hard on Marc, Clara. He couldn't have known this was going to happen."

"Can't he? You don't know Marc like I do. He's a professional mischief maker. Still, you're probably right. This seems too devious even for Marc. I just wish he would think of the consequences of his actions before he jumps into something feet first."

"I suppose Renault will have seen it. I wonder what Allan will say tomorrow."

"It's what he will decide to do that matters."

"He's been very pleased with my work, so at least I can feel okay about that."

They spoke about other things, trivial things and about how much they were missing each other. "I'd better go now," Clara said finally. "Good luck tomorrow. Stick up for yourself. You've done nothing wrong. You're still the same worker you were yesterday."

"Thank you, my love. Look after yourself. I will come to Paris next weekend. Hopefully, this nightmare will be over by then."

No sooner had Huey returned to his room than the supervisor knocked once more.

"Monsieur Tate," he complained. "These stairs are not easy for a man of my age. I wish you would book your calls so that you can answer them yourself."

"Another one?"

169

"Another one. Same phone." It was Allan from Renault

"You don't make it easy for me do you, Huey?"

"I'm sorry Allan. I've only just heard."

"Don't come in tomorrow. And keep away from the college. We'll let this calm down and then hopefully we can all get back to work. These politicians flit from one thing to the next. Moreau will be on to something else in a week's time. Besides, I despise the man. He's a murderer and a traitor. If you were the worst worker in the company I wouldn't fire you on his recommendation. But there are people higher up than me who might be happy to appease him. So, lie low until I get in touch."

Huey moved out of Montpelier in a mood of depression. He told himself that he was no worse off than he had been before Marc had introduced him to Allan and Renault, but his expectations had been caused to rise so sharply that he was miserable at the loss of this opportunity. Although he trusted Allan, he could not be sure that Allan would be able to swing the board round to his side.

It was raining when he stepped out of the Gare de Lyon onto the Paris streets. It wasn't heavy but it came from a glowering, doom-laden sky which emphasised Huey's low mood. Indifferent to his increasingly dampened condition he walked the long distance back to his apartment. He was in no hurry. He felt that he was returning as a failure.

The scraping of his shoes on the stone stairs leading up to his floor could not obscure the shouts that were emerging from inside his apartment. He first recognised Clara. And then Marc. He let himself in and followed the sound of the argument. They were so engrossed in their conflict that Huey

170

was able to stand and watch them from the living room doorway for several minutes.

"You are a selfish fool," Clara yelled. Huey could tell that they were well into this argument. It had reached a high pitch of antagonism. "You knew Moreau would retaliate and you didn't care who suffered."

"You're over-reacting," Marc responded. He reached out to take Clara's elbow but she snatched it away violently.

"Don't patronise me, Marc. I know you. You think Huey is necessary collateral damage. Just like in the war when the Nazis took reprisals."

"Don't be ridiculous," Marc shouted back. "You and I were the same in the war. We did what we had to."

"You infuriate me, Marc. What is Huey going to do now? His hopes are dashed."

Marc moved closer to Clara. With his open palms he aimed to placate her. She turned her back on him and he moved to wrap his arms around her, pulling her tightly to him. Huey watched in shock and confusion. Clara shook herself free of Marc and, turning round, caught sight of Huey in the doorway.

"Huey!" she exclaimed. "You're here. Oh, thank heavens." She pushed her way past Marc and threw her arms around Huey. He held her lightly for a moment and then walked past her into the room, placing his bag beneath the window.

"What's happening here?" he asked calmly.

"I am arguing with this fool of a man," Clara hissed. "He has no thought for anyone other than himself."

Huey looked at Marc. The picture of him standing with his arms round Clara was burned on his retina. Marc shrugged. Clara's words were literally being shuffled off his duck's back. Huey was annoyed with Marc, but he had to remember that Marc had been the one to get him the position in the first place. Huey had the realisation that if he was not careful, he would let all kinds of speculations in, and they would poison his thinking. They tripped through his head as he tried to dismiss them. Had Marc fixed him up with Renault to get him out of the way? Why was he here with Clara now? Does Clara allow him to embrace her in the way he had just witnessed?

"What are you doing here, Marc?"

"I came because Clara called me and accused me of every crime under the sun. I wanted to calm her down and explain things to her." He paused and moved across to Huey.

"Anyway, is this how you greet an old comrade. Come here. Let me embrace you." The men stood in a comradely embrace as Clara stared in disbelief.

"Explain what?"

"Pardon?"

"You said you came here to explain things to Clara. What did you mean?"

"I wanted to tell her that you would be all right with Renault. Apart from Allan Gachot, who will fight to keep Huey, we have plenty of leverage we can use."

"What do you mean?"

"Look, shall we sit down. Clara, get us all a drink and I will explain in full."

Exhibiting her extreme exasperation at Marc's presumption that he can take charge and dish out the instructions Clara, nevertheless, did his bidding.

"My law firm," he began, "is pursuing a long game against those we know collaborated with the Nazis. There are so many low-level collaborators that it would be impossible to prosecute them all. But people like Moreau will definitely face justice one day. We have a growing file on him, and it is my ongoing task to continue to build it. There are members of the Renault board who have war secrets they would rather leave in the dark. We have issued enough discreet messages to warn them off victimising Huey and others like him. Moreau thought he was onto a vote catcher, as well as a way of hitting back at me personally, but he's having second thoughts now that people we have been in touch with are distancing themselves from him. As far as we know he's moving on to the issue of Algeria. He'll be finding demons there to excite his voters with."

"What does that mean for Huey?" Clara asked.

"It means he will have a nice little break, and in a couple of weeks Allan will call him and he will return to Montpelier as if nothing had happened. You should be thanking me, Clara. You'll have the unexpected bonus of Huey's company with you for a short time."   Later that evening, after Marc had left, Huey and Clara sat at opposite ends of their sofa. The dishes from the meal they had shared lay around the uncleared table. Huey was reading an edition of Le Monde which was a few days old. Clara shuffled closer to him and leant her head against his shoulder.
"Huey, what's the matter?"

"What do you mean," Huey asked by way of reply without looking up from the paper.

"You hardly spoke during the meal. Are you upset? Is it Marc? Is it me?"

Huey folded the newspaper and placed it on the floor beside him. He struggled to find a way to express what was bothering him. He had never thought himself a jealous man but there was something about Marc that wound him up.

"Marc's been a good friend to me," he began.

"So, it is me, is it?" Clara interrupted.

"No, let me finish. I was saying – Marc has been a good friend to me. But there's something about you and Marc. You are so close. I sometimes feel like an interloper. Like the odd one out. Like three's a crowd and I'm number three."

There, he'd said it. As close as he could to the truth without blurting out his creeping jealousy.

Clara sat up in surprise. "I can't believe you are saying this!" she exclaimed. "I left Marc for you. He didn't throw me over, I ditched him. Why are you feeling insecure?"

Huey felt embarrassed and a bit ridiculous at this. "I don't know," he said. "Marc seems to think you are still his and it makes me wonder if he is right."

"You were upset with the way he put his arms round me. But you saw me push him off. He takes liberties like that with all women."

"Yes, I know. But he thinks you and he are special. I know he doesn't like it that we are together."

"That's the way Marc is. He manipulates; he controls. He doesn't really want me. Maybe he wants to prove to himself that he could win me back but it wouldn't make him faithful. Please Huey, this isn't like you. Doesn't that prove that it's Marc manipulating things? He's made you think in ways unnatural to you. Come here."

Clara slid onto Huey's knee and wrapped her arms around his neck. They kissed. It was the clearing of the air as much as the kiss that relaxed Huey.

"I'm sorry," he whispered. "You must think me a fool."

"No I don't. But I don't ever want you to feel insecure. If I ever intend to leave you, which I won't, but if ever I did intend to, I promise you won't have to wonder or guess or speculate. I will be the first to tell you."

That made Huey laugh softly. Clara kissed him again. She eased herself off his lap and, taking him by the hand, led him to the bedroom.

Thirty

Clara woke in her hotel bed. She reached over to touch Huey but his side was empty. She rolled into the space he had vacated and fell into the warmth he had left behind. She inhaled his former presence and smiled. With eyes closed she let her mind dwell on last night and the pleasure it had brought. Her heart fluttered as for a moment she imagined he had gone for good. What if he didn't return? Where, in fact, was he? She sat up and looked around the tiny room. There was no written message on the bedside table. Huey had obviously dressed himself in the clothes she had relieved him of last night. His shoes were gone. But there was his canvas bag with his spare items and toiletries. She lay back again and luxuriated in the warmth that only the 'in-love' feel. Why the moment of insecurity? she wondered. Was this love so precious that she would live in constant fear of losing it? She had returned from the bathroom along the hall and was dressed and drying her hair when Huey came in. He leaned over her and kissed her lips. Every time he kissed her it was like the first time. She wondered if she would ever get over the intense thrill of it. Would she always be as helpless as this?

"Hey, sleepyhead, what time do you call this," he whispered into her ear.

She turned over and tasted his sweet breath. "You were up early. Where have you been?"

"I've been to the town hall; sorry – hotel de ville. I've confirmed our time with the deputy mayor. He will be conducting the ceremony. I took all the necessary papers with me and everything is ready for 12 noon. Do you think you'll be ready by then? Or are you having second thoughts?"

Her only answer was to stand and kiss him. "Hey, hey, slow down," Huey laughed. "If you get started on that we'll miss our slot."

Clara chuckled. "Okay, but don't think you're going to escape. I'll get you later."

"I'll make sure you do. Come on, we've time for breakfast before they close the kitchen." They had come to Evreux the previous afternoon. It had been a pleasant two-hour train ride just about a hundred kilometres west of Paris. Apart from a short walk to a nearby restaurant the previous evening they had seen little of the town.

"Come on babe. It's a lovely day out there," Huey said when they had finished eating. "We mustn't waste it sitting around here. It's only a ten-minute walk to the town hall. There's a lovely riverside route that will take us there."

The mid-July weather was in sympathy with them. A kindly but insistent breeze was moving the tiny clouds across the sky. But the sun was becoming hotter and fiercer the higher it climbed. They walked between the lines of maple trees that bordered the riverside path. Bursts of sunlight sparkled on the surface of the river and flickered through the whispering leaves. The couple attracted lots of attention. Huey in his suit, with his white carnation buttonhole. And Clara in her plain, white, knee-length dress, with bouquet in hand. They were obviously on their way to their wedding. The strangers' reactions varied from the puzzled to the delighted with a small sprinkling of distaste. Nothing more than Huey expected. Clara was too excited to notice anything.

"I'd have preferred the purple carnation," Huey had complained. "It perfectly matches the silvery-grey of my suit."

"Don't be ridiculous," Clara had laughed. Don't you know a purple carnation symbolises capriciousness."

"How can that be? It's just a flower"

"Nevertheless, that's what it means."

"Well, what about the white?"

"Pure love and good luck."

He stared at her in disbelief. She laughed at him.

"Are you sure this is how you want it?" Huey asked.

"You mean, the wedding?"

"Yes. Wouldn't you have preferred guests and a nuptial breakfast. All your friends gathered and your mama smiling, proud of her daughter. Should I have invited Marc?"

Clara froze. "You haven't, have you?"

"No. I was just asking if you would have preferred a grand traditional wedding." Clara sighed with relief. "Thank God. If you had invited Marc, I would have left you standing at the altar."

"Oh, come on. He's not that bad."

"You don't know him. No. In answer to your first question, I wouldn't prefer a grand traditional wedding. This is exactly how I want it."

They turned off the riverside path and crossed the boulevard towards the town hall. The alleyway they were walking along was narrow and ahead of them, going at a snail's pace, was an elderly couple, whom they could not pass. They were probably in their mid to late eighties. They walked along hand in hand, with the woman leaning her head against his shoulder. From time to time they stopped, unaware of Huey and Clara and kissed. Huey and Clara shared a glance. Their expressions seemed to say, 'Ah, how sweet.'

The old man heard them as they came up close behind and he stopped his wife and stepped behind her. "Let these young people pass," he said. She stopped too and they both smiled at Huey and Clara. Close to, Huey could see that the man was about five-five tall and his wife came to his shoulder. She had a lined, but pretty face. Age had pinched it but the bone structure was still there. She wore an ankle length summer skirt and a cotton jacket, both of which covered her slender figure. She obviously didn't feel the heat of the day to the extent that Huey did. Her husband had a full crop of white hair that covered his large head. Sun-damaged blotches were dotted around his face and his thick framed glasses gave him the appearance of extreme seriousness. His smiling comment immediately dissolved that impression.

"Ah! The lovebirds. Let them through my sweet. They must be on their way to the hotel-de-ville for their nuptials."

"You are exactly right," Huey laughed. He looked at Clara, as if trying to decide something. Without speaking to her, he turned to the couple and asked, "Would you like to come with us?"

Clara's initial surprise was dissipated when it dawned on her what he was asking. The couple looked at each other not sure how to respond. It was the wife who guessed first. She whispered to her husband. He smiled and nodded at her. She looked at Clara and said, "Your man wants us to come and act as witnesses. Am I right?" "Yes," Clara smiled.

There was only the slightest hesitation and then the woman replied, "Of course. We would love to."

The hotel de ville was a beautiful stone building set back from the main thoroughfare. It had expansive stone steps leading up to the main entrance of the three-story building. In front, a row of flagpoles waved the Tricolour and flags of the town, the region and the province. Beds of shrubs and summer marigolds decorated the area around the bottom of the steps.

"Oh wow!" said Huey. I've been here three times now and every time this building takes my breath away. It must have been some old aristocrat's mansion before the revolutionaries guillotined him."

"You are probably right," Clara replied.

They took the steps slowly. They were wide enough for the two couples to ascend side by side, and the wedding couple were happy to keep pace with their witnesses.

The old man turned to Huey, halfway up and said, "Look, the sun is out for you. It's a good omen."

True enough. Huey blinked a glance at the fiery ball overhead, which was by now gently cooking the town, throwing their deep shadows onto the steps in front of them. A solitary white cloud hung motionless a small distance away. With hardly a breath of wind it would not cross the sun anytime soon. "You must be a lucky man," the old man added.

Thirty-one

Paris, November 1952

Clara sent the waiter away explaining that she was waiting for a friend. When Marc came into the café, she watched him scan the room looking for her. A flurry of rain that swept in with him was silenced by the closing of the door behind him. She thought his face looked fierce. When he spotted her, he smiled briefly and then joined her. They ordered coffee and a baguette each. "How are you? Why haven't I seen you for so long?" Marc asked after the waiter had delivered their order.

The tension between them flowered spontaneously as soon as the question was asked. Marc's tone immediately made Clara's hackle's rise. There was too much propriety in it. 'He still thinks he owns me,' she thought.

"I'm very well. And you? What did you want to see me about?" she asked.

He sat back in his seat and coughed a humourless laugh. "Do I have to have a reason now? Can't I spend some time with you? Or is he jealous?"

"Don't be ridiculous. Huey is not the jealous type. Besides, he has nothing to be jealous about."

Clara played with a spoon in the sugar bowl. Marc lit a cigarette. She looked across at him, seemingly hesitant in what she was about to say. "We're married."

The shock that struck Marc froze his face. He stared at her in stunned silence. Eventually he spoke.

"You can't be." He crushed his newly lit cigarette in the ashtray. "You can't be," he repeated. His brain swam with so many conflicting ideas that the connection between it and his tongue was compromised. "You can't be. Why didn't I know?" There was no anger or officiousness in his tone. It was a desperate plea.

Clara laughed. "I'm a big girl you know. I am old enough to marry."

"I don't believe you. You can't be."

Clara was beginning to feel a little discomfort. She became accusatory. "Why?" she demanded, "Is it because he's black and I'm white."

"Don't be silly," Marc retorted, affronted.

"Well, because I'm French and he's American?"

"Now you're being ridiculous. We don't think that way. We never have."

"Are you sure?"

Marc's annoyance betrayed a tiny amount of self-doubt.

"Well," Clara continued, "It must be because you still think I belong to you."

"Why didn't I know about it? Why no invitation? What about your parents?"

"We did it without all of that fuss. We asked a man and a woman passing in the street to witness it and it was done. We didn't invite anyone, so you don't need to be insulted." She paused before going on. "You know how much I loved you. There was never going to be anyone but you for me. But you don't make me happy. I think I've grown up. I think of you as a schoolgirl crush. The war was different. We shared so many dangers. We lived on a diet of high excitement. It was thrilling and terrifying at the same time. Huey has won me. I love him now."

"I don't believe you. We meant so much to each other. We still mean so much to each other. You and I are more intimate than you can ever be with him. We've shared everything a man and woman can share. For heaven's sake, Clara, we have killed together."   Clara knew that it was pointless to try and argue with him. She dipped her buttered baguette into her coffee until it was soft enough to eat. She wondered how Marc would react to her latest news. She wasn't totally sure she would tell him today. But if not today, when?

"I'm pregnant," she stated, matter-of-factly.

Marc's coffee cup paused halfway to his mouth. "When?" he stammered. They both laughed at the stupidity of his question. "I didn't mean that," he went on. "I mean, wow! Congratulations. When's the baby due?"

He was never a good actor, thought Clara.

"I'm nearly five months. So, March or April if all goes to plan."

"Well, congratulations again. Huey must be a very proud man. How is he, by the way? I always liked him you know. Even if he did steal my girl."

"He didn't steal me. You lost me. Something happened to you during the war. You became self-obsessed. It made you the great resistance fighter you became. But it did not help your personal relationships."

"Thank you for the personality dissection. But I'll ask again, how is Huey? Is he still with Renault?"

"He's doing well. He's been in Flins since September."

"Ah! The new factory. So, his wartime experience as a mechanic has come good."

"He knows he owes a lot to you Marc. If you hadn't put him in touch with Allan Gachot none of this would have happened for him. He is very grateful to you. We both are. But, yes, his wartime mechanical experience has been vital. He's been appointed senior supervisor of the engine assembly line. He stays in Flins during the week and comes home at weekends. We're going to be moving to Flins once he has found a house good enough for three. He has been with a three-piece band there, playing jazz standards in cafes around the region. He's very happy. We are very happy."

Marc smiled. "I'm pleased for you both. I really am."

Clara reached forward and took hold of his hand. "We really are very happy, Marc. I hope you find happiness soon. The right woman is waiting to meet you."

Marc's smile was a straight line drawn on an empty page. "I found her a long time ago. I let her go." He stood to leave. "I've got a case coming to court this afternoon. A Free French veteran, an Algerian, accused of burglary. He did it but I must do my best to get him acquitted. Monsieur le Juge will be annoyed if I am late. I have to go. I hope we can keep in touch."

"Of course. Good luck."

Two weeks later.

"I saw Marc today," Huey said. He shook the rain from his coat and hung it in the hall. It had started in Flins when he had left work, had continued throughout the train journey to Paris and soaked him as he had hurried from the Gare Du Nord all the way to their apartment. Sometimes he believed it only rained on Friday evenings in France.

"Oh?" Clara mumbled. She stood to meet Huey and they hugged and kissed in the hallway. His hands came around from her back to gently caress her petite swelling. "Where did you see Marc?"

"He was in Flins for a court hearing and he came out to the factory during recess."

"What did he want?"

"Just wanted to catch up. Congratulated me on our forthcoming baby. Said he'd like to come see my band playing sometime."

184

"Come on, let's get you dry." Clara unbuttoned his shirt and tugged it from him.

"You're soaked," she complained. "Go and bathe. I'll warm up the meal. We're having beef casserole."

"My favourite," Huey called as he ran his bath. As the water poured into the bath, he came back into the living room with a towel around his waist. "How did Marc know about the baby?"

Didn't I tell you? He asked me to meet him a couple of weeks ago for coffee. I told him then."

"What did he say?"

"You know Marc. He doesn't like anything happening that he doesn't know about. He was shocked. He was just as shocked when I told him we'd married."

"Poor Marc," Huey laughed. "If he's not in control he's not living."

Thirty-two

The move to Flins had been easy to accomplish. Neither of the newly-weds owned much in the way of possessions and so the move had been completed in one trip. Like most of their contemporaries, Huey and Clara rented their house. The monthly cost was much less than they had been paying in Paris and Huey's income from the Renault factory had easily covered the cost of the basic furniture they needed to make their house a home. They decided on a terraced property on Rue Maurice Berteaux. Number 147. It stood in the middle of a network of narrow streets. The properties varied in size but Huey's and Clara's was possibly the smallest. No front garden; a front door which opened onto the street; a yard at the rear. But it was three storeys high with two adequate rooms at the top. Clara thought it was the best house in the world.

Both Paris and Flins had seen thousands of G.I.s during the liberation, many of them black. But in Flins it was harder to be anonymous. People knew each other. They knew who the strangers were. They all soon knew of the new French woman with the black American husband. Even when they didn't disapprove, they found it impossible not to stare. For Huey that was not a problem. Compared to Alabama this was freedom. For Clara it became annoying. She wanted to stare people down. She wanted to ask them what they were looking at. Huey dissuaded her with a laugh and a tug on her arm. Soon they built up a circle of friends, mostly around Huey's workmates. Clara got to know neighbours through Ana, who was now almost two months old. Women stopped Clara in order to look at Ana and stroke her cheeks. They struck up conversations with her whilst they cooed at Ana in her pram. Soon people had warmed to the couple and their new baby.

They became a feature of the town that people mentioned to visiting relatives or friends. When Clara pushed Ana round to the boulangerie for croissants or the charcuterie for the evening dinner, she could be out for a long time.

Thirty-three

Flins, May 1954

Huey stood at the door to the shower room. He could see Clara soaping her body under the spray. He was still in awe of her beauty. She sensed his presence and turned. She could not resist raising her arms above her head and striking a provocative pose. Huey laughed. "Hey, come on, "he said. "we've no time for that. They will be here soon."

He went into Ana's bedroom and spent ten minutes talking to her in English. His French was fluent by this time but he was keen for Ana to have both languages. He told her a Brer Rabbit tale that his Mama had often told to him. The one where Brer Rabbit fooled his friends into filling his pond for him while he watched them do all the work. "Brer Rabbit is clever, isn't he," Ana said.

"He sure is."

"Papa," she enquired tentatively, "Is he a bit naughty as well?"

"Well, maybe just a little bit. But he never harms anyone, so I suppose it's all right." He folded the blanket around her, kissed her and whispered goodnight. Just under an hour later Huey answered the buzz at the door and opened it to welcome Marc and Felicité, Marc's new partner. Felicité was carrying a large bouquet of flowers and Marc held two bottles of champagne.

"Come in," Huey said. Felicité stepped in and stood on tip-toes to kiss Huey in greeting. Marc pushed one of the bottles under his left arm and shook hands with Huey.

"Something smells good, "Marc said. "Who's been cooking?"

"Not me," admitted Huey. "We've got Clara to thank for tonight's fare."

Over a starter of garlic escargots and battered mushrooms they chatted generally about the state of France. There was still some rancour from both Clara and Marc about the post-war treatment of the Resistance fighters.

"They have air-brushed us out of the narrative," Clara complained. "I don't want a medal or my picture in the newspaper but I would like the true story to be told."

"I thought that you were awarded pensions?" Felicité ventured.

"Don't start me on that," Clara laughed. "That's an insult.

"I don't understand," Felicité said.

Marc chimed in laughing. "It's Clara's ultimate bugbear. You shouldn't have brought it up."

"Someone please explain?"

"It's all right for Marc to laugh. His pockets are swollen." Clara turned to Felicité. "I get half of the amount he gets. Because I'm a woman."

"What?" she squealed. "That's absurd. No, it's not absurd, it's obscene. Is that President Coty's doing?"

"No," Marc jumped in, "It was President Auriol's work. Straight after the war."

Felicité was several years younger than the rest. She had been a child during most of the war and evacuated to Vichy. The ex-combatants soon steered the conversation onto other subjects. It was Marc who led the conversation.

"Any news from home, Huey?"

Huey paused his fork on its way to his mouth. "I had a letter about 4 months back. Everything seemed okay."

"What does okay mean for your mother and your sisters?"

Clara gave Marc a searching look, not sure where he

189

was taking this.

"Well, you know," Huey grimaced. "Alabama is Alabama. It sure ain't Paris."

"I've been reading some American newspapers. There's been a judgement made by the Supreme Court. Have you heard of this man, Oliver Brown?"

"Of course," Huey replied.

"Well, the case he brought in 1951 against the Board of Education in Topeko, Kansas has just resulted in a judgement. Apparently, your constitution has a Fourteenth Amendment and that has won his case for him. It's over three years late, maybe, but it's a big win for your people, I think."

"What do you mean, his people?" Clara bridled. "We're his people."

"Yes, I know that," Marc conceded, "But Huey knows what I mean."

The conversation paused for a moment or two. Huey was feeling uncomfortable and he couldn't figure out why. Marc wasn't saying anything he didn't know but he somehow felt he was being made to feel different. It was a feeling he'd rarely been affected by in France. People here tended to think of him as 'the American', not as 'the black'.

Marc picked up the conversation again as they began their main course of beef bourguignon. "Is Alabama far from Kansas?"

"Oh, I don't know," Huey replied, "Maybe as far as from here to Poland – give or take."

"Are the circumstances similar? For the black people, mean?"

"I guess so. Jim Crow laws apply all over the South."

Felicité looked up. "Jim Crow? Who is this Jim Crow?"

"Oh, Felicité," Huey sighed. "The term is used to describe the segregation laws that were enacted after the slaves were freed by Lincoln. They were supposed to keep the blacks and whites apart but equal."

"That's the crucial point," Marc interjected. "That's how Brown won. The Supreme Court ruled that the law dictating separate schools for blacks and whites are unconstitutional because the schools are demonstrably not equal."

"But I want to know who Jim Crow is," Felicité complained.

"Oh, for heaven's sake, Felicité, Marc jibed. "Do you have to be so irritating?"

His tone was so dismissive that Felicité was visibly hurt by it. She wiped her mouth with her napkin to hide her embarrassment.

"Okay," Huey said to break the atmosphere that had sprung from nowhere. "He was a character invented by a theatrical performer in the nineteenth century. This man, whose name was Thomas D Rice, used to black up his face and dress up like a farm nigger. He would dance and sing and fool around and talk like an ignorant halfwit. The whites loved him. They believed all negroes were like that. It made them feel better about keeping them as slaves. When the slaves were freed, they decided down south that they couldn't have no Jim Crows voting or getting educated so they brought in the segregation laws. Separate schools, separate churches, separate benches in the parks, separate parks sometimes. And, most important of all, no mixed marriages. Clara and I would be criminals in Alabama and the rest of the south."

"That can't be true," Marc said leaning forward to place his elbows on the table.

"Oh my God," Felicité groaned. "What is the matter with America?"

Huey sat back and drained his wine glass. "Now you know why I decided to live in France."

Marc drained his glass too, looked from Huey to Clara and shook his head as if in disbelief. During the rest of the meal the talk ranged over Ana; work; one of Marc's cases; Felicité's parents who lived in French Indo-China. As Clara and Huey got up to clear the dishes, Clara said, "And now, no more depressing talk. Let's move into the living room. I'll bring coffee and cheese through. We can share some music."

Soon the air was thick with smoke and they sang some Billie Holliday songs to Huey's guitar playing. Marc and Clara's harmonies were just as good as in the old days. Huey could not help but admire them. It was after midnight when Clara noticed that Felicité was falling asleep. They brought the night to a close. Huey took the tray of coffee cups out to the kitchen whilst Marc followed Clara into the hall to collect the coats. He slipped his arms around her waist from behind and whispered into her ear, "It's been so lovely to see you."

Clara pulled herself sharply away and turned to face him. "What are you doing?" she hissed. "You have no right."

Marc held up his hands. "I'm sorry," he grinned. "Just an affectionate embrace between two comrades-in-arms."

"Don't be cheeky," Clara snapped and dumped the coats into his arms. She hurried off into the kitchen.

"Huey, darling," she shouted. "Come and say goodbye. Marc and Felicité are leaving."

They all came through to the hall. Huey opened the front door as they slipped into their coats.

"Thank you for a wonderful evening," Felicité said over tired eyes.

Marc and Huey walked out to Marc's car. Clara hugged Felicité and whispered, "Are you alright?"

Felicité produced a smile that was half grimace. "I'm fine," she said. "He always treats me like a child. I'm having to get used to it."

Clara thought of a thousand things she could say to advise Felicité but she held her peace.

"Yes," Marc was saying to Huey. "She's a great little motor. I think she was built before your time at Renault. Anyway, she keeps going. So, thank you. It's been a wonderful evening." He pushed his hat to the back of his head and said to Huey as a parting comment, "I hope your family remain safe. Good night. Come on, birdbrain," he called to Felicité as he held the passenger door open for her. She raised her eyes at Clara before scooting lightly down the path. With a wave from Marc they were gone.

A little later, as Huey stood at the sink and Clara took the washed dishes from him to dry and put away, she asked, "Are you all right, my love?"

Huey didn't answer immediately. He stopped swirling the water over the dishes and stood deep in thought. "Yeah. I'm fine. It's just....."

"What? Is it what Marc has been saying?"

"Well no, not entirely. Then again, yes to some extent. But I do worry sometimes about Mama and my sisters."

Huey dried his hands on a towel and came up behind Clara who was leaning into a cupboard, putting away some dishes. He reached his arms around her and caressed her breasts. She stood upright and leaned backwards, her head nestling into the crook of his neck. She strained her head around and their mouths met. She laid her hands on top of his and guided them under her blouse. Reaching behind her back she unhooked her bra, allowing his hands to reach inside and cup her naked breasts. Still with her back to him she reached behind her and began to tug at his belt. Her attempts to undo him were unsuccessful so he turned her round to face him and whispered, "Now then, Madame Tate, what was it you were so keen to do earlier this evening."

As she murmured a reply he reached down, lifted her skirt above her waist and slipped his hands inside. The silky smoothness of her skin excited his passion. He lifted her onto his shoulder in a fireman's lift. She beat playfully on his back as he walked to the bedroom.

Thirty-four

Flins. 1955

Allan Gachot approached Huey on the workshop floor. Huey was no longer engaged in the assembly of the cars. His expertise with engines had soon been spotted by Pierre, his immediate superior, and he had been moved to engine development. An engine, in Huey's hands, was as supple as his guitar. His hands seemed to know what to do before his mind could think. He seemed to see in the contours of an engine the corners and turns that could be introduced to make it even more efficient or powerful, quieter or durable.

"Allan, ca va?" Huey asked as he wiped his oily fingers with a rag.

"Come up to my office," Allan said. "Away from this noise."

Allan handed Huey a cigarette as he beckoned him towards a chair facing the desk, which stood diagonally across the far corner, in front of the picture window.

"The engines we provided for the pumps in Rotterdam."

"Okay? What about them? Problems?"

"Nothing massive. But there's nobody up there knows them well enough to prime or maintain them. Pierre Noyer has been on to me. I've read his reports on your work. He made a recommendation that I wholly agree with. We're sending you up there to put in some training. No-one here understands these engines like you do. Also, you know how important the Port of Rotterdam can be to us if we keep them happy. I can depend on you to do that."

"Wow, Allan. You've thrown me a bit. That's a big responsibility. Are you sure I'm your man?"

"I'm positive. And I know it's a big job. Pierre has convinced the bigwigs that you're the man for this job. You will be well recompensed for your work."

"Well, what can I say? I'm very grateful. How long do you think I will need to be away?"

"We have provided for one month. We think that you can train up six of their staff in that time. We've booked you into a good hotel near the waterfront."

"But I haven't said I'm going yet."

"Listen, you will enjoy this. It's a suite of rooms and we've budgeted for Clara and Ana to join you each weekend if they like. Train fare, transfer to and from stations. We even have provision for a chaperone to accompany them if you so wish. It's also been hinted at that if you do a good job there's a promotion and pay rise in the pipeline for you. Now, what do you say?"

"You're a very persuasive man, Allan. I have to talk it over with Clara but you can be pretty confident that my answer is yes."

Thirty-five

Rotterdam. 1955

The company had booked Huey into the Grand Hotel adjacent to the waterfront, but far enough away from the docks for it to be a pleasant base. All expenses paid. The work was tough but rewarding. He worked on site with six men. One of them had been dismissive of the black man at first but he had soon come around. His name was Robert and he seemed to want to make up for his initial attitude by befriending Huey. He was the first to invite Huey and Clara and Ana for a meal when she came to visit. Robert and his Swedish wife Beatrice welcomed them into their home and they became friends. Apart from dreadfully missing his home life Huey couldn't have been in a happier work situation. To spend all day with his head inside an engine with top men hanging on his every word was a kind of bliss he never expected to experience. He thought back to his life in Alabama. He could scream for the constraints that way of life had placed upon him. His abilities and potential crushed. He thanked his stars every day for the war and where it had delivered him to. And then he berated himself with guilt for thanking the evil of war for anything.

One night, when his driver dropped him back at his hotel, the one thing Huey was looking forward to was a long hot bath and early to bed. It had been a hard day. The men were getting the hang of the engines now, but Huey was stretching them by positing breakdown situations for them to rectify. They were quick learners but very demanding.
He was startled out of his long, dozy soak by the
sound of his telephone ringing. Convinced it must be Clara he leapt out of the bath and dripped his way to the phone.

"Hi, Clara, is that you?"

He recognised Marc's voice immediately. "Hey, Romeo, not so fast. Sorry to disappoint you but it's only me, Marc. Your old buddy. Remember?"

"Sorry, Marc. I wasn't expecting you. I wasn't expecting anyone as a matter of fact. I just assumed it must be Clara."

"Clara not calling tonight? You've not had a tiff, I hope?"

"Don't be silly. She can't call every night. She has Ana to care for and the nearest telephone is in Café Rimbaud, on the corner. We speak Mondays and Thursdays. Saturdays as well if she's not coming to stay over for the weekend."

"Anyway, don't worry about her. I saw her last night."

"Oh. Where was that?"

"I saw her as I was driving to a court hearing. She was with Jean-Paul having a coffee in Café le Treize. You know that one near Sacre Coeur."

"You mean she was in Paris?"

"Certainly. Is something wrong?"

"No, of course not. I'm just surprised. It's a longish trip from Flins. Did she have Ana with her?"

"That I can't say. I didn't see Ana but she could have been there. I went past quite quickly."

"So, getting back to you, Marc. Why did you call?"

"I'm here in Rotterdam. I'm serving extradition papers in front of a Dutch judge tomorrow. There's a war criminal living here. He was a torturer for the Vichy regime. He thinks he's escaped justice but I'm here to see that he returns home."

"Good luck with that. I hope he gets what he deserves."

"So, I was thinking, how about we two meeting up. You can show me the Rotterdam night life."

Huey's heart sank. His hopes for an early night were lost. There was no way he could say no to Marc, so he agreed to meet him in the lobby of his hotel in an hour.

Marc held Huey in a tight embrace when they met.

"Huey, you look great. It's so good to see you. We miss you and Clara in Paris. They were great days weren't they. When the band was in its heyday."

"Good times. They certainly were. What do you want to do tonight?"

"Well, I thought we'd start with a few drinks and then you can show me to some music dive. There must be somewhere in Flins where music is being played."

"Okay. We can do all of that. Let's go."

Marc suggested they eat in the first bar they entered. Huey had eaten earlier. He joined Marc, who ate a steak with steamed vegetables by ordering a small portion of fried sardines with a basket of bread. They both drank wine. By the time they reached the music venue Huey had chosen, they were drinking beers. Marc added the occasional brandy chaser, but Huey, mindful of work the next day, resisted his constant urgings to join him.

"Not bad."

"What's that?" Huey responded.

"The band. They're not bad."

"I like them. I've seen them a few times now. I'll introduce you to them when they take a break."

They were in a smoky basement called The English Bar. There was nothing English about it if Huey's recollections of Lancashire were representative of that country. Its walls were painted black, there were posters of the American greats on the walls – from Count Basie to Louis Armstrong - and the Belgian beer they served was very strong.

The band was a four piece – piano, bass, trumpet and clarinet. There were, in addition, two female singers. They did most of the backing vocals for the piano player who did most of the lead singing. During a cigarette break the piano player whose name was André, and one of the backing singers Martine, came over. Huey did the introductions and they chatted music for five minutes or so. André asked Huey about the sound and the arrangements. He chided Huey for not bringing his guitar along. Huey had talked about his involvement with Les Libres many times with André and he congratulated Marc as the leader of that excellent band.

"Alas, no more," said Marc as he excused himself and moved across to chat with Luka, the other backing singer who was sitting alone on the edge of the stage having a cigarette.

When the band got up to play again there was only one backing singer on the stage and Marc was nowhere to be seen. As the first number came to its conclusion a commotion erupted to the right-hand side of the stage and a door to the rear of the building slammed. Luka came storming through followed by Marc. She turned and hurled abuse at him. Phrases like – who the hell do you think you are? You have no right – poured out of her. She was furious with him. She stormed up to André and remonstrated with him, turning and gesticulating constantly at Marc. Marc walked over to Huey and picked up his beer. He sipped at it. He was calm and unruffled. André came over. He gave Marc an iron stare. Marc returned it. André spoke to Huey.

"Your friend is not welcome here, Huey. I'm surprised you hang around with his type."

"Hey, you," Marc interjected. "What do you mean, my type?"

He made a half-hearted effort to lunge forward but Huey easily restrained him. The other guys in the band were beginning to lay down their instruments and make as if to come over.

"Get him out of here," André suggested.

"No problem," Huey said. He took a hand to Marc's back and began to push him towards the door. Marc resisted, shrugging Huey off.

"If your friend doesn't mind, I'll finish my drink first." He took his time sipping his beer, all the while staring at the girl who had by now resumed her place next to Martine at the microphones.

"Come on, Marc. Don't be an asshole. Let's go."

As they walked the dark streets back towards Huey's hotel, Marc began laughing. "Well, what a night this has been. I came close there. I was sure I had dropped lucky."

"What do you mean? Lucky?"

"Well, why did she come outside with me? She obviously wanted something. What's the point of coming outside and then saying no? No means nothing from a woman like that."

Huey looked at Marc. He wondered how drunk he was. "What do you mean, 'a woman like that'?"
"You know exactly what I mean."

"No, I don't. I've known Martine and Luka for several weeks now and 'a woman like that' seems a poor fit."

"Look," Marc said. "Let's forget it. It's meaningless." Just a misunderstanding." They split up at Marconiplein where they took separate trams.

"Thank you for a great night, Huey. I've really enjoyed myself. I'll make sure I call in on Clara when I'm next in Flins."

"It's been good catching up with you. Are you sure you'll find your way back to your hotel?"

"Absolutely. My tram stops outside the front door."

Huey's tram came first but he let it go. He waited and made sure Marc boarded the correct tram headed in the right direction. On his own tram ride back, he started to brood. He felt uncomfortable about the confrontation in the bar. He would have to make a point of checking with Luka soon and making sure she was all right. He knew of Marc's reputation but if his behaviour hadn't shocked him, it had annoyed him. But he was most bothered by the fact that he was repeatedly pondering what Marc had said about Clara and Jean-Paul meeting up. It wasn't so much what Marc had said as the way that he had said it.

Thirty-six

Clara and Ana came to Rotterdam that following Saturday morning and stayed over until Sunday afternoon. Ana finally fell asleep on Saturday night after a tiring day. It had included a visit to the zoo and later, after something to eat, a stroll along Lijnbaan, the only city centre, pedestrian promenade in Europe. With the reconstruction of post-war Rotterdam in full flow, there was plenty to see and do. And as they listened to Ana's gentle breathing, they smiled at the success of their tactic.

Once Clara was in his arms, Huey felt all concerns fall away. Beneath the cotton sheets he felt Clara clinging to him. Her skin against his made his heart take flight. Their lovemaking was gentle but intense. Clara's breath enveloped him as she repeatedly breathed, 'I love you'.

Sunday was spent walking to the playground area in the park and eating at the English Bar. The band didn't play on Sundays but André was there with Martine and Luka.

André invited Huey's family to join his table. Martine smiled kindly and rose to shake hands with Clara and fuss Ana. Luka did not look pleased to see Huey. When the noise in the bar made it possible for Clara to speak to Huey without the others hearing she asked what the matter was.

"It's nothing. She got upset last time I was in here."

"With you?"

"No! Not with me." Here Huey was in a dilemma. He could easily tell Clara about Marc's behaviour but he didn't want her to think that he liked to run him down. He had a pretty clear idea of the wartime relationship they had had. They were comrades in arms. If he constantly criticised Marc, Clara might become resentful. Marc may have been boorish and arrogant, but nothing serious had happened. He wanted to drop the subject.

"I was with some guys and one of them insulted her. She took offence. Quite rightly. She probably associates me with his behaviour."

"Oh," Clara remarked, unconvinced.

Luka warmed to the company as the meal progressed and Clara put it out of her mind. In the end it was a very pleasant afternoon. Later, after collecting Clara's overnight bag from the hotel, he walked them to the station.

"Did I mention that Marc visited me?"

"What on earth for?"

"He was here on legal business. An extradition case. He stayed over one night. We had a meal and some beers."

"That must have been nice for you. I bet you get lonely."

"It was good. The guys at the works are fine but it was good to see a familiar face."

Huey was contemplating whether to say more. Before he knew it, he had. "He said he'd seen you."

"Did he? I don't think so."

"Café Le Treize, Sacre Coeur."

Clara's expression cut Huey. Her head dipped and she blushed. "What's the matter?" he asked.

"Nothing. Yes, I did go there."

"Was Ana with you?"

"No. She spent a night with my mother. She likes it with her. She gets spoiled a little."

"So why were you there?"

Clara stopped and tugged Huey's arm. "Why all the questions? Is something the matter?"

"Not at all, I'm just interested."

Clara said nothing. They walked on in silence for a while.

"Well?" Huey eventually persisted. "Why were you there?"

"I will tell you but I don't like the way you're interrogating me. I don't ask you to account for your every move while you are here. I met Jean-Paul."

"I didn't know you were still in contact with him. He was badly injured in the war, wasn't he?"

"Badly injured makes him sound like some honourable battlefield casualty. Jean-Paul was tortured. Brutally tortured. But he refused to give up our names to the French gestapo. It's because of him that I am alive to be here with you today. He has never truly recovered from the trauma."

"Oh, that's terrible. I'm sorry to hear it. But why did he want to see you?"

"That's enough Huey. I've never known you like this. Are you becoming jealous?" This question brought Huey up sharp. Was he? He immediately relented.

"Forget it," Huey said. He reached down and swept Ana into his arms. He pulled Clara to him. "We are silly to spoil our last few minutes together getting in a bad mood with each other. Come on, let's have an ice cream before you get your train."

As the train moved away from the platform, Huey watched and waved. His mind niggled at the exchange he had had with Clara about Jean-Paul. Why had she been reluctant to talk about him? Then he became annoyed with himself, probably making something of nothing.

On board the train, with Ana settled at the window beside her, Clara felt dejected at the way the weekend had ended. She knew that it was a sense of shame that made her so reluctant to fully explain to Huey her relationship with Jean-Paul. She felt responsible for Jean-Paul's ongoing trauma, his night terrors. They all went back to the night when he and Marc had failed to save her from Moreau and his accomplices. She owed him her life and she loved him. He was the brother she had never had. Whenever he wanted or needed to meet and talk, she knew she would always go at a moment's notice. She couldn't bring herself to give Huey the gory details of what happened to her that night. To explain about Jean-Paul would inevitably lead to her revealing the worst details of the rape. How would Huey cope with such knowledge? She felt bad for thinking the worst of him – that his love for her would be tainted. But she knew she would always find it too difficult to share that dreadful experience with him.

Thirty-seven

Flins, 1955.

On a Monday morning, after a fond weekend in Rotterdam with Huey, Clara awoke in her bedroom in Flins feeling refreshed and happy. She crept through to Ana's room to check on her without waking her and then continued on downstairs. On her way to the kitchen, she picked up the post that lay on the doormat. She placed it on a worktop unopened, while she filled the kettle. She would make coffee and then get Ana ready to go to the market and buy breakfast of cheese and ham and baguette. She would also buy some croissants. As she waited for the kettle to come to the boil, she absent-mindedly picked up the envelopes and opened the one that lay on top. She unfolded the paper and was immediately shocked by the script. It was written in shaky capital letters and spaced erratically down the page. It read:

It is illegal in France to procure an abortion.

I know what you did.

You will pay me or you will regret it.

Wait for my instructions.

A panic began to rise inside her. Her happy existence had suddenly been wrenched out of her control. She forgot about the singing kettle as she repeatedly re-read the note. Clara's mind was flooded with the morbid thoughts that had swamped her when Marie Louise Giraud, the woman who had helped her, had been executed. Her mind raced headlong over the events of the rape and the abortion. She'd always assumed that Marc was the only person who knew all the details. But perhaps that was silly. Jean-Paul probably worked it out. Many of her Resistance comrades could have

207

discovered the truth. Maybe intimates of Marie-Louise Giraud were privy to her activities. It was unlikely she had worked completely alone.

Her first instinct was to telephone Huey. The thought of doing so actually made her shudder. Her memory of the multiple rape she had suffered was so distressing she had done her best to block it. Life with Huey had been a fresh start. She had believed it was behind her and over with. The shame and dirtiness she had felt had faded. Now, suddenly they were back. If she had to tell Huey what had happened to her, she knew it would sully their relationship. The past would stain their future. And what would Huey think of her after discovering that so many men had used and abused her? Could he still love her? She wanted to believe that he would, but her insecurity made her decide not to tell him. She picked up her telephone and called Marc.

"Ah! It's Clara. I thought we were no longer friends."

"What do you mean?"

"Well, how long is it since you called me? How long since we saw each other?" As Clara absorbed his comment, she could picture Marc's grin flickering on his lips.

"Marc, don't be silly. And please don't tease me. I need your help."

"Oh, I see. It's not me you are keen to see, it's my help you are after. Well, I don't suppose I can deny you. What can I do for you?"

"If I wasn't desperate, I wouldn't have called you."

"So, you're desperate. You'd better tell me all about it." Clara explained the situation to him. As soon as Clara had finished he said, "Stay where you are. I'll come straight to you."

As he replaced the receiver into its cradle he slid open his desk drawer and pulled out an unsealed envelope. He took out the sheet inside and read it once over. He slid it back inside, licked the envelope and sealed it. The address was already in place. He licked a stamp and stuck it on the corner. On his way to the Metro station he dropped it into a mailbox.

Clara was anxiously waiting for Marc to arrive. She opened her door as soon as he knocked and before she knew it, she was in his arms, overcome with relief.

"Where's the note," he asked as he kissed her forehead and cheek. She handed it to him. He sat down, reading and re-reading it. He rubbed his hair and hummed introspectively.

"This could be bad," he said. "We can't take this to the Gendarmes."

"Oh my God! No! That's the last thing I want," Clara gasped.

"You'll have to leave this with me," Marc decided. "What did Huey say?"

"I haven't told him." Clara's embarrassment was obvious. To admit to Marc that there was something she could not tell her husband was to share an intimacy with him. It made her uncomfortable.

Marc stood up and went towards her. "You can rely on me," he whispered as he wrapped his arms around her. "I'll keep your secret from Huey. He doesn't need to know anything about this."

As he whispered, he placed his cheek against hers and before she knew it, he was kissing her mouth. After a moment's surrender she drew back. He resisted her withdrawal for a moment, kissing her more fiercely, but then released her.

"I've made us some lunch," Clara said. She backed off into the kitchen.

"Where's Ana?"

"She's in kindergarten."

"So, it's just you and me. How fortunate."

"Please Marc. Don't do this."

"Don't do what?"

"Manipulate the situation to get what you want."

"Huh! Is that what you think? You really do think the worst of me, don't you?"

"I asked for your help as a friend. You're the only one I can turn to."

"So, I am more useful to you sometimes than even your husband?"

Clara had no response. She laid two plates of sandwiches on the table and poured coffee from a pot.

"Can you help me?"

Marc stared at her. He chewed on his sandwich. "It felt good. Holding you. It felt natural. Like it used to." He took a slug of coffee, washed down the sandwich. Clara looked down at her plate. "I'll have to think about this," he continued. There's not much to go on with this note. We'll have to wait for another message. Whoever it is wants money. Whoever it is knows about your wartime past. It could be one of the rapists. I'll take the note with me and begin investigating the people who could have known about the rape and the abortion."

"Apart from you and me, I can't think who else could have known."

"You weren't the only woman amongst the comrades who suffered the same fate. It didn't take a genius to work out why a female comrade disappeared for a few weeks. The

210

other women could be the first to speculate. It wouldn't take long for a rumour to turn into an agreed fact. The blackmailer could just be taking a guess on you. You could bluff it out. Ignore the threat."

"But what if they carry out their threat. I'll be investigated."

"What could any investigation find? Nothing."

"But I couldn't have an investigation. Huey would find out the terrible details. I don't want our relationship sullied by the past. I want us to be new."

"Okay than. We'll do as they ask. Leave it to me."
They chewed on their sandwiches until their plates were empty.

"Do you really know why you haven't told Huey?"

Clara's face displayed the distress she was feeling. "I could. I know I could. I'm sure he would understand and support me."

"So?"

"I've told you. I just don't want to bring that into our relationship. Huey has been a new start for me. We're clean. We're fresh. This would make everything dirty."

Marc's tone altered. "I'm glad you called me. I would do anything for you – you know that. I'll always be here for you. If ever you tire of ....."

"Please! Stop! I don't want to hear you say that. If you can't help me as a friend, well, I'm sorry I called you."

Marc stood up and went around the table to her. He took her by the hand and pulled her upright into his arms. He kissed her neck. He kissed her lips again until she turned her face away. "I'll help you," he said.

Thirty-eight

"So, another note has come." Marc sat beside Clara in her Flins home. She was crying as he read the note.

"It's the same writing," he said.

Bring 100,00 francs to the Gare du Nord
Tuesday coming 19th 10.30
Stand opposite the barrier to platform 8
Carry the money in a red bag
Wear white gloves
You will be approached by a man with a bicycle
Hand over the parcel

"What am I going to do? This is ruining my life. I'll lose Huey and Ana." Marc took her in his arms and kissed the top of her head.

"Hey," he urged." Have I ever let you down? I'm going to deal with this. You will be able to forget about it and get on with your life. I'm not going to let anything happen to you."

"How can you be so calm?" Clara asked looking up into his face. Marc smiled. He kissed her forehead, her eyes, her lips.

"Trust me." He whispered.

"But Marc, I don't have that amount of money. If I did, it would be mine and Huey's. I couldn't just hand it over to a blackmailer without asking Huey."

"I will get the money. I will arrange for the handover. You won't need to be involved at all."

"Won't he be expecting to see me? He obviously knows who I am."

"Don't worry. In my line of work we deal with this sort of thing. I have people who can do this. A woman with your build, in sunglasses and a tight headscarf, will pass as you. A man collecting 100,000 francs will not be hanging around to check identity papers."

"Oh Marc," Clara sighed, "I can't thank you enough. Without you I would be lost." Sha sagged in his arms and he held her tightly to him.

"We are for each other forever. We were in the war and we always will be." As he spoke he caressed her back. She could feel his passion beginning to arouse. She drew back slightly and looked at him.

"Do you want to make love to me? Is that the price I must pay?"

Marc released his embrace. He contemplated her visage. His face was unreadable.

"Of course not. I'm sorry. I'll get going." He pulled away from her and headed for the door.

"Marc?"

He stopped with the door half open. "Yes?"

"Thank you," he shrugged and left.

The nineteenth came and went without any word from Marc. Clara called his office but his secretary informed her that he was out of town on business and was not expected back that week.

Thirty-nine

Rotterdam, 1955.

"What's the matter, Clara? You seem distracted." Huey came into the hotel bedroom from the en-suite. He was drying his hair after showering. Ana was in the living room of the suite of rooms Renault had provided for Huey during his stay in Rotterdam.

"I'm sorry," Clara replied, shaking herself out of her reverie. "I was thinking, wouldn't it be nice to live here in Rotterdam. We could make a fresh start. The people here love you."

"But my work is with Renault. I'm needed back in Flins."

"I know. I think I'm missing the excitement of a big city. Rotterdam has some of the life that Paris had and Flins doesn't."

"I thought you liked our home in Flins?"

"Oh, I do. I guess I'm just daydreaming."

"What about Ana and her education? How would she cope with a new language?"

"You're right. It's a pipe dream. It's an urge I sometimes get to travel. To experience something new. To get right away from the past."

She stood up and wrapped her arms around Huey's trunk. She looked up into his face. "I love you," she whispered. "Wherever you are is where I want to be. I suppose I sometimes feel that if we move, I'll leave any worries behind."

"What have you got to worry about?"

Clara felt herself blushing and hid her face against his chest. "Nothing really. But if you are a worrier, you don't need something to worry about. Worrying is what you do."

"I didn't know you were a worrier. You're more a warrior than a worrier. That's the girl I met in Paris knocking hell out of the Nazis."

"Things were different then. I had nothing to lose. Now I've got everything to lose."

She clung tighter to him. He felt her rush of vulnerability. He was confused. All he could think to do was hold her, caress her hair and hush her. "Has something happened?" he asked.

Clara seemed to make a decision. She shook herself free of him, stood up straight, smiled into his eyes and said, "There, that's over now. Take no notice of me. It's only a passing mood. Melancholy is a French thing. We like to indulge ourselves sometimes but we never let it last. Tell me what we are going to do tomorrow in this great city."

The summer had rolled on into autumn before Clara caught up with Marc. It had been a dreadful period of anxiety for her. No more notes had come. Did that mean that the blackmailer had been satisfied? Had Marc done as he had promised and sorted the whole thing out? Or were the gendarmes preparing a case against her and her arrest was only a matter of time? Not knowing was the worst of it. One minute she felt safe; the next minute she was filled with dread. She lost weight. She was short-tempered – sometimes with Huey but mostly with Ana.

Huey came down the stairs from Ana's bedroom to the living room. They were all permanently back in Flins. Huey's time in Rotterdam had been successful and he had been given a promotion with a pay rise.

"Ana is settled now. She's stopped crying."

Clara shook the magazine she was reading, folded it

and lifted it closer to her face.

"You didn't need to shout at her like that," Huey said. "She only came back down for a hug from you. She thought she'd done something wrong and wanted to say sorry."

Clara dropped the magazine to her lap. Her eyes were moist. She blinked away a tear.

"What's the matter?" Huey asked. "You seem to be on edge all the time these days. Has something happened?"

"Nothing's happened," she answered, but the catch in her voice gave the lie to her answer. Huey put his arm around her shoulder. "If there's something wrong, you can tell me, Clara. I'll do anything to help you."

"There's nothing the matter." She pushed herself out of her seat and said, "I'll go up and see Ana. I'll tell her I'm sorry for shouting."

Huey listened to her footsteps on the stairs and the click as Ana's door closed. He puzzled over Clara's current moodiness. He worried that it had something to do with him – or their marriage. He remembered a conversation he had had with a G.I. named Miller at the top of a church tower in a Normandy village. He shook his head in an unconscious attempt to free himself from an irrational worry. He and Clara were forever. He knew that. He just wished he knew what was bothering her.

"I'm going to Paris at the weekend."

Huey turned and looked questioningly at Clara, who had just returned to the living room.

"I haven't seen my mother for weeks. I need to check on her."

"Oh. Okay. Will you take Ana with you?"

"No. It's better if she stays with you. She's with me all week. She needs some time with her papa. It will be good for both of you to have time without me. I'm going to have a bath and then I'm going to bed."

Huey watched her go through the doorway, down the hall to the bathroom. He thought about Miller. He had to stop himself wondering if Clara was really going to visit her mother. Or was there some other point to her Paris trip? He thought about going after her to the bathroom to have it out with her. But he was scared. Scared of saying something irretrievable or opening a box that couldn't then be closed. He would have to trust her.

The prettiness of Paris in the autumn assaulted Clara with pre-war memories, when she was a girl about to leave school with hopes of a carefree student life. The orange and yellow leaves carpeted the pavements and crisped beneath her feet. She had spent Friday night with her mother who had been thrilled to see her but disappointed not to have also seen Ana and Huey.

"I'm meeting some friends this morning," she had said to her mother, before departing for the Metro.

"That will be nice," her mother said, "Will you be seeing Marc?"

"I don't think so."

"Good," her mother replied "Me and your father never liked him. He was too cocksure of himself."

Clara smiled wryly and kissed her mother's cheeks.

"I'll have dinner ready for seven. Will you be back by then?"

"Oh yes. I'll be back well before then."

Marc's new apartment was in the 16th arrondissement, Paris's richest district. She walked along large avenues, past ornate 19th century buildings. Marc's

217

apartment building overlooked the Bois de Bolougne and from his second floor living room he had a view into the park. A young woman of around twenty-five or six answered her ring at the door.

"Hello. Is Marc in? Will you tell him it's Clara?"

The woman disappeared down the hallway. Clara heard indistinct voices and then Marc appeared in the hallway. He wore trousers and a sleeveless vest. He disguised his surprise with a pencil line smile. "Clara, how lovely to see you. It's a bit inconvenient at the moment. Why don't you walk across to the park? There are benches along the main path opposite here. I'll join you in ten minutes."

Clara watched couples and dog-walkers ambling past. She saw Marc before he saw her. His face betrayed his annoyance. She interpreted it as his hatred of being wrongfooted. He was never happy if the other person initiated an encounter.

"Ah, there you are," he said, changing his expression.

"How lovely to see you."

"Marc, where have you been. I've been going mad with worry."

"Why on earth would you be worried. Has Huey done something?"

"Don't be ridiculous. And don't pretend you don't know what I'm talking about. The last time I saw or spoke to you, you were leaving to meet someone who was blackmailing me. Don't you think I wanted to know what happened?"

"Oh, that!" he shrugged. "That's all sorted."

Clara swung at him and punched him hard in the chest. "Don't you 'oh that,' me!" she yelled. People turned to stare but Clara was oblivious to them. "Why did you do that to me?

218

I have been living in anxiety. Not knowing if the next knock on the door would be the police. Not knowing if the whole sordid story would be in the newspapers. Not knowing if my life was about to be turned upside down. How could you be so cruel?"

"Cruel, am I? The one who dealt with your problem? The one who made it go away? The one who let you go back to your mundane little life?"

Clara was furious with the tears that pricked their way out of her eyes. At first they had been tears of anger. Now, with the slightest of chances that Marc could be telling her the truth, they became tears of relief. She sat down on a nearby bench. Marc sat beside her. "Tell me what happened," she demanded.

"I can't."

"Why an earth not?"

"It's better if you don't know."

"Oh my God! Did you kill him?"

"It's better if you don't know. All you need to know is he will never bother you again. Forget him."

Clara inspected Marc's face. She searched for signs that would convince her he was telling the truth. Marc lit a cigarette. He offered her one but she declined. He drew on his cigarette, bringing the smoke deep into his lungs. He held his breath for a few seconds. As he exhaled, he smiled. "Nobody knows your secret now. Just you and me."
Clara could not ignore the mischievous taunt contained in that comment. "Are you blackmailing me now?"

Marc stood up and crushed the cigarette beneath his shoe. His reaction startled Clara. Not many things sparked such a response from Marc.

"You demean yourself with your ingratitude," he spat. "You'd better get back to your little life in Flins and the husband who is too pure to know your past."

Clara got to her feet. "Marc, please, don't be angry. I have been at my wit's end." It was pointless continuing. Marc had turned and strode back towards his apartment.

Forty

Dallas, 1957

The overnight flight from New York had encountered heavy turbulence. Marc had been quietly terrified. He had chain-smoked and drunk several glasses of Bourbon. Fortunately, the conference on 'War Criminals and the International Justice System' would not commence until the following morning and, having arrived at his hotel by two in the afternoon, he had had time to sleep off his hangover.

At seven in the evening, he went down to the hotel restaurant where the delegates were gathering for the first of the five nights of the conference. He was one of the last to turn up and all the tables were occupied with sharp-suited men, eating American beef steak and engaging in rapid fire conversation. Marc collected a tray and went to the serving hatch. There was a choice of turkey, ham or steak. To a Frenchman the steaks all looked burnt so he chose turkey. 'Turkey is an American bird. When in Rome,' he thought.

He wandered the aisles between the tables until at last he found an empty place. He excused himself and asked one of the delegates on either side of the space if it was indeed vacant. The giant of a man sitting there rotated in his chair and turned what was obviously a stiff neck to look up.
"Why sure there, young fella. Help yourself."
"Thank you, Monsieur," Marc replied and slid into the seat.
"A Frenchie, huh?"
"That's right. Whereabouts in this amazing country are you from?"
"I'm from the beautiful state of Georgia."
Ah, Georgia. Georgia On My Mind. One of my favourite songs. I always wondered if the Georgia in the song is a girl or a State."

"Story goes," the big man said as he chewed a chunk of his steak, that Hoagy Carmichael was challenged by a band member to write a song about my beautiful State. It's said he boasted he'd got Hoagy started with the first two words."

"But the first two words are 'Georgia, Georgia."

"Exactly. But anyway, Hoagy took up the challenge and with his roommate who wrote the lyrics, he finished the song. A good guy was Hoagy. His roommate who did the lyrics never got on the royalties contract but good old Hoagy sent him a cheque for half every time a royalty payment came in."

"It's a lovely song."

"You a musician, Frenchie?"

"Before the war it was my life. Even during the war, we kept the band going. It got more and more difficult as we got dragged into the conflict."

"So what kinda music you Frenchies play?"

"Well, mostly American, believe it or not. Louis Armstrong, Duke Ellington, Benny Goodman, Count Basie. Singers like Billie Holliday and Ella Fitzgerald too."

"You got a lotta nigger music going on there. Surprised you Frenchies like that stuff. Bit too jungle to my taste."

"Mmm. That's what the Nazis said too. We had to hide our favourite stuff in amongst some awful German propaganda tunes."

"Well, maybe the Nazis were evil bastards but their taste in music, as far as nigger music goes, weren't all bad."

"We had a black G.I in the band just after the war. Very good guitarist."

"You see what's happening over here now. All these niggers getting up demanding civil rights. Demanding to eat and drink in diners and bars where we do. Demanding to drink from the same water fountains and use the same bathrooms as whites. Next, they'll be demanding to marry our women and then all hell will break loose."

"It's interesting you say that. The G.I. I told you about is married to a white French woman. And they have a child."

"Oh my sweet Jesus! Another piccaninny in the world. How come you Frenchies put up with it? If that so-called G.I. was over here, he'd be strung up sure as my name is Buster Lordan. And too good for him, I'd say."

Marc fell silent. He concentrated on his meal. His thoughts ranged over the Georgian's comments. What an appalling racist, was his first reaction. He then wondered what an attitude like his would bring to a conference on international justice. He would keep a keen interest in his contributions to the discussions. But then there was something that excited him. On a personal level. He paused in his thinking. He was not sure he wanted to allow it in. In fact, he kept it at bay all through dinner and through the rest of the evening in the bar.

It was as he lay in the dark of his room, thinking back to his homeland, where Clara and Huey would be sharing their lives; sharing their daughter; sharing their home; sharing their bed. That was when the thoughts came charging in like a train entering a tunnel at top speed. His hatred of Huey had never diminished. After first being charmed by the slick black G.I. with the magical fingers on guitar, he had developed a seething desire to destroy him. How could he, Marc, have been the one to lose his lover to a black foreigner? He had done nothing wrong. What Frenchman did not take the occasional mistress? It didn't disqualify him as a lover and a husband. But along comes Huey the Yankee hero. What terrible timing for Marc. How Huey must have seduced her. Pretending to be Marc's friend and all the while pursuing his lover behind his back. If they lived in America it would not have happened. After everything he and Clara had been through together in the war. He had always thought of the two of them as soulmates. His bitterness welled and flowed. As he imagined Clara back in his own arms, his mind recollected the words of Buster Lordan. He hung onto those words as a justification for his righteous resentment. Buster would see things his way. He resolved to seek out Buster and probe him further. Hearing the man's completely unselfconscious bigotry somehow helped to soothe Marc's wounds. It allowed him to excuse his bitter resentment. Maybe the opportunity would arise for Marc to tell Buster his story.

The conference schedule was tightly timed and the delegates had some free time only after the third session of the day, which ended at eight in the evening. At that time the delegates gravitated towards the bar to wind down. Predictably the men, (all the delegates were men) clustered together in their national groups. For this reason, it wasn't until the third evening that Marc was able to make contact with Buster again.

Marc re-filled their drinks – Marc on Cognac, Buster on beer – and began the conversation by showing interest in Buster's opinion of the conference so far. His views were almost diametrically opposite to those of Marc, but Marc nodded in agreement with every statement he made.

"Nuremberg was a mistake," Buster drawled. "We wasted time hunting Nazis when they were our natural allies. Post-war, I mean."

Marc bit his tongue, sipped his Cognac. He thought of the ravages of his continent. He thought of the oppression the French had lived under and of his comrades tortured or murdered. But he pursed his lower lip as if acknowledging the sense in Buster's comments. "It's the Commies we should have gone after. Look where we are now. The Russians own half the world and we can't get a toe-hold in eastern Europe."

Buster could expound on the evils of Russia and the idiocy of the Nuremberg war crimes trials endlessly and Marc began to despair that he would. However, the moment came for him to shift the subject when it was Buster's turn to replenish the drinks. As soon as he returned Marc jumped in.

"I was really interested in what you were saying the other day about inter-racial marriages and the laws over here in America."

"Oh, they ain't all over America. Most northern States and those out west have acquired some sloppy European values. Niggers do most what they want in them places. It's the South I was talking about."

"So, when you say the South, you mean the old Confederacy States."

"That's right."

"This friend of mine in France, he's from Alabama. What would happen if he decided to come home with his new wife and child?" Buster spurted out a mouthful of beer. He laughed as he wiped the dregs from his suit trousers.

"You better tell your pal he'd better not do that. He wouldn't last five minutes."

"What do you mean? He's a legally married man under French law."

"I don't care if he's legally married under every law on goddam Earth. In Alabama he's a dead man."

"Do you mean he'd be arrested?"

"Could happen. But I doubt it."

"Why?"

"It wouldn't get that far. A lynch party would have him before the legal system could get going."

"You still have lynchings here?"

"No. Of course we don't. When we cut 'em down we find they died of misadventure or something like that."

Marc was thrown by that reply at first but Buster's big wink and twisted grin clarified matters.

"Oh. I see. You do but you don't."

"Exactly."

"But if he came back alone, to see his family, say, he'd be safe?"

"Depends."

"On what?"

"On how much the local men round here knew about him."

Marc swirled his cognac in its glass and contemplated the ideas Buster's comments were planting in his mind. He shifted track slightly.

"I heard your contribution in the Q and A session after the main lecture today," he began.

"Oh yeh. Which bit?"

"Where you accused the Allies of their hypocrisy over the so-called racial crimes of the Nazis."

"Go on."

"Well - correct me if I got you wrong – but you seemed to me to be saying that many of their policies were not too far from those practised in many other countries; highly civilised countries, you said. You mentioned the eugenics policies of Scandinavia, the developing apartheid in South Africa, the racial immigration policies in Australia and last but not least the segregation laws here in the United States, which no self-respecting American would disagree with."

Buster nodded and took a long slug of his beer.

"You said that international law was not being levelled against these countries and therefore it is hypocritical to single out the Germans for punishment."

"You got that right, Frenchie. I also said that the mass murder of the Kulaks by Stalin and the massive network of Gulags across the Soviet Union are much more a threat to international justice than any of the Nazi's behaviours."

"That's right."

"So, what's your point, Frenchie?"

"My point is, I was wondering if these are your held beliefs or were you playing devil's advocate?"

"Well, if any one of the higher ups was asking, I was playing devil's advocate, but between you and me I couldn't believe in anything more strongly than I do in the innate superiority of the white Caucasian male and the imperative that we fight tooth and nail to maintain it – no matter what."

"So, the gas chambers?"

"Hey, Frenchie. We ain't going there. There's a time and a place for those truths to come out. But I still got a career to think about. It don't do to lay all your cards on the table at once, you know."

"Got you."

Marc's heart was pounding. He was right at the point when the question he really wanted to ask was the next to come, or he would just put the idea to bed and never raise it again. Almost before he could stop himself, he had plunged on. "You personally find the marriage between black and white abhorrent?"

"Absolutely."

"And if an individual who had committed such a crime was known to you, you would act?"

"Most certainly."

"For example, if my friend in France returned home to visit his family and you knew he was here, what would you do?"

"This the fella married to the French girl?"

"That's right."

"And she ain't no half-caste, North African nor Polynesian? Nothing like that?"

"No. She's one hundred per cent European, white French."

"Well, I'd see to it that the people who deal with those matters are fully aware of his presence back in our country."

"And?"

"And leave them to do their business."

"Okay. Meaning?"

"Meaning he ain't gonna need no return ticket."

Buster laughed out loud at his own remark and Marc joined in nervously with him. "Before the conference breaks up, we must swap addresses. I would very much like to stay in contact with you."

"A good idea, Frenchie. We can learn a lot from each other."

Forty-one

It was only three days after Clara and Ana had waved au revoir to Huey at Paris Gare du Nord station that Marc turned up in Flins.

"Well, hello," Marc called, lifting his hat. "Fancy meeting you here," he added cheekily.

Clara had been pushing Ana along in her buggy. The three-year-old Ana looked up at Marc. She scrutinised his face with an intensity of curiosity. Clara leaned in towards Marc and they exchanged cheek kisses.

"Well, I live here. It's me who should be saying, 'fancy seeing you'."

"I'm here on business."

"Tracking a collaborator?"

"Not this time. We've already got him. I'm supporting the prosecutor with documentary evidence. What about you? Where are you going to?"

"Ana has had her morning in kindergarten and so I was taking her for a walk along the river and to play on the swings."

"Mind if I tag along?"

"Not at all. It will be nice to have some adult company."

"Is Huey busy at work? Neglecting you?"

"No, not at all. He's actually gone back to Alabama. I thought you must have known that. Your news about his mother worried him. He decided he had to get back to see her. He did write but got no reply. Post takes such a long time and he knows his mother is not a great writer. He left three days ago."

"No, I didn't know he had gone although I'm not surprised. That kind of news would worry anyone."

Turning to Ana, Clara stooped and said, "We went with Papa to the railway station, didn't we?"

Three-year-old Ana's face lit up at the sound of Papa's name. She looked around her as if expecting him to be approaching.

"Ah, I'm sorry darling, did I raise your hopes?" Clara lifted Ana out of the buggy and held her tightly. "Papa will be home soon."

Marc took charge of the empty buggy as they walked together along to the riverside. "It's lovely to see you again," Marc said as they stood beside the swing that Ana was riding.

"You too. Will you be in Flins long?"

"I'm not staying over but I will be here regularly, as long as this trial lasts."

"How long might that be?"

"It's not an easy case. It is about collaboration but most of the prosecution evidence is about tracking the movement of stolen Jewish funds managed by the accused. Financial and fraud cases are notoriously difficult. It could take months."

"Oh. We'll be seeing a lot more of you then."

"Hopefully. If you don't mind me being around?"

"No, it will be nice to meet and chat. We shared a lot during the war. They are not the kind of thing we can talk about with anyone else."

"When do you expect Huey to be back?"

"That's very difficult to say. He's going to be six weeks aboard ship, heading for Halifax in Nova Scotia. Then it will take time to get from there to Alabama – perhaps another two or three days. Then it will depend on his mother and how ill she is. If she is dying, Huey may well want to stay with her until the very end. You know more about his Mama's illness than we do. What did you think when you were told?"

"The man who told me was from Georgia whose company had done the legal work for the housing development where Huey's mama lives. His company maintained an office in the town and kept in touch with the situation there. He had had dealings with Huey's mama's purchase of her property and had picked up on the news of her illness. Cancer, he reckoned. Pretty far gone. I'd say Huey will be home pretty soon."

"Oh, what a terrible thing for me to think, but I was going to say, 'I hope so'."

"Don't be hard on yourself," Marc said. He reached out a hand and placed it on Clara's shoulder. She smiled at him but pulled away to push Ana in her swing.

As Marc accompanied them on their way back to their house, they spoke little. Clara's thoughts went back to an incident they had shared in the war.

Clara watched the hands of the clock on her living room wall. They read 25 minutes to nine. It was a fine Sunday morning in May. Her hand closed around the butt of the pistol in her mac pocket. Although it was warm in her apartment, she was dressed ready for the outdoors in a thin summer dress and a light mackintosh. Her hair was hidden by a tightly tied headscarf and she wore sunglasses. The hands had moved on to a quarter to nine. She strained her eyes to identify every movement forward as it clicked slowly on. The moment the hand reached ten minutes to the hour, she stood up, left her apartment and began her perfectly timed walk to the rendezvous point. The Paris streets were beginning to welcome the early risers. Clara knew that her walk to the rendezvous was potentially dangerous for her. If she was stopped and searched her gun would be found and it would mean immediate death in front of a firing squad. A close call was avoided when she heard the sound of soldiers' boots approaching around a corner. She stepped into a café doorway and kept herself hidden until they had passed.

This pause in her progress made it important for Clara to hurry now, to the junction of Rue Galande and Rue Saint-Julien le Pauvre. She approached this point from the south end of Galande which was much narrower than it became after the junction. Galande also made a sharpish bend to the left at the junction, making it a three-way position. As she drew within one hundred metres of the meeting point, she caught sight of Marc. He sat on a bench, smoking a cigarette and reading a newspaper. She scanned the street looking for Jean-Paul. She couldn't see him. This was a worry. His reliability was in question. Michel Gagné had been adamant that he should be stood down and take no further part in operations. It had been Marc who had persuaded Michel to allow Jean-Paul to take part in this attack. Jean-Paul had begged Marc to get Michel to include him. He believed taking revenge on Moreau and any of his co-fascists who happened to be with him would free him of his depression and guilt. In the end Michel had relented under Marc's persistence.

Marc shifted the hat on his head to let Clara know he had seen her. She crossed the street to be almost opposite him and took up her position in the doorway of a tabac, which was closed for Sunday.

Still no sign of Jean- Paul. The unmistakeable sound of a Carlingue van ignited their senses. Both Marc and Carla, tightened their grip on their pistols. True to the intelligence Patrick had provided them with the van stopped almost directly opposite Carla and about fifteen metres away from Marc on his side of the street. Moreau's cohorts climbed out of the vehicle. According to Patrick, it was their habit, after a long night of interrogating and torturing suspected Jews or communists or social-democrats, to take over the café bar and drink and play cards all day long. There were five of them. They stretched themselves on the pavement waiting for their boss. Moreau had been driving and was slow to emerge from the van. Carla looked at Marc in consternation. What should they do? Moreau was the prime target. By the time he alighted most of his crew would be inside the café and too hard to get at. As Carla watched, Marc made his decision. He got up from his bench. Raised his pistol and began firing as he ran towards the men on the pavement. Carla immediately swung into action. She raised her pistol and aimed at the driver's window. Her first aim was wayward and hit the bottom of the door. Her second aim shattered the glass of the driver's window and her third brought forth a scream of pain from Moreau. But as she rushed across the street to fire again, he slammed the vehicle into gear and scorched erratically away. Carla fired three more shots after the van but had little hope of hitting him. The absence of the van now opened her view of the pavement scene. Three of Moreau's colleagues were lying dead. As Marc aimed his pistol at the fourth who was bleeding from the shoulder but very much alive, his pistol jammed. The wounded fascist pushed himself up between two of his dead colleagues and drew his own weapon. Marc was helpless. He was less than two metres away. As she strode towards the collaborator, she raised her own pistol and began firing. She hit him three times, the last time in the head. Blood burst out of his temple like water from a hose. He

233

slumped back into the heap of bodies. With an appreciative glance at each other, Carla and Marc turned in opposite directions and walked hurriedly away. Retreating the way she had come, Carla caught a tram on Rue Dante and rode it all the way to Quai de Montebello. As she alighted, she handed her mackintosh, which she had rolled into a neat bundle, to the elderly madame serving at a magazine kiosk. The old lady took the coat and stored it safely inside the kiosk under stacks of old magazines. Thus did Carla relinquish possession of her pistol. She crossed the boulevard, entered Notre Dame brasserie and ordered a large brandy. Twenty minutes later, as arranged by Michel, a driver collected her from the brasserie and drove her to her parents' home in Saint Denis.

"Jean-Paul was stopped and searched on his way to the rendezvous. They found his pistol."

"Oh my God. Has he been executed?"

"Not according to Patrick. He is at 93, Rue Lauriston. He is being interrogated. Tortured, no doubt. We all need to be more than careful. It's more than likely that he will give up our identities to them. No-one can endure their techniques without succumbing." Michel Gagné, Marc and Clara were together in the basement of Le Sous Sol. Marc and Clara were being de-briefed by Michel.

"I warned you that he was not fit for operations," Michel fumed. "I blame you for this Marc. I let you persuade me against my better judgement."

"That has nothing to do with his capture. It could have happened to any of us," Marc argued. "Random stops are a calculated risk. Jean-Paul was just unlucky."

"You make your own luck in this game," Michel raged. "Jean-Paul's ragged nerves would have given him away. I'm as furious with myself as I am with you. And after all that, you failed again with Moreau."

Michel paced angrily to and fro, thumping his right fist into the palm of his left hand. After several minutes of this, with Marc and Clara wondering what was coming next, he calmed himself and began to order his thoughts. Eventually, he looked at Clara and said, "Your parents' home is no longer safe for you, Clara."

"You're over-reacting, Michel," Marc interrupted. The Allies are only fifty miles away. The Paris uprising is planned. The Nazis are ready to pull out any day. We can move between safe addresses here and be ready to play our part in the uprising."

"Nobody knows when the Allies will get here. They don't want a battle for Paris. They want to destroy the Germans already retreating eastwards. If DeGaulle can persuade them to attack Paris, maybe. Maybe, if the uprising starts, Eisenhower won't want a massacre similar to the one in Warsaw. But it's all speculation. They could be here tomorrow, but it might be next month or the month after. Plenty of time for Jean-Paul to succumb and see us all snatched and executed."

"But why?" demanded Clara. "Nobody could have identified me."

"Didn't you just hear what I said. Jean-Paul is bound to give us up under torture. You and Marc and everyone else that Jean-Paul could point the finger at must disappear. We have safe houses arranged for you two."

"Houses?" queried Marc. "Are we not going together?"

"Of course not. And if I discover that you have made any attempt to communicate with each other, never mind see

each other, I will have you both court-martialled and shot."
Clara and Marc looked at each other. Clara shrugged.

"Where are you sending me?" "Marc," Michel said.
"You must not hear this. Go over there," he said pointing to a
table at the far end of the basement. I'll call you back when
I've finished with Clara" Marc shuffled reluctantly away and
slumped into a chair at the farthest table.

"You are going to stay with a shopkeeper and his
schoolteacher wife in Dreux. It's an area the Germans have
withdrawn from in order to fortify Paris. The couple have
been volunteers since we were invaded and they have hidden
several Jewish orphaned children from the Nazis. They are
completely reliable."

"What will I do there?"

Michel slammed his fist on the table. "You will do
nothing," he hissed. "You will live in total lockdown. They have
a secret room where you will stay until it is safe for you to
return. You will be well-looked after. They will instruct you in
every detail of how you are to behave. You will be putting
their safety at risk if you don't follow their rules to the letter."

"When do I go?"

"Now."

"Now? How can I go now? I don't have any of my
things."

"You go now," insisted Michel. "There is a grocery
truck waiting in the alley outside. The driver has a delivery for
the shops in Dreux. Go upstairs now and get in the truck. We
will message you when it's safe for you to come back."

Clara heaved a frustrated sigh and turned her back on
Michel. Marc stood up as she passed his seat and took her in
his arms. "What did he say?" Marc whispered.

Clara put her finger over his lips. Then she took it away and placed her own lips there instead. They kissed passionately.

"Enough!" shouted Michel eventually. Clara pulled herself away, climbed the stairs to the alley and clambered into the truck, where a round-faced, bald man smiled at her as he slipped the engine into gear and drove away.

"You've been daydreaming." Marc smiled.

"Yes, I was thinking about one of our missions. When we failed to get Moreau. He got away. Poor Jean-Paul was captured."

"It's not something we're never likely to forget."

"I was thinking about Dreux and the lovely couple who hid me away. I was only there for three days. I got there on August 12th and the rebellion started in Paris on the fourteenth. By the fifteenth I was on my way back. I had very little chance to get to know them. I often thought of going back to look them up and thank them for their bravery."

"Same here. Michel had me billeted in Chambourcy with a retired headteacher. He allowed me the run of his big house. Did you stay hidden in the safe room?"

"Yes. I was allowed to join my hosts for twenty minutes or so at night. Usually around eleven o'clock. But that only happened twice. When the uprising began, Eisenhower changed his mind and sent Patton towards Paris."

"Those days of the uprising were tremendous days for France. How humiliating it would have been if we had sat back and let the Americans and the British do all the fighting for us. At least we could hold our heads high and say we played our part. They were dreadful days too. We got back together on the sixteenth and immediately began planning to launch an attack on Lauriston to release Jean-Paul and all the other prisoners. When we saw Moreau and a handful of his men pour out of there, we thought it was a godsend for us. The only pity was we weren't ready and they escaped. We did release Jean-Paul and killed those who had been left behind. But we didn't know at the time that Moreau and his men were setting out to ambush thirty-five young Resistance fighters in the Bois de Boulogne. Betrayed by a Frenchman. All gunned down. All those young lives lost. When we finally laid siege to the building we were joined by the Americans. Remember? That's where we first met Huey." Marc nodded pensively. Eventually he added, "And Jean-Paul had withstood their torture. He had not revealed one name to them."

"Poor Jean-Paul. His bravery was unsurpassed," Clara reminisced. "But his health was broken. He has never recovered."

"I know it's a strange thing to ask," Marc wondered, "but – do you ever miss those days?"

Clara was surprised by the question. It was something she had often pondered. She smiled affectionately at Marc. The intimacy of their relationship had been beyond the normal. Lovers they had been. That was behind her. But the danger and excitement they had shared would never be matched.

"No," she replied eventually. "It would be selfish and foolish ever to wish those times back. I understand what you are saying. We lived a heightened existence and, with luck, we'll never experience anything as intense again. But we should be glad of that."

Forty-two

As the weeks dragged into months and still no word from Huey, Clara's anxiety became extreme. She became mildly depressed, which meant she managed to function enough to do the basics, but she became short-tempered with Ana and neglected lots of the things around the house that had once been second nature to her. Marc visited almost every day. He had taken to spending the weekends in Flins, staying at a nearby hotel. He would arrive in Flins on Friday morning, check into his hotel and then go immediately to Clara's house. If Clara was having a low episode, Marc would take Ana to the park and buy her ice-cream. He would post any of Clara's mail and buy in some provisions. He also arranged for a baby-sitter with the daughter of a colleague in the Flins legal office. He and Clara would go for a meal and a stroll along the river. Eventually, Clara's anxiety turned to hurt. She could not understand Huey's desertion. Everything between them had been perfect. He was a good husband. He was attentive and loving. And he was a great father. His disappearance was inexplicable. The hurt she felt was unbearable. She was sometimes troubled by the memory of a comment Huey had once come out with after they had made love. He had said he once knew a man who believed that a marriage between a black man and a white woman could never last. What did she think of that? She had thought he was having a momentary rush of insecurity. She had asked him how he could even think such a thing never mind ask her. She remembered taking his face in both her hands and looking deep into his eyes. "You tell me my answer," she had said. He had smiled as he rolled her over in the bed and kissed her.

"Clara!" Marc shouted up the stairs. "Ana and I are going to the park. When we get back all three of us are going to take a ride in my car. By the way, shall I post this letter for you?"

"Yes please," came a faint reply.

With Ana facing forward in her pushchair, she didn't see the letter being deposited into the first waste bin inside the park. The address had intrigued Marc. Until now Clara had addressed her latest enquiry to the authorities in Alabama. This time she was writing to the American embassy in Paris. It would find its resting place in the same litter bin as the others. That night he took Clara to La Restaurant Marseilles. They both started with escargots followed by coq-au-vin for Clara and steak tartare for Marc. Clara became more talkative after her second glass of wine and even began to enjoy herself.

"I'm so grateful to you Marc for everything you are doing for me, and especially for Ana. She really likes you, you know. You're becoming the father figure she lacks."

This was a lead in Marc had hoped for. "I was looking at some American statistics for a client who is aiming to market his product in America. Did you know that the proportion of black American males who desert their wives and children is much higher than in any other racial background?"

Clara's tears began to well up. The memory of Huey's question re-surfaced. "I'm so sorry," Marc said. "I shouldn't be so thoughtless."

"It's not your fault, Marc. You've been more than kind. You can't help it if Huey tired of me."

"Oh, come now Clara, you can't say that. I can't believe Huey tired of you."

"Well, how would you describe what's happened?"

Marc grimaced. "It is difficult, I agree. Maybe it was a bit of 'out-of-sight, out-of-mind' syndrome. Maybe he realised he missed his American home more than he'd realised .Maybe his mother put her foot down. Who can say?"

"It really upsets me. It makes no sense. He loathed the circumstances for black people in Alabama. He detested the life he had been forced to live there. He was so successful at work here. They absolutely loved him at Renault."

"Look, I'm sorry I mentioned those statistics. Please don't upset yourself. Maybe he couldn't help himself. If it's in your nature, what can you do about it?"

"I would never have believed that of Huey. But perhaps you're right. After all, there's no fool like a lovesick fool."

"Which of us can tell where our racial instincts will take us?"

Clara gave Marc a curious look. Marc thought he might have pushed it too far. He decided to row back a little.

"It's not just black GIs who have left single mothers. There is a whole generation of illegitimate, half-American children all over Europe."

He diverted attention from the topic by calling the waiter over and asking for the dessert menu. He changed the subject. "I saw Jean-Paul on Wednesday."

"Oh. Is he well?"

"Not so good. He has digestive problems. It all goes back to Moreau and his gang. He still struggles to cope mentally."

"How is his drinking?"

"Heavy. But he handles it. He says sometimes it's the only way he can get through a day."

"His suffering now is why you and I and many more are still alive," Clara fumed. "He didn't give away one name to those bastards."

"I know. He still carries guilt for what happened to you."

Clara considered this but she did not voice her thoughts. Marc had been with Jean-Paul the night Moreau and his men raped her. They were both equally involved in the failure of the mission to kill Moreau. But how differently it had affected them. For Jean-Paul it had defined the rest of his life. For Marc, it was as if it had never happened. What a curious character her friend had! But now she thought about it, he had always been that way. Nothing seemed to affect him. Maybe that was a good thing. He wasn't going to be blown this way and that by events. Emotions were firmly under control. It had been what had made him so successful in the Resistance. "Huey will come back," she asserted with confidence. "I know him. He will definitely come back."

Forty-three

Alabama, 1959

Huey stood on the porch in front of his Mama's house; the house she had bought with the money he had sent back over the years. A single-story timber frame house. Two bedrooms, a bathroom, living room, kitchen and indoor toilet. Paradise compared to the shack she had raised her four kids in. He could hear her now, humming away as she pottered around in the kitchen. It was wonderful to see her and be with her again after so many years. But he didn't know whether to be grateful or angry for the deception it seemed Marc had played upon him.

Flins, two years earlier.

"That will be them."

Clara untied her apron and hurried through the house from the back yard to the front door. The chimes of the bell rang once more.

"I'm coming," she called.

On the pavement outside their door stood Marc and Angelique. Angelique and Marc had been living together in Paris for two months or so. Angelique worked as a secretary in Marc's law firm. She was twenty-two years old and smitten with Marc.

Clara and Angelique exchanged cheek kisses. Marc leaned in to kiss Clara. With a slight tilt of his head his lips glanced against the edge of Clara's. Knowing that this was typical of Marc, she dismissed it and welcomed them in.

"Hey, you guys," Huey called as they stepped into the yard. "Welcome to Bistro Huey."

He turned away from the barbecue he was working at and embraced them in turn.

"This is how American men cook," Huey joked. With his flowery apron and his French beret, Huey looked absolutely the part. "Sort out drinks for our guests, Clara. This meat will be another ten or fifteen minutes."

Marc and Angelique seated themselves at the small table in the only sunny corner of the yard whilst Clara went to fetch drinks. Ana came through and climbed onto Angelique's knee to show her some stones she had collected from the riverbank. When Clara had returned with the drinks, the two women fell into conversation and played with Ana. Marc got up and walked over to join Huey.

"How's the chef getting on?" he asked.

"Won't be long now. These just need turning one more time. Pass me that beer, Marc. It's just there on the wall." The men sipped their drinks and looked at the sizzling meat.

"I don't know if this is a good time" Marc ventured. Huey looked at his friend and asked.

"For what?"

"I heard news from a colleague I met at the Dallas conference."

"Oh?"

"It's about your mother."

"My mother? What could a guy from the conference know about my mother?"

"It's a strange coincidence, but his law firm did the work for the housing development you bought the house on. He's still involved with ongoing legal work there."

"And......?"

Huey had placed his meat tongs onto a plate and was looking at Marc. "He's heard that your mother is seriously ill. It's a very callous business but they keep tabs on news like

244

that so that they are aware of any sales that might be coming up. Of course, they will be keen to cash in on any conveyancing."

"Sales? What do you mean? My Mama isn't thinking of selling. Unless?"

"I'm sorry Huey. It's pretty serious so I'm told. She might not have long."

"Oh shit. I can't believe it. Mama is as strong as a horse."

"I'm really sorry to be the bearer of bad news. I'm only passing on what I've been told."

Huey reached out and rubbed Marc's shoulder in a brotherly show of affection. "Hey Marc, I appreciate you telling me. It would be dreadful if something happened and I never got to hear about it."

Huey turned back to the meat. He gripped it in his tongs and stacked it onto a plate. "Come on," he said. "Let's enjoy today. I'll tell Clara about this later."

The men walked over to the table. Clara came from the kitchen with potatoes and salad and they enjoyed a pleasant meal in the afternoon sun.

Forty-four

Warrington, November 1958

It was the Glasgow train from Euston which called at Warrington. Huey told himself he was aiming to catch up with Maggie. He had never received a reply from her after he wrote telling her of Marvin's death. Was she okay? Had she had Marvin's baby? What was she doing now – married maybe? Maggie was the real reason but he was also curious to discover how Betty's life had turned out. What was it? Thirteen, fourteen years since they had been a young couple in love?

With his room booked at the Patten Arms Hotel next to the station, Huey had Maggie's last known address in his pocket. He checked in around two in the afternoon. It was a cloudy, showery Tuesday and he was glad he didn't have far to lug his suitcase from the station to his hotel. The male clerk at the desk was very helpful in directing Huey to the correct bus to take out to the district of Latchford where Maggie had lived.

He wandered into the town centre to catch his bus. The memories of his Burtonwood days re-surfaced, especially when he caught sight of current day G.I.s from out at the Burtonwood base, where a few thousand U.S. troops still lived and worked. The streets were different. The endless queues outside of the shops were gone. He had read that the food rationing system had ended and the shops were full of goods again. Nights with Marvin and the girls came back to him. There was a strange familiarity about everything – almost but not quite right. The clothes people wore were different from back then – and very different to clothes worn in Flins. The young were much more confident and distinctive looking than during the war. They wore their fashions proudly and they no longer dressed like their parents.

He thanked the conductor for shouting out his stop for him and hopped off the bus on Kingsway South. He orientated himself, checking the address and skipped between the cars to the opposite side. Behind him, vast areas that he remembered as fields, were covered with hundreds and hundreds of new houses. Houses with front and back gardens, spacious sidewalks out front and tree-lined grass verges. They delivered a newness to the area that the residents seemed proud and protective of. He'd read of the phenomenon of council housing that the post-war government had spread across the country. The French newspapers had reported on it extensively.

Leaving Kingsway, he tunnelled into an old street of pre-war terraced houses, where Maggie had lived with her mum and dad. He stopped at number 93 and rattled the knocker. The door opened and in front of the gloom of the passageway stood a small, stooped man in an old worn suit.

"Yes?" he grunted, looking Huey up and down.

It took a while but Huey finally recognised Maggie's father - "the old bastard." "You won't remember me," he began.

"I remember you all right," he interrupted. "Soon as you opened your Yankee gob. You're one o' them bloody G.I.s came over 'ere takin' our women. What do you want?"

"I was looking for Maggie."

"You won't find her 'ere. Disgraced us she did. Good riddance."

He began to close the door but Huey put his foot in the way. "Oi!" the old man shouted, "What d'you think you're doing?"

Just then a woman's voice came down the passageway. "Percy, what is it? Who's there?"

"Some bloody blackie. Won't let me shut the door."

"'Ere, come out the way. Let me deal with it." She pushed past him and shoved him back along the passageway. "What d'you want, Mister?"

"I'm trying to find Maggie," Huey said.

"What for?"

"I was Marvin's best friend. I was with him when he was killed. I know it's been a long time but this is the first opportunity I've had to come back and see how she's doing."

"Well, you're going to be disappointed, Mister."

"Oh, why's that?"

"We ain't seen her since the war. Not since all the trouble with that fella she hooked up with."

"Do you mean Marvin?"

"That's him."

"Did she, I mean? Erm, I'm not sure how to put this..."

"You want to know if she had the baby."

"Yes."

"Yes, she did."

"So, the kid will be thirteen or fourteen?"

"Thirteen. But they're not here." The woman's voice thickened. She sniffed and played with the hem of her apron. "We've never seen the child. He won't allow it," she said glancing back along the passageway. "So where is Maggie?"

"No idea. But her friend Betty will be able to tell you. They've kept in touch over all the years."

Huey's breath caught in the back of his throat when he heard Betty's name.

"Where can I find Betty," he asked.

" 'Old on," she said and turned back into the house. In a moment she had returned with a scrap of paper. On it was scribbled an address. He looked at it carefully.

"Is this her name now? Lythgoes?"

She nodded.

"How do I find this?" he asked.

"Easy. Just carry on up Kingsway, cross over the canal by the swing bridge and at the grass triangle take the second left. Betty's is the big house on the corner. You can't miss it. It's a mini mansion. Only a few hundred yards apart we are, but it might as well be a million miles. Cheek by jowl with the nobs he calls it."

Huey hadn't gone far when he heard breathless footsteps hurrying after him. "Wait, love," a voice panted. He turned to see Maggie's mother running to catch him. " 'Ere, please take this. If you ever see Maggie please give it to 'er."

It was a sealed envelope. From its bulkiness Huey could tell there was more than a letter in there. He knew it contained some money. His look told her he knew.

"For the child. You know. Her chin wobbled. It would have been comical if not so pathetic. "I've never seen her. It's 'is fault," she added nodding back to the house. "Tell Maggie I love 'er."

With that she turned and ran back to her front door.

As he crossed the grassy triangle Huey could see the house looming up in front of him. He began to get cold feet. It was impressive. A large bay window, upstairs and down, either side of the double front door. Large bay windows upstairs and down, along both sides too. Stone pillars held iron gates which guarded a gravel drive leading around a grass circle. He stood before it in awe. Reminding himself that his purpose was not to see Betty but to discover the whereabouts of Maggie, he steeled himself and crunched up the drive to the door. The porch was about the size of the first apartment he and Clara had shared, he joked to himself. He lifted a weighty knocker and banged it three times against its base. He waited. As he was about to step into the porch and knock again, he heard a lock turning. A woman in her twenties appeared. She was wearing a pinafore and her head sported a turban. She failed to hide her shock at his appearance.

"Yes?"

"Is Mrs Betty Lythgoes at home?" The woman relaxed a little when she heard the American accent.

"D'you mean Elisabeth, the mistress?"

"I guess so."

"Who shall I say is asking?"

"Huey. Huey Tate."

"Does she know you?"

"She did. I'm pretty sure she'll remember me."

"Wait here."

The door was closed and he was left standing and wondering if it would ever open again. When it did, Betty stood before him. She was visibly shocked. Her face had reddened with embarrassment and her hands had flown to her mouth. She almost bent double in a mixture of fear and astonishment. Huey turned his open palms out to her in a gesture that said, 'hey, it's only me'. "Mrs Lythgoes, I presume,"

Betty gathered herself, straightened and allowed herself a smile. But she was obviously put out and not sure how to behave. "You'd better come in," she said, and stepped aside to let him pass. Huey took off his hat and looked around. Betty pointed at a hat stand against the wall and he popped it onto a hook.

"Alice!" Betty called and led the way into a large reception room which Huey guessed he had seen behind one of the great bay windows fronting the house. Looking around, Huey found it difficult to pinpoint an item of furniture that looked as if it could have been bought for less than a two or three hundred bucks. Betty went to the door and called Alice again. The girl came and Betty ordered a tray of tea and biscuits. She shooed the girl away, closed the door and walked straight up to Huey and threw her arms around him. She clung on tightly to him, like a drowning man clings onto a log. Huey froze. He kept his arms behind his back and waited for Betty to release him. Betty looked up into his face and smiled. "Oh my God, it is so good to see you. And you're safe and well. Say something."

"Hello Betty, or should I say Elisabeth now?"

"Yes, I'm afraid so. We're all very posh now, you know."

She directed him to a deep leather three-seater settee and she took a seat in an identical one facing him. Her hair was no longer in a shoulder length bob as it had been, nor did it hang and sway naturally. It was styled in a waved coiffure, highly lacquered and stiff, as was the English fashion. She wore a knee length dress and nylons. Her high-heeled shoes were not entirely compatible with the deep pile carpet but she had clearly learned how to manage the terrain. Alice entered with a tray, placed it on the coffee table that stood between them and asked if she should pour.

"It's all right, Alice. You can leave us. I'll pour."

Betty got up, smoothed her dress down over her flat stomach with both hands and poured two cups. "I don't know if you take milk and sugar or not."

"Milk and two sugars please."

After handing him his cup and saucer she sat down, pulled her hem down over her knees and picked up her own drink. She took a sip.

"It's amazing to see you again," Huey beamed.

"Likewise," she replied. They both chuckled at her use of an old Americanism she had picked up from Huey.

"How are you? You look great."

"I'm smashing, thank you. What about you? You look quite prosperous yourself."

Huey thought about Clara, Ana, his life in Flins. He felt blessed. "I'm doin' okay. They sipped their tea and smiled at each other over the rims of their cups. "How's your Pop? Are you both still mad keen on that rugby game?" She lowered her cup to the saucer. Her face became slightly more serious.

"I've stopped going actually."

"Oh, how come?"

"It's just the way Saturday works out really. It's not so convenient anymore." "Oh?"

"Well Dad plays golf with Gerald on Saturday mornings and after a drink in the clubhouse they go straight on to the match. It doesn't work if they have to come back and pick me up. The golf club doesn't admit women – so there it is."

"Gerald's you husband, I take it?"

"That's right. We married in '46. Dad introduced us at a golf club dance." Another sip of tea and a proffered biscuit.

"Thank you. These are nice. You can't get them in France."

"So, you are a Frenchman now?"

"Very much so. In a macabre way the war turned out to be good for me."

"What do you want?"

252

The way she suddenly sprang the question popped the bubble of niceties they had been swapping. Huey swallowed a mouthful. He coughed. "Well," he began but was interrupted.

"What's past is past, you know. I'm happily married now. What happened in the war was, what shall I say? Very romantic. But we all had to grow up, didn't we?"

"I got your letter, Betty. You don't need to try and explain. Maggie filled in the gaps that you left out of your note."

"What do you mean? What gaps?"

"Nothing." Before she could jump in, he quickly added, "I'm married. I have a daughter. A beautiful daughter. Her name's Ana."

Betty's head shook uncomfortably. "Oh. I see." She looked around the room – anywhere but at Huey.

"And you?" he asked. "Have you got children?"

"No," she laughed dismissively. Their eyes locked for a moment. "It's just never happened." She paused and sipped her tea before continuing. "And your wife, what's her name?"

"Clara."

"That's a nice name. Unusual. Is it American?"

"No, she's French – a Parisian. We've settled in a nice small town called Flins. It's not too far from Paris. I have done okay since the war."

Betty placed her cup noisily on its saucer. "No," she uttered. She looked as if something had escaped her grasp. "I never thought ..."

"What?"

"Oh nothing." She stood up, went to the door and called for Alice. Alice cleared away the pots and went out.

"You'll have to be going soon."

"Is your husband due home?"

"No, no that could be any time tonight. I never know when he's going to get back. He's a busy man. It's not that," she protested. "I have to go out."

Huey sensed that this was a white lie; that she wanted him to be gone. His revelation about Clara and Ana had affected her.

"You haven't told me why you're here," she added as she stood to signal that it was time for the meeting to end.

"Well, I foolishly thought you might be pleased to see me. For old time's sake?"

"I am pleased to see you. But I thought you might have another reason."

"Well actually, I do. My mother is seriously ill and I'm on my way home to see her. I decided that this could be my only chance to visit here again and I am looking for Maggie. I've been to her parents' house and her mother sent me to you. It seems she doesn't know where Maggie is currently living but thinks you might."

Betty's face softened. "Poor Maggie. She desperately loved Marvin" She stopped herself suddenly and looked away embarrassed. "I do have an address for her. She's moved away from Warrington. Things were hard for her when the baby came. People are so stupid. We write to each other."

Betty moved to a sideboard and returned with a sheet of paper on which she had written an address. She handed it to Huey. "Maggie met a man at a wedding in Manchester. One of our friends from the munitions works invited us both. The girl's husband had invited some ex-war comrades and Maggie got lucky with one of them. He was an ex-Spitfire pilot from Antigua. He was living in Leicester. She's married now and living there. Seems very happy."

"Oh. Okay."

The conversation died right there. A bubble of silence rose up between them. In an embarrassed demeanour, Huey edged his way to the door. He aimed a tight-lipped smile at her and nodded as he backed out of the room. Alice was in the hall and she escorted him out. It was only when he reached the bottom of the gravel drive that he realised he had forgotten his hat. He crunched his way back to the front door. Passing the bay-window he could see inside the room they had occupied. Betty was sitting on the edge of the settee her face in her hands, sobbing. The front door opened and Alice handed his hat to him. He turned and crunched his way down the drive.

Forty-four

Leicester, November 1958

The next morning Huey checked out of his hotel and caught a train to Leicester. Changing at Nuneaton he had an hour to wait for a connection which he filled by walking around the town centre. He was glad to get back to the station after spending a complete hour without seeing one other black face and trying to pretend that he wasn't perturbed by the stares of all passers-by.

Disembarking at Leicester, London Road, he immediately felt better when a short fat West Indian ticket collector welcomed him at the barrier with a beaming 'good afternoon, brother'. The man checked the address on Huey's paper and gave him directions.

"You can take a number 33 bus, or you can walk it easy in fifteen minutes, if you care to stroll."

There was blue sky showing between strings of white clouds so he decided to walk. At the park gates he turned off London Road, into Evington Road. Instinctively, he knew he was in the right area. The number of black faces rose from one in fifty to easily three or four in twenty. He felt more comfortable. The verbal music swung between the flat Leicester vowels of the whites to the staccato tumbling of the West Indians. He looked at his address and turned into St Stephen's Road. There, six houses in, halfway along a terraced block, stood number 73. He pushed open the little gate and took the one and a half strides to the front door. There was no bell. No knocker. He lifted the letter box and rattled it. He checked his watch as he waited. It was two-thirty in the afternoon. Would Maggie be in? Maybe she worked. Just as his hopes began to decline the door opened and there stood Maggie.

They both froze. Maggie's astonishment was a sight to behold. Huey couldn't help but grin. Maggie's mouth fell open her eyes popped out and she curled up as if recoiling from a physical blow.

"Huey," she screamed. She fell down the doorstep into his arms and virtually danced him around in a circle. They were both laughing and gasping with delight. A figure appeared in the doorway. A tall, thin, muscular West Indian male. He sucked his teeth as a puzzled expression flickered across his face.

"Who dis now, dancin' wid me wife?"

Maggie pulled away from Huey and fell against the man. "Ray," she insisted, tugging his arm. "Come here. This is Huey. You know, the Huey I've told you about – from Burtonwood in the war."

Ray looked momentarily unsure. "Ray," she demanded. "You know. Betty's boy. The one I told you about." Realisation dawned on Ray. "Oh dat Huey. Well, what you keepin' him in de yard for? Bring de man in de house."

Maggie slapped his arm playfully and she pulled Huey into the house, pushing Ray before her as they went. They passed directly into a front room, through one door into a tiny space and immediately through another door leading to a living room with a dining table and a couple of easy chairs. The contrast with Betty's room could not have been greater. "Come in, come in."

Ray disappeared into the kitchen beyond, while Maggie sat Huey down in one of the easy chairs and pulled an upright chair right up close to him so that they sat knee to knee. She interrogated him about his life and times since they had parted. She was furious to hear about the assault upon him in Paris. Then she was delighted that it caused him to miss the rest of the war. Poetic justice she called it. She had to know everything about Clara and Ana. Most of her contributions began with – do you remember when? – and went on to cause bouts of laughter when they recalled some scrape or other they had got into in Burtonwood or Warrington.

"You two look as if you're having fun," a voice said.

Huey looked up in surprise. Ray had come back in. His Antiguan accent had disappeared and he spoke the way Huey had heard British officers speaking or one of those radio announcers on the BBC. It was a way of speaking he had never heard an ordinary Englishman or woman using. Maggie laughed at Huey's expression.

"Posh, ain't he."

"Well he sure surprised me. What's going on?"

"He was in the RAF in the war. Flew Spitfires, didn't you, my hero? They teach you to speak like that in the RAF. They're a cut above the other services."

"Flew Spitfires? I didn't know they let people like me and you do that, "Huey said.

"Oh, they did when they were running out of bodies to fly them," Maggie interjected. Not that they were grateful when it was all over. They won't even let him drive a bus now."

"Is that right?"

"Too right, I'm afraid," said Ray. "I applied for a vacancy with Leicester Transport. They wanted drivers so I went for an interview. When I arrived, I could tell by their faces as soon as they saw me, that I wasn't welcome. A man came along the line and called my name. When I stood up, he hesitated, checked his list, asked me my name again and then told me to wait while he returned to the interview room to check something. He came back out a few minutes later and told me that all the vacancies had been taken. I knew he was lying and he knew I knew. There were twelve others waiting and two of them got up to leave with me when they heard that the jobs had gone. He quickly turned to them and said they could stay, along with all of the others because they had been selected."

"That stinks," said Huey.

"It's worse than that," Maggie blurted. "And the unions are as bad. They've said they'll strike if any blacks get jobs there."

"So, what do you do, Ray?"

"I make typewriters. Imperial Typewriters has a gigantic factory here. I work maintaining machinery. Maggie works there as well, on the assembly line."

"How come you two aren't working today?"

"If you work Saturday afternoon you get Wednesday afternoon off," Maggie said.

Ray poured coffee for Huey and himself and a cup of tea for Maggie. "It's all a man can do to get a decent drink of coffee in this country. They're drowning in tea but they don't know how to make coffee."

Huey savoured a sip of the strong black brew and nodded in appreciation. He was thinking of Miller again. He wished Miller could be here now to see Maggie and Ray. He thought it might change his opinion on mixed marriages. Or would it? He reached into his inside pocket and pulled out the envelope Maggie's mother had given to him. He handed it to her. He and Ray watched as she opened it.

"I saw your parents yesterday," he explained.

"How was the old bastard?" Maggie asked.

"Pretty much the way you described him. Your mom gave me that."

Maggie pulled the contents out of the opened envelope and spread them on her lap. Twenty one-pound notes lay there along with two sheets of note paper. Maggie gasped. Suddenly she was crying. Ray reached an arm around her shoulder. "Hey, what's the matter?" he soothed.

"My poor mother. Married to that useless, useless man. How could she afford to do this?" She sobbed some more.

"Her words were – for the child," Huey said.

This caused more tears from Maggie. "Poor mum. She's never seen Lizzie. And she doesn't even know about our Angela. What a shame. What a damn shame!"

"Oh, you have two children?" Huey asked.

"Yes," Ray said. "We have Angela and Lizzie. They should both be home from school soon. Lizzie is at high school but she finishes twenty minutes before Angela and gets to the primary school in time to meet her sister." He looked at his watch. "Yes, they should be here anytime."

Ray turned to Maggie. "Hey, love," he said. "Don't cry. We could go and see your mother. Marshall has said I can borrow his car anytime. We could do a nice cross-country trip to Warrington. You could see Elisabeth too."

"Betty? Do you think we could? Would Marshall's car get us there?"

"Now you're being cheeky," Ray laughed. "Wait till I tell Marshall what you said about his car."

The sound of a gate opening in the back and then voices coming in through the back door told Huey that the girls had arrived home. "Hey girls," Ray called, "Come and see who is in here."

Huey leaned forward and whispered to Maggie. "Does Lizzie know about Marvin?"

Maggie touched his knee with affection. "Yes, Huey. It's thoughtful of you to ask. But yes, she knows all about her father. Ray's her dad but Marvin is the father she never met."

"And Ray ......?"

Maggie knew what Huey was attempting to ask but struggling to formulate the words for. "Ray is wonderful. He treats both girls exactly the same. I'm a very lucky woman, Huey. And I know it."

Lizzie came through the door from the kitchen first. Huey had to stop himself gasping. He looked back at Maggie. The look she returned told him that she knew exactly what he was feeling. She smiled. It was a proud motherly smile. Huey looked back at Lizzie. He stood to greet her. He held out his hand. There was a slight tremor for an instant. It was as if Marvin had jumped back to life. The girl was beautiful in her own right but her inheritance from Marvin was in her eyes, her movement, her smile, even her hand gestures. Huey found his heart filling with warmth for this child and regret for the fate of her father, his buddy Marvin.

Lizzie was bumped from behind, which snatched Huey out of the spell he had been under. Angela squeezed into the room. "Come on Lizzie," she teased. "you're standing there blocking progress." Like Lizzie, she was dressed in her gingham school uniform dress and a dark blue blazer. The blazers were the same, apart from the badges on the breast pockets but the dresses were different colours – Lizzie's green, Angela's blue. Like Lizzie, she pulled her straw, wide-brimmed hat from her head and threw it onto a shelf.

"I hate that hat," Angela exclaimed.

"You say that every afternoon," Maggie teased.

"That's because I hate it."

"So do I," Lizzie added, throwing hers to land on top of Angela's.

Maggie spent some time explaining who Huey was and how they knew each other. Lizzie's eyes widened when she realised that Huey had known her father. Angela sat on Maggie's knee and Lizzie curled up on the floor beside her chair to listen to Huey reminisce about his and Marvin's exploits back in their Burtonwood days.

"Aww, Dad," Angela complained when Ray called them.

"Never mind, 'Aww'. You've both got that dentist appointment and we'll be late if we don't set off now. It's a good ten-minute walk. And we should leave your mother to have some good catch-up time with her friend."

"Wait!" Lizzie shouted. "I've got to change out of this horrible uniform."

Both girls jumped up and ran up the stairs, which appeared from nowhere through a door behind where Huey was sitting. When they could be heard bumping down again, Ray took Huey's hand and shook it. "It's been a pleasure to meet you. It would be nice to have time for a long talk. I'd particularly like to find out more about life in France. Maybe the next time?"

"My pleasure too. You have a great family here, Ray. You should be very proud."

"I have my moments," he said.

"So long girls."

"Bye Huey."

"Bye Huey," said Lizzie. "Look forward to seeing you next time you call."

"Au revoir, Lizzie," Huey added.

The door slammed and the buzz that the girls had brought was gone. Maggie and Huey looked at each other, adjusting to the quiet. "How was Betty?" she asked eventually.

Huey recounted his visit. He included the detail about his view through the window of her crying. Maggie pondered this for a while. She sighed.

"Betty is in a loveless marriage. She did it to please her father. He's happy. He's got son-in-law Gerald to go golfing with and boozing with and talking business with. Poor Betty has nothing."

Maggie paused. She looked fiercely at Huey. "Betty made a terrible mistake, you know." She didn't need to say anything else. Huey knew what she meant.

"I would have come back for her – if she'd wanted me. I thought she was the one for me."

"She was," Maggie squealed. "And you were the one for her. She just didn't have the damn courage. It's such a damn shame."

Huey began to feel a little uncomfortable. "I must tell you about Clara and my Ana," he said. He took out a couple of photographs from his wallet. Maggie studied them.

"They're both beautiful, Huey. No, I mean it. They are really beautiful." Huey told some of the details of Clara's war.

"My God, not only is she a stunner but she's a war heroine too. You're a lucky fella, Huey." She stopped and reached out again to touch his knee – as if reassuring herself that he was really there. "But you deserve it. You're a good man."

She got up from her chair and walked to the window overlooking the tiny rectangle of backyard. "I'm lucky too," she said in a quiet voice. "I met Marvin and I have our gorgeous daughter. And now I've found Ray. He's every bit as wonderful as Marvin was and he's made my life." She turned round suddenly and looked at Huey. "I loved Marvin," she said, "and in some way I always will. But it doesn't stop me loving Ray. Ray is the love of my life."

Miller's words came into Huey's mind again. He mentally berated himself for allowing that man's cynicism to force its way in despite the evidence before him. Emotion welled up in Maggie and a rogue tear ran down her face. "Listen to me," she squawked. "Sentimental old fool, that's what I am."

"It's great to see you so happy. You have a wonderful family. Seeing Lizzie walk in was like seeing the ghost of Marvin."

Maggie laughed. "I know. It's uncanny isn't it. She lifts my heart every time I look at her. Life's good here in Leicester. We're not the only mixed couple. There's been a big influx of West Indians, filling the vacancies in the factories. The city is booming. Lots of them are from Antigua too, which is nice for Ray."

Huey couldn't say what he had worried he might have found. Maggie and Lizzie alone and in poverty. Maggie alone or married to an Englishman with Lizzie in foster care or worse, a home for unwanted children. He should have known better of Maggie. "Lizzie? Betty? Elisabeth? Lizzie?" he asked in a roundabout way.

"Of course," Maggie replied. "Who else could I have named her after?"

Huey felt it was time to get going. The girls and Ray would be back from the dentist soon. He didn't want to intrude on their hospitality any further. "No, please don't go. You must stay and eat with us."

"I'm sorry, Maggie, I can't," Huey lied. "I've got an appointment for a telephone call with Clara and Ana. It's booked in at the hotel for six-thirty. I need to get going. I can't miss it."

"Oh, that's such a shame. We had so much more to talk about."

"Maggie, there's something I want you to do for me."

"What?"

Huey took a small package out of his inside pocket and handed it to her.

"What's this?"

"Please don't embarrass me. I didn't know how I was going to find you. I feared for your baby. I remember what it could be like here for coloured people. I want you to have this anyway. For the girls. Buy them something you couldn't afford." "I can't accept this," she said.

"Please, Maggie. Marvin was my buddy. He saved my life more times than I can count. Let me do this for his memory. If you don't want to tell Ray about it you don't have to. I would understand if he was annoyed with a stranger giving you money. But please. Keep it for the girls. For when they need something you couldn't afford – a new dress or new shoes. I'm doing good now. Better than I ever hoped. My company is good to me. And I haven't forgotten how you made me feel welcome when I came here. Please?"

Maggie relented. "I'll put it with mother's. And thank you." She reached out and put her arms around him. She held him tightly. She kissed his cheek.

"Go on then," she ordered. "You mustn't miss your phone call. And keep safe. Don't hang around in Alabama any longer than you have to. Get back to Clara and Ana and your life in France as quickly as you can."

Forty-five

Alabama, 1959.

Swarms of mayflies hovered above the pond in the field across the street. The sun on his face was like a childhood memory. The French sun was never as fierce. "I got you some breakfast here, Huey son."

"Okay, mama. I'm coming in."

"No. You sit yourself down on the porch and I'll bring it out." She came out carrying a tray with a coffee pot and a plate piled high with eggs, pancakes and fries.

"There. Ain't no French cooking can beat an American breakfast like that."

"You're right mama. They don't know how to eat breakfast. Buttered croissants dipped in coffee. Yuk!"

The smells and the tastes transported him back. There had been happy times in his childhood. His mama, his brother and his two sisters and the highs and lows they had shared. His thoughts filled him with nostalgia.

"How's the girls, Mama? I ain't seen nothing of them."

"Ceceline done married. Gone off to Hayneville. Got a good man, I reckons. Works hard at a fruit factory. Got a little boy name of Joey."

"Sounds good. How about Mary?"

Mama sucked her teeth. "Don't ask me about her. Mary acting like a darn fool. Got herself a no-good nigger from Monty. She livin' over there with him. I don't know what she gets up to." Mama rubbed her hands on the dishcloth she was holding. "Now you gonna ask about Danika. Well Danika doin' the best of all. She moved up to Chicago, soon as she could. She workin' for the railroad. Accordin' to her, she runnin' Union Station – single-handed." Mama cackled at the thought and Huey laughed along with her.

"Well I'm pleased for her," he said. "And for Cissie. You want me to go to Monty to look up Mary."

"Don't you do no such thing. That feller she with – I don't trust him. Like as not he put a bullet in you. No. Mary made her bed; she can lie in it."

"How you been keepin', Mama? I heard you not been too well."

"I don't know who been tellin' you them stories. I never been fitter."

She pulled out a chair and sat down beside Huey. She reached over and rubbed her hand up and down his forearm. "I miss you, son. Everyday I have a little cry for my Huey. But everyday I stop myself and I thank the Lord that you no longer here. I'm so happy you livin' in France, where people treat you decent. Don't you ever think about coming back to Alabama. It ain't no place for a colored person to live."

"Why do you stay, Mama? You could move to Chicago. Get a place near Danika. Make sure she's doin' a proper job at that there Union Station."

"I could sure do that," she smiled. "But I'm too old to uproot myself now. Anyways, I've got this lovely house you bought me. Why would I go and leave a beautiful house like this?"

"You know what's best for you, Mama."

"And I know what's best for you, son. It's been the joy of a lifetime to see you again but I want you to get back to your wife and baby in France. You made the right choice. Don't you let nobody nor nothing change your mind."

"Well, I've only got 'til the weekend, Mama. My boss been very good to me. But he wants me back at work."

"Good. I'm glad. But why you not send me more pictures. I'd like to see your baby growing up. And it would be nice to see more photos of your wife. You could post me some, on birthdays or at Christmas?"

Forty-six

Paris, December 1962

"Come here, Ana." The voice came from the living room of the Montmartre apartment. A five-year-old dark-haired girl came running down the stairs and leapt onto the man's lap. They rolled on the sofa in a wrestle for a few moments until she fell onto the floor giggling. "What do you want, Papa?" she spluttered.

"I want to show you my new toy."

She got up on her knees, all ears now. What was this new toy? Her brown eyes shone with curiosity and her ebony skin glowed with the oils her mother had just massaged into her following her bath.

"It's here, look. In the corner."

Ana followed her Papa's eyes until hers rested on a square item of furniture standing there."

"Oh my," she exclaimed. "It's a television. When did you get it? Does it work? Can we watch it now?"

Papa looked at his watch. Yes, we can put it on now. There might be something interesting to watch. He walked over to the box in the corner and turned a large knob. The resounding click made Ana gasp theatrically. Papa came and sat beside her on the sofa.   After a few moments she looked up into his face and said, "It's not doing anything."

Papa smiled and whispered, "Be patient. Shh! Here it comes."

The square window gradually lit up and some lines darted across it. Ana was amazed. When the picture resolved itself into images of people moving and talking, she gasped again. She looked at Papa. Her hand covered her mouth which was agape. She looked back at the screen. "What is it?" she demanded. Papa looked at a magazine which was lying open next to him. He scanned the page. "It's called 'La Boîte à Sel'," he answered. "Listen," he continued. "It's funny. It will make us laugh." Clara came into the room. "What is all the fuss about?" she laughed. "I can hear you two upstairs."

"Mama, look. It's our new television. Papa has bought it for us."

Clara sat herself on the sofa between them. She reached out and took his hand. She lifted it and kissed it. "Oh Marc," she said. "You shouldn't spoil us. I'll never get her to go to bed now."

Marc reached across and wrapped his arm around Clara's shoulder. He pulled her to him and kissed her lips. "We can't be the only family in Montmartre without a television can we. Ana would be laughed at in school." They kissed again.

"All right, little mademoiselle princess Ana. But when this programme ends it's bedtime for you."

"Thank you, Mama." She climbed in between her Mama and Papa and snuggled down inside their warmth. Marc gazed over her head into Clara's eyes. He mouthed, "I love you."

Clara smiled in return. She leaned over Ana to meet his lips. She got up from the sofa and walked to the door of the room. "Send her up when this is over. I'm going to carry on working."

As she climbed the stairs, Clara rubbed a knuckle into an itchy eye. At the top of the stairs she went into the spare bedroom. This was the room they kept for guests if ever they should have any. Occasionally, Clara's mother stayed a night or two. Even less frequently, an itinerant lawyer from the provinces would arrive home with Marc. She sat at a dressing-table and pulled open the bottom drawer. Inside there were several scrap books. Clara was beginning to recognise the triggers that sent her to this place. Hearing Ana call Marc 'Papa' was one. She loved the fact that Ana was so happy with Marc, but it always conflicted in her when Ana said it. The second was whenever she said, 'I love you' to Marc. It wasn't that she didn't mean it. But she suffered a flicker of guilt each time as she recalled saying it to Huey. It had meant something different then and her guilt was about being inwardly deceitful. She selected one of the books and let it fall open at the place where she always went to first. Her heart sagged as she affectionately rubbed her hand over her favourite picture of Huey. Resplendent in his U.S. Army uniform and holding his guitar, his smile made her believe she could hear his laugh. A tear ran down her cheek, tumbled onto her lip. The same mantra repeated itself in her head. 'Why did he have to go back? Why?' As soon as it started, she upbraided herself. Of course, he had to go back! What kind of man would not return for his mother when he knew she was dying? Certainly not the kind of man Huey was. The next step in her thinking was too painful to allow. She always stopped herself here. They were so in love. What had made him fail to return? Was she just another G.I. bride – a foreign adventure? She closed the album and slid it back into the drawer as she heard Ana's footsteps running upstairs. "Mama, Mama!" Ana called. "It was so funny. You must watch it too next time."

Forty-seven

Alabama, 1959

After showering and putting on a clean T-shirt, Huey told Mama he was heading into town for a look around the old spots. He reminded himself with each step, that he was in Alabama and not Flins. He needed to adopt his "good nigger" persona. Leaving the black area where Mama's house was, he felt the change in atmosphere immediately. If anything, it was worse than it had been before he left. There was a tension in the air. The "uppity niggers" were making a noise all over the south. They were being echoed in the northern liberal areas, like New York and Chicago. The southern whites were bristling. De- segregation was a word you didn't whisper in these parts. What was happening? He was tempted to play the innocent Frenchman and keep to the sidewalk when a white woman approached. But he always lost his nerve. Cops stopped him twice to ask what he was doing. He explained that he was looking for the Starburst club where he had played guitar before he moved away. Each time they let him move on with a warning to watch his step.

The old Starburst building was boarded up. Wild dogwood shrubs were growing out of the tarmac in the front lot. The timber cladding was peeling and some slats had fallen off. It was a sad sight for Huey. He stood out front and shook his head.

"Hey nigger, what you doin'?" It was two white guys, with their girlfriends. Huey turned to look across the street to them. The men walked over. "I asked you what you doing, nigger?"

"I'm sorry. I was just going down memory lane. I used to play guitar here before the war."

The shorter blond guy laughed and nudged his buddy. "Get that Pete. Nigger's goin' down memory lane." He lunged at Huey and punched him in the chest.

"Hey, what's that for? I don't mean no harm."

The blond guy lunged again. Huey stepped back and his assailant stumbled. "Hey," he yelled. "You see that? Nigger tried to push me over." He was working himself into a fury caused by his embarrassment.

Pete took his buddy's arm. "Calm down, Adam. We don't want this. Look our gals are waiting across the street."

"Hey, boys, whatcha all doin'?" one of the girls called over. "You gonna leave us waitin' here all day?"

"Come on, Adam. We ain't come out to do this. What's the matter with you anyway? This guy ain't done nuthin' to you"

"Hell, he could be one of them civil rights niggers."

"So what? Come on, we got better things to do. I'm going."

Pete walked across the street to join the girls. Without his six-foot buddy Adam looked less intimidating. Huey knew that it was more than his life was worth to even defend himself, never mind take the offensive. He just stood his ground.

"You're a lucky nigger," Adam snarled. "You won't be so lucky next time I catch you out where decent folk live."

Huey watched him walk over to his friends. He didn't move until they were out of sight. Part of him wished his friends and workmates in France could have been there to witness the scene. He knew they wouldn't believe him if he told them.

He decided to get back to Mama's before anything else could occur. He thought he'd made the right choice when he crossed the street to avoid passing some white schoolgirls but it took him to the side where an old white guy was sitting outside a bar. He was sinewy and grizzled, but he smiled through yellow teeth. He stuck a leg out and stopped Huey. Huey went to step off the sidewalk and go around but the guy spoke in a friendly manner. "Hey buddy, no hurry. Ain't you that Huey Tate? Used to play decent guitar at the Starburst?"

Huey smiled. "That's me. I just been out to look at the old place. All boarded up. Gone to hell."

"That's right. Didn't last the war. Nobody seems to want to take it over and do something with it. I reck'n it will just rot away to nothing but dust. Say what you doing around here? I ain't seen you lately."

"No, sir. I don't live around here no more. I been back to see my Mama. She's getting' on. You know."

"And where's she at?"

"Oh, out on the Prescot development."

"Very nice. She doin' right well. I bet you had somethin' to do with that." Well, maybe," Huey laughed. This old guy wasn't a bad old feller. He seemed personable enough anyway, especially to a stranger nigger.

"She in one o' them single storeys?"

"That's her."

"Well you take good care yoursel'. These is strange times. Ain't nobody knows what's gonna happen next."

"Sure will, mister. Nice talking to you."

The old guy dropped his leg from the post. Huey decided to head back to Mama's. He had thought about going to a bar in the black downtown district over the tracks. But he decided against it. He was feeling good. The old guy's friendliness had given him some of his French confidence and he wanted to spend time with Mama. As he walked, he nostalgically breathed in the old Alabama air of his childhood.

The vast, endless sky out beyond the tracks took him back to years roaming with Clarence and his buddies. There were good times too – so long as they kept away from whitey. He was confused about Marc. Here he was on a false errand. Mama was more or less like her old self. Sure, she was older, a little stiffer, a little creakier but she sure wasn't suffering no terminal illness. What had led Marc to believe that? Did the lawyer guy he met at the conference confuse his Mama with someone else? Anyway, whatever, here he was and thanks to Marc he was spending precious time with his Mama. Time, he thought he might never have had. So, in that way he had to be grateful to Marc. Without his intervention Huey would never have got to see his old Mama again, this side of the grass.

That evening Mama cooked fried catfish followed by banana pudding. She invited her new neighbours, Joe and Marlene Cole over and they all sat on the porch in the pure still evening. Joe was a black Alabaman, descended from slaves, just like Mama and Huey. Marlene was from Kingston in Jamaica. They had met during the war when Joe had been deployed to Jamaica. He had been based in Vernam Field, the U.S Army Air Forces airfield located 50 or so miles out of Kingston. Marlene had worked in the canteen.

"So, you're living in France now," Joe commented.

"That's right," Huey responded.

"Got yourself a nice French lady?" Marlene chuckled.

"Right again," Huey laughed.

"Too right," Mama, butted in. "An' I got me a French speaking granddaughter. I never knowed I was so clever."

Their laughter echoed along the street, Mama's self-deprecating chuckle the loudest of all. They finished eating and they all carried some pots inside. Mama found a cardigan for Marlene to wrap around her shoulders and they all sat back out on the porch. The men had beers, Marlene had a rum and coke and Mama had a finger of the cognac that Huey had brought with him. It was as pleasant an evening as Huey could ever remember having on his native soil. The silence of the street was only broken by their soft chatter, the odd clink of glasses and the sometime distant call of a child or bark of a dog.

They leaned forward when the sound of a car drifting closer grew in their ears. It was a red 1950 Chevrolet Styleline with a black soft top and it came at a slow pace but it kicked up a cloud of dust from the dry street as it cruised by. Huey loved the shape of that car and he followed its progress fondly. He had a momentary wish that he was back amongst the Renaults he spent his working days with. He recognised the face in the passenger seat. He waved. He guessed the old guy from this afternoon hadn't recognised him. He stared at Huey and mouthed something but he did not wave in reply.

"That's the old feller I was tellin' y'all about. In town today. The guy I was chattin' with. Right friendly."

The sound of the engine faded to nothing and the silence fell once more. The four neighbours sat back in their chairs enjoying the silence and savouring their drinks. Huey's mind flew back to Clara and Ana. He was enjoying this moment but he was longing to be back with them. He had been ruminating on a plan to get Mama to join them in France. She wouldn't be able to go back with him this time. He was booked to fly out from Montgomery in three day's-time. He hadn't even mentioned the idea to her yet. But he would plant it in her head over the next few days. He would let it stew there and then when she was good and stewed, he would send for her. He could just see her with Ana. He could imagine her on the streets of Flins. Oh, how she would marvel

277

at the life Huey had made for himself. And oh boy, how she would love the way she could walk around the shops and the cafes at will. No more 'No Coloreds!' or 'Whites Only!' signs to beat her down.

The sound of a car struck them again. This time it was sharper, faster, more urgent. Angrier! It beat a tornado of dust into the air as it skidded to a halt outside their porch.

It was the red Styleline as before, but this time Huey couldn't see the old man.

Four whites got out. Three carried baseball bats, one had a pistol. The one with the pistol was shorter than the other three. He was mid-thirties with wispy red hair and maple syrup freckles. They walked quickly towards the porch and bounded up the steps. Joe and Huey got to their feet. Marlene pushed her chair over as she struggled to stand. Mama, put her glass down on the table and pushed herself slowly upwards.

"What d'you want?" she hollered. "What you doin' on my porch?"

"Shut up bitch!" the one with the pistol said. "We ain't here for you."

Huey stepped forward. He was totally perplexed. Nothing had gone on. He had only been home just over a week and he hadn't seen nothing or no-one. What was this all about? "Hey guys," he said placatingly. "What's all this about? Ain't nothing going on here."

"You Huey Tate?" the guy with the pistol asked.

"I sure am."

"You a Frenchie now?"

"I live and work in France, sure. But I'm still an American."

The white guys next move shocked Huey to his bones. He pulled a sheet of paper out of his back pocket. Huey looked at the three guys with baseball bats as the piece of paper was unfolded. Their faces were impassive – as if they were carrying out a common procedure down at the town hall or somewhere. The guy held out the paper. This is what shook Huey. On it was a picture of himself, Clara and Ana.

"This you?" The face was getting redder and the freckles more syrupy.

Huey suddenly realised where this was going. He knew he was in deep. Deeper than he could have ever imagined. Should he lie? "Where d'you get that?" he said before thinking it through.

"So it is you. Take him boys."

Before he could move, two of them had grabbed him. When Joe stepped forward the third guy let swing with his baseball bat and cracked him on the shoulder. Marlene screamed and Mama pushed forward. The guy who had hit Joe punched Mama in the face leaving her out cold back in her chair. Huey's anger rose but it came too late. He was held fast. As he struggled the third guy again let loose. He whacked Huey three, four times across the legs with his bat. Huey's shins and knees were battered. He struggled to stand. Huey was dragged down the steps of the porch to the car. The freckled guy waved his gun around the porch.

"Don't get no funny ideas niggers. We only upholding the law. We don't have no niggers takin' white women and producing half-breed children. An' we don't care what country they in."

As they dragged Huey to their car all he could think about was the picture. He knew it. Marc had taken the shot with his camera when he had visited them in Flins. He had posted them a print a few weeks later from Paris. It stood in a frame on their sideboard in his home. It had been there the day he left for Alabama. This was another copy. There's only one person who would have had another copy of that picture and that was Marc. So, what was it doing in this man's hand?

Thrown onto the back seat, his hands tied behind his back, in between the two who had held him, freckles sped away. As they passed the far corner of the street and turned out of the coloured district, the driver waved to someone standing there. It was the old guy from downtown. He waved back, shook his head, turned and walked off.

Four days later Huey's body was found by a share-cropper who had come to investigate why the meagre trickle of water from the creek, that his crops depended on, had near enough dried up. Huey was lying face down, impeding the flow. When the coroner examined his body, he determined that, due to the battering his face had taken, rendering it unrecognisable as human, and the mass bruising all over his body, he must have been kept and abused for several days. However, the cause of death was not drowning in the creek or assault with one or several blunt instruments, but strangulation consistent with lynching. Due to his conclusion of 'death by misadventure' it was not deemed necessary for the police to investigate the death.

Forty-eight

Chartres, March 1963

Marc grabbed his briefcase as the train shuddered to a halt in Chartres. As he walked in the shadow of the magnificent cathedral, he re-read the address on the slip of paper he clutched in his hand. Henri Corbin was the name at the top of the slip. En route he entered the police station. He ran up the three shallow steps to the door, nodded to the gendarme on duty there and entered the lobby. He was expected and quickly ushered through to a sleepy office where several men at typewriters, paused to look at the stranger entering their domain. A door at the far end opened and a shirt-sleeved, large-bellied man with a moustache and a balding head beckoned him forward. Marc ploughed his way through the low-hanging cloud of tobacco smoke. Inspector Desmarais closed the door behind him and pointed towards a chair in front of his desk.

"Henri Corbin," the inspector grunted. He studied the file that Marc had handed to him. He looked up at Marc through the blue smoke swirling from the cigarette that remained glued to his bottom lip throughout the conversation that followed. "Are you sure about this?"

"Definitely. He's our man. He's the last link in the chain. It's the chain that will ensnare Moreau once and for all."

"So, this is about Moreau? He is a member of the National Assembly. He has twice been a member of the Cabinet. You don't go fishing for small-fry, do you?"

"Moreau is a big-fry criminal who has escaped justice for far too long. We should have got him when the Allies liberated Paris but he always slipped through our fingers."

"You are mad, Monsieur. Corbin is a big player in this town."

Marc grimaced. "Corbin will be all right if he plays along. He was one of the 'go along to get along' cowards who collaborated. But this is different. I have irrefutable evidence of war crimes against Moreau. If I get him inside a courtroom he will get the justice he deserves. The French judiciary know that if they let someone like Moreau go free the International Court of Justice will move against him and make our system look pathetic. Now, can we get on."

Desmarais continued to look doubtful. "Henri Corbin is a well-respected man in Chartres. He is chairman of the Chamber of Commerce and he is deputy mayor."

"He hunted French Jews throughout the occupation and sent thousands to their deaths."

Desmarais shrugged as if this was a petty commonplace. "But this was a long time ago, Monsieur Durand. Have we not moved on? Surely, it is time to forgive and forget."

"Inspector Desmarais," Marc said, pointedly leaning closer to the round-faced policeman over his desk. "I fully understand why you would want us to forgive and forget."

Desmarais sat back. Marc's indication that he was fully aware of Desmarais's own war record had shocked him. "And you see yourself as the avenging angel, I suppose, righting all wrongs."

"Think what you like, Inspector. But I've told you, we don't want Corbin for his crimes," Marc continued. "Unfortunately, there are too many ex-collaborators in high office even today. So, we close our eyes to the activities of so many. But we do want Moreau. And Corbin is going to give him to us or Corbin will pay the price. Now Inspector. If it's not too much trouble I request the team of officers I was promised and I will carry out my duty." The inspector closed the file and tossed it over the desk to Marc. He pushed himself with difficulty out of his seat and opened the door to his office. He yelled two names and a couple of uniformed men hurried between the desks to him.

"Go with Monsieur Durand. Follow his instructions. Report back to me when you have completed this task."

The men grunted assent and followed Marc out into the Chartres sunshine. Marc instructed his accompanying officers to wait outside the Hotel de Ville where he had arranged to meet Corbin. The interior of the building was tiled with patterned marble. Footsteps and voices echoed around the high-ceilinged vestibule. A receptionist asked him to sign a register and then led him up a grand staircase to a landing which led through to rows of offices. She stopped outside a door labelled 'Deputy Mayor' and pointed to a seat opposite. She went into the room, reappearing moments later. "The Deputy Mayor will let you know when he is ready." She offered him a fleeting smile and walked back to her post. An hour later Marc's patience was not diminished. He was wryly amused by Corbin's impertinence. But he was not going anywhere. Fifteen minutes later Corbin popped his head out of his doorway. He glanced up and down the corridor. When his eyes fell upon Marc disappointed annoyance flickered across his face. He half stepped out of his room and spoke.

"Ah, you are still here, Monsieur. I apologise for keeping you waiting. However, I must tell you that we cannot meet today. I have urgent council business which will keep me busy all afternoon."

Marc stood, gathered his brief case and smiled. "That's perfectly all right Monsieur Corbin."

Without another word he walked past Corbin and hurried down the stairs. Outside, on Rue de Maire, the two Gendarmes inspected the document that Marc had handed to them. When they had finished, he just said, "You know what to do."

They looked at each other and grinned. Then they nodded at him and went into the building. Three minutes later they emerged with a jacketless, handcuffed Deputy Mayor between them. His struggles were useless against the strength of their grip. He was furious. He yelled threats at Marc and the gendarmes but they were deaf to his abuse.

Inside the police station, Corbin vented his fury. Inspector Desmarais stood and took the blast of Corbin's ire full in the face. He remained expressionless throughout. Corbin had to be forcibly taken to an interview room where Marc left him to stew for an hour. Petty - but sweet revenge.

"You will regret this!" was Corbin's first remark when Marc entered to commence the interview. "Who do you think you are? What gives you the right to treat a senior member of the government of Chartres in such an outrageous manner?"

"I'll tell you who I am. I am Marc Durand and I am here under the auspices of Monsieur le Juge Patrice. He is leading the investigation into certain war crimes. I am here under his authority to interview you."

"I know you. You are an assassin. You are the one who should be investigated."

"If you and your Nazi friends had won the war, I am sure that would have happened. But unfortunately for you, you didn't."

"How dare you call me a Nazi? I am a French patriot."

Marc leaned over the table between them and whispered, "I know exactly what you are."

Leaning back, he opened a file and took out a series of photographs. "You will know these people," Marc said.

"Take your time. Look at them carefully. We have all the time in the world."

Corbin glanced at the first two or three and then turned away.

"You are not looking at the photographs, Monsieur Corbin. Why is that? Are you refusing to co-operate with the judge and his investigation?" Corbin folded his arms, turned sideways in his seat and said nothing.

"This first one is Luis Berger. He was taken by Jacques Moreau and his department at the Carlingue. He was taken into the Rue Lauriston building on 27th January 1942. His body was found ten days later. Records show that you were on duty for all of those ten days. You will tell us everything you know about what was done to Luis."

"Luis Berger was a criminal. Like you – an assassin. He got what he deserved." "Ah. At last. We are getting somewhere. So, you admit your involvement in the kidnapping and murder of Luis Berger."

"I do no such thing." Marc slid another photograph across the table.

"Here is Marie Voland, a French patriot who worked with an underground organisation to hide Jews from the likes of you. She was arrested on 14th May 1943. You accompanied the SS party that seized her from her home at 11.45 pm. She suffered multiple rapes and was tortured during her interrogations. We have witnesses who saw you and can testify to your crimes against her."

Slowly and methodically, over the next two hours, Marc went through eighty-one cases, each of which, it could be proved, Corbin had some involvement with. As each case was related in detail, Corbin's shoulders sagged even further.

"What do you want from me? That was wartime. We all did things we're not proud of."

"Some more than others, don't you think, Monsieur Corbin?"

Marc gathered up his papers, slid them into his briefcase and stood to leave. "I am not satisfied that you have co-operated fully with my investigation. Therefore, I require that you be arrested and taken to Paris to be interviewed by Monsieur le Juge."

Corbin jumped to his feet. "You can't do that," he yelled. "I am the Deputy Mayor of this town. I will not be treated this way."

Marc smiled at him, opened the door and left. Minutes later the same two gendarmes came in, handcuffed Corbin and accompanied him to a police van. Marc watched them drive off for Paris before heading to his hotel for a night's sleep.

Forty-nine

Paris, September 1963.

The telephone ringing interrupted Clara in her brushing of Ana's hair. At first this hair-brushing had been a trial for them both as Clara had only learned slowly, under Huey's guidance, how to groom Ana's Afro/French hair. After they had acquired the correct oils with which to massage it before brushing, it had become a routine they both loved. So few of their friends had telephones that Clara was pretty sure it would be Marc, calling from work about something. It was usually important, so she stopped brushing and went into the hall to pick up the receiver.

"Clara, it's me, Marc."

"I guessed it would be," Clara laughed. "What have you forgotten today?"

"The jury is deliberating. They have sent out a request for some incident dates. It's buried amongst papers that are back at the prosecutor's office. We thought our involvement was over and all we had to do was wait for the verdict. His clerks are struggling to find it amongst the mountain of paperwork that was returned for filing. It's easier and quicker if I retrieve it."

"Well, you need to know you have upset Ana and me. We were hair brushing. You will have to pay a forfeit when you get in tonight."

Marc laughed. "I will look forward to that. Now the incident dates are in my diary for 1943. You'll find the diary in my desk drawer."

"But you always keep that locked. You always say that I am not to meddle with your professional papers."

Marc laughed again at the tease in Clara's voice. "Now, please hurry,"

"You'd better tell me where the key is."

"Right. Of course. The key to my writing bureau is in our bedroom. You'll find my trumpet case inside my wardrobe. Inside the case, there's a section with a lid for mouthpieces. Stuck to the lid is a key. It has a blue ring."

"Well," exclaimed Clara, "what a lot of secrecy?"

"I learned to be careful during the war. We all did. And you know how confidential my law work is."

"Of course. What next?"

"Go into my office and unlock the writing bureau. When you unlock the lid the drawers will open. The diary is in the second drawer down on the left side."

"Marc, I can't believe you kept a diary throughout the war. Do you know how dangerous that was?"

"Of course I do. But I was very careful. Careful enough for it not to be found. And useful enough to have helped me track and prosecute the number of murderers and traitors I've so far managed to catch. Now hurry up."

Clara headed upstairs to Marc's office. After collecting the key from Marc's trumpet case, Clara skipped through to his office. Ana trailed along behind her and stood at the door. Although it was always open and Marc was not precious about it, it was a room Clara hardly ever entered. She hurried to his bureau and unlocked the lid. Just as he'd said, the drawers were now unlocked. Beneath three manilla folders she found the diary. Clara hurried downstairs, passing a bored looking Ana who was making her way up.

"I won't be long, Ana. I'll call you when I've finished on the phone with Papa. We'll carry on with your hair then."

As Clara was passing on the dates to Marc, Ana was wandering into Marc's office. She rarely came in here and was intrigued to see the writing bureau with its lid down. 'It looks like it is sticking its tongue out,' she thought.

"Excellent," Marc breathed. "I've got the bastard. Clara, I can't wait to see you tonight. All those comrades and innocent civilians he tortured and murdered will be avenged."

Clara breathed excitedly. "Oh Marc, I hope so. Good luck and be careful. We're both longing for you to come home. Love you."

The phone went dead. Clara replaced her receiver. The inevitable pang was fainter now but still there. No matter how she tried she could never prevent an image of Huey appearing to her whenever she said those words. His desertion had broken her heart and embittered her towards him. But she could not stop loving him.

"Ana," she called as she walked back into the living room. "Where are you? We haven't finished your hair."

"I'm up here," Ana called back. "In Papa's office."

"Just a minute," Clara said. She looked around and spotted Marc's diary where she had laid it down. She picked it up and headed up the stairs to replace it in its hideaway. "I'm coming," she said. "I have to put Papa's things back in his desk." Clara came to the open door of the office and stopped.

"Oh, my word, Ana, what are you doing?"

Ana was sitting on the floor, her lap covered in papers which she had lifted from a drawer that Clara had not noticed. "How did you get into this little drawer?" Clara asked as she noticed that its frontage perfectly merged with the wood which surrounded it when closed. A secret drawer.

"It's really sweet, Mama," Ana replied. "Watch."

Ana scrambled onto her knees and closed the drawer. The drawer became invisible. She then reached under the shelf and pressed a hidden button. It shot out again. Ana giggled and Clara could not help smiling. She got down onto the carpet beside her daughter and together they sifted through the papers that Ana had taken out.

"I hope you can remember which drawer each paper came from. Did all of these come from the secret drawer or have you taken some from one of the others?"

"They're all from the secret drawer," Ana replied. "The one with the picture of my first Papa."

Clara felt a shock of electricity shoot through her.

"What did you say?"

"My first Papa. Look!"

Ana held out a small square photograph. Clara took it from her and found herself looking at herself and Ana and Huey. Clara skimmed the papers scattered around Ana and her shock was intensified when she glimpsed a name on a newspaper cutting which was jutting out from the bundle. The name was Tate.

Clara took Ana by the arm and pulled her to her feet. She became very business-like. "Go to the living room. Wait for me. I will have to tidy this mess up. If Papa finds out he will think you are very naughty."

"But Mama……"

"Go to your bedroom," Clara shouted. Ana began crying as she turned and ran.

Fifty

With every page she turned, Clara's heart beat harder against her ribs. For all the years of Huey's absence she had harboured a deep resentment for his desertion. It had affected her self-esteem. How had she failed him? She had believed in the love they had shared. The fact that he had so casually tossed her aside had made her feel worthless. Seven long years now and not a word. She had been so grateful to Marc for rescuing her; making her feel valued and loved again. In the solitary hours she had pictured Huey back in the United States, living a new life. Maybe in Boston, maybe New York. Sometimes she imagined him in California. He had even talked of Canada as a place where he would be happy to live. He would never have gone back to live in Alabama or any of the other southern States. She thought about the woman he might have taken as his wife. She wondered if she was black or white? She pictured him with new children, wondered what kind of house they lived in and if he was a successful mechanical engineer, as he had been in France. These thoughts, which recurred endlessly, left her empty. Answers to the infinite number of questions she could contemplate were impossible to find. That part of her life, which had brought her the epitome of happiness, had become a vacuum.

Ana's voice became tired of calling through. It seemed an age since her Mama had shouted at her and her boredom had turned to fatigue. She walked from her bedroom to the living room mirror and began to brush her own hair. She struggled with its tight curls and eventually gave up. She walked slowly along the passageway, dragging her fingers along the dado rail, as if trying to make the walk longer. She came to the doorway of the office and leaned against the frame.

"Am I going to school today?" she asked.

Clara turned to the door. She could see Ana standing there but it was as if the significance of her existence could not register. Clara's face was a mass of tear-stained blotches. She constantly wiped her nose with the back of her hand.

"Mama?" Ana questioned.

"No, ma petite. Not today. You are staying home today. You can play in your room or read in the living room. Mama is busy. Now go away."

Ana obediently left and Clara continued to scrutinise the papers Marc had hidden for all these years.

After Huey had failed to come home, she had written to the address of his mother's house. She had written twelve times. No replies came. Now she thought about it, Marc had always taken the letters to the post. Even in the early days, when he had begun to reappear in her life in Flins, he had offered to take letters for posting. He claimed he was saving her the expensive international postage and would put it through with his lawyers' mail. Now she wondered if those letters had ever been sent. Marc had been the one to explain the process of annulment that was available to her due to Huey's desertion. And she remembered how he had proposed marriage on the very day the annulment came through. But here was the proof that Huey had not deserted her. He was dead. He had been brutally murdered. And Marc had known all along. Why hadn't he told her? Wanting to think the best of Marc she speculated that he might have wanted to protect her feelings. But after a little thought she knew that didn't make sense. As soon as Huey had gone, Marc had turned up.

Fifty-one

Clara felt her limbs go lifeless. Her energy supply evaporated and she fell backwards onto the rug. All over her lap, newspaper cuttings and letters lay scattered. She felt a boiling rage well up inside her. At the same time, she felt helpless, a complete loss of control. A sudden thought shot a bolt of energy through her. She sat bolt upright and began ferociously scrabbling her way through the papers all around her. She seized upon the item she was looking for and jumped to her feet. In an instant she had grabbed her coat and rushed out of the apartment. It wasn't until Jean-Paul opened his door and said, "Where's Ana?" that she realised she had left her alone in the apartment.

As Jean-Paul rushed with Clara back to her place, she poured out her heart to him. Passers-by stared at the woman in floods of tears verbally bombarding her companion as they hurried along.

Clara surprised Jean-Paul when they arrived back at her apartment. She went straight to the pile of papers littering the floor and did not think to check on Ana. Jean-Paul supressed a coughing fit before going into Ana's bedroom. He found the girl curled up on her bed and sobbing. He spent ten minutes consoling her, all the time half listening to the rampaging Clara slamming through the apartment shouting obscenities about Marc.

"I'll go and talk to Mama now," Jean-Paul said to Ana. "Everything will be fine. You'll see." He hugged Ana. She felt comforted, despite the scraping of his chin stubble on her cheek and the scent of brandy on his breath. It somehow reassured her that she was under the protection of an adult. He left her and returned to Clara.

Jean-Paul took Clara firmly by her elbows and pulled her face close to his.

"Clara, Clara, Clara! You've got to calm down. This is getting you nowhere." He led her through to the living room and sat her down. As he took control, she succumbed to that feeling of lifelessness again. She trusted Jean-Paul and was content to have him guide her. He poured two glasses of brandy and sat beside her on the sofa. Clara seemed to catch her breath and compose herself. The brandy seemed to strengthen her. Before he knew it Jean-Paul was listening to the whole story of Huey again.

"Read this letter," she demanded of Jean-Paul. He took the sheet of paper that she waved at him and sat back to read it.

The letter was from a Buster Lordan, Attorney-at -Law, Dallas, Texas. With offices in Atlanta, Georgia; Montgomery, Alabama and Louisville, Kentucky. It was crystal clear from the letter that Marc and this American had conspired to get Huey to return to Alabama. It was also clear that they had made sure that white supremacists were made aware of his return and of his marital status in France. Clara then forced Jean-Paul to read the newspaper accounts of Huey's murder.

"I can't believe I've slept with this man. How could he do it? He tells me he loves me. How could he do this to someone he says he loves?"

"Love is a strange thing, "Jean-Paul whispered, half to himself. "Marc is a very determined man. You remember how he was in the war. He let nothing stand in his way. He was bitterly disappointed when you chose Huey over him."

"But he had no intention of being faithful to me. I doubt he would have asked me to marry him."

"He saw you as his. He always did."

"He took me for granted, you mean."

"Perhaps."

Clara was crying again now. "My poor, poor Huey. And all these years I have doubted him, thought of him as just another unfaithful G.I. I feel so guilty to have let those thoughts enter my mind. It's all Marc's fault."

"I don't know how I can help you, Clara. He's not broken any laws here in France. In America there has been no case to answer."

"When you read this letter, what do you think?"

Jean-Paul read through the Lordan letter again.

Dear Marc,

With reference to our mixed marriage business. The information you provided has been more than helpful. Our miscreant has been apprehended and dealt with.

The brothers of the organisation send their thanks to you for your small but significant contribution to curing this pernicious disease.

I have included a report of the incident from the Montgomery Star.

As you will read the investigation began and closed on the same day. Misadventure.

Decent laws still apply here in the South.

Maybe we'll meet up again at a conference sometime down the line.

Bonne chance mon ami.

Your good friend,

Buster.

Jean-Paul shook his head as he handed the letter back to Clara. She pushed a newspaper cutting into his hand as she retrieved the letter.

Jean-Paul reluctantly glanced at the cutting. "Don't ask me to look at that again," said.

"It's too terrible," Clara groaned. The pattern of Huey's shirt, one she had bought for him, was just visible above the mass of blood stains that had soaked the rest of it. His face was unrecognisable. She wiped tears from her eyes and looked pleadingly at Jean-Paul.

"What has he done?"

With a sudden change of demeanour, Clara got up from her seat and went to a desk by the window. She sat down and began writing furiously on a sheet of paper. When she had finished, she picked up the letter from Lordan, pulled Jean-Paul by the arm and dragged him to the telephone.

"What are you doing?" a startled Jean-Paul asked.

"You are going to speak to this Buster Lordan. You will say you are Marc and you will say, more or less, what I have written here."

"But why would Marc be ringing him after all these years?"

"Read through that," she commanded, pointing at her sheet of writing." Jean Paul read carefully. "So, I am Marc and I will be travelling to the States next month and suggest we meet up. Flying into Dallas on the 16th."

Jean-Paul looked at her in despair. "This is insane, Clara. It won't work."

"All you have to do is end the conversation by saying this." She pointed at the end of her scribble to where she had written – YOU DID A GREAT JOB WITH THAT HUEY GUY -.

Jean-Paul looked at her as if she was insane. She ignored his silent accusation and added, "We'll just see how he responds."

She dialled the number and listened to the slow clicking of the international connection struggling its way under the Atlantic Ocean. After over a minute the connection jumped into life and a female voice with a strong southern States accent said, "Lordan, Chesney and Dacre, Attorneys at law, how may I help you?"

"I have a long-distance call for Mr Lordan. This is Marc Durand's secretary speaking. Monsieur Durand and Mr Lordan are acquainted."

"Hold the line please. I'll see if Mr Lordan is free to take a call right now." The line went silent. Clara and Jean-Paul held their breaths. Eventually the secretary came back on the line.

"Mr Lordan has a free moment or two I'll put you through now."

Click and ratchet followed ratchet and click. Finally, the sound of heavy breathing and, "Hi there, Marc. What a pleasant surprise. To what do I owe the pleasure?" Clara nudged Jean-Paul who reluctantly began. "I wanted to let you know that I am going to be in Dallas on 16th June. I was hoping we might be able to meet."

"That's a marvellous idea. What is the purpose of your trip this time?"

Jean-Paul looked at Clara. She pointed to the word 'vacation' that she had written on the sheet.

"Nothing to do with work this time," Jean-Paul said. "I'm bringing the family for a vacation." Clara and Jean-Paul both had their ears pinned to the receiver.

"Well, that sounds just dandy," Lordan crooned. "You bringing that nigger kid you told me about? Not sure that would be too wise."

Clara and Jean-Paul looked at each other. Jean-Paul's face contorted in disbelief. Clara's boiled up in anger. Before Jean-Paul could respond, Lordan was continuing. "You'll be held in high esteem for helping us deal with that Tate fella. You wouldn't want to run into trouble by walking around over here with a nigger child." Clara snatched the phone from Jean-Paul and slammed it down.

"You heard him," she yelled. "Marc had Huey killed."

"I heard him alright," Jean-Paul replied. "The thing is, it makes no sense. Marc was never in favour of race discrimination. He was furious at the end of the war when the North African troops were hidden away from the triumphal parades. He liked Huey. He hung out with him during the days the band was in full swing. He was passionately opposed to the Nazi race laws. He despised the Vichy for sending Jews to the death camps. I don't understand it."

"I think it's worse than that. He is almost worse than that despicable Lordan character. You are right, he was against all forms of racism. But think of it. In order to win a personal battle – to get Huey out of the way so that he could take possession of me – he was prepared to betray his own beliefs. What kind of a man does that make him?"

Jean-Paul had no answer. He shook his head. The fury he witnessed in Clara's face frightened him. "I don't see a way out of this," he whispered. "Are you going to leave him?
As I've said, he hasn't committed an offence that he can be investigated for here. In Alabama it's been ruled that no crime was committed. It's a wicked stalemate." Clara paced the room. She clenched and unclenched her fists. She crushed the fingers of one hand inside the other. Her face was contorted in deep thought.

"Jean-Paul," she said at last, "I want you to take Ana home with you tonight." Jean-Paul started to interrupt but she continued.

"Marc and I have too much to talk about. It will get noisy. Ana will be upset. It's better that she doesn't hear what might be said."

Jean-Paul reluctantly saw the merit in her comment and agreed to take Ana home for the night with him. Once this was decided Clara couldn't get the two of them out of the apartment quickly enough.

Fifty-two

Marc came in late. He had achieved a success he had been working towards for years. It was the reason he had entered the legal profession in the first place. When Corbin had spent two nights in a Parisian cell, and he had heard from his lawyer the press treatment he was getting and the reactions back in Chartres, he had caved in. In exchange for an agreement with the judge on which charges would be brought against him, he had provided all the evidence needed to bring about the arrest and charging of Jacques Moreau. Marc had been in court for the last two and a half weeks and today Moreau had been sentenced to death by firing squad. A military execution.

Marc was elated. The man they had failed to gun down, after three assassination attempts, was finally going to get the bullet he deserved.

"Ana, Clara, where are you?" he tossed his jacket over a hook inside the hallway and dropped his briefcase onto the wooden floor. A kindly light shone from the living room and he passed along the hallway to it. There was no-one inside the room but he heard a sound from the kitchen. It was a secretive sound as if not meant to be made. He wondered if the two of them were hiding in there to surprise him. Supressing a smile, he tip-toed to the kitchen and slipped in. Clara was there. She had her back to him and was reading a piece of paper.

"Clara?" he queried. "What's going on? Where's Ana? Have you heard our news? It's the firing squad for Moreau". He walked over to her. Joy and relief, a fantastic sense of achievement filled him. He reached out his arms to embrace Clara from behind. As he reached towards her, she turned and plunged a shining blade deep into his heart.

They are standing face to face. From fleeting moment to moment, she sees changing emotions in his eyes. Or thinks she does. Surprise. Pain. Shock. Sadness. Regret. Shame. At any given moment it could be any of those. Or it could be fear. She looks for love but cannot be sure it is there. In her left hand the piece of paper. He glances at it, then looks straight back into her eyes. Is that understanding she sees emerging in him? She hopes so.

Fifty-three

Jean-Paul had just got Ana off to sleep when his front doorbell rang. He silently cursed it but luckily Ana remained asleep. He opened the door to find Clara standing there. It was a warm night and she was wearing a cardigan but he could see that she was trembling.

"Come in quickly," he urged.

"Where is Ana?" she asked as soon as they were in his living room.

"Don't worry about Ana, She's fine. She's fast asleep."

"I have to wake her."

"Why?" Jean-Paul demanded restraining her by taking hold of her elbow as she passed him.

"I have to go to the police. I must get Ana to my mother. I have to be sure she is in safe-keeping when they ...." She tailed off.

"Clara?" Jean-Paul asked. "What have you done?"

Her trembling intensified. She looked down at her hands and then up into Jean Paul's eyes. "I've killed him," she whispered.

Jean-Paul was visibly taken aback. His mouth twisted in a macabre reflex. They stood in silence. Jean-Paul stared at Clara. She was unable to hold his gaze. Her trembling seemed to be getting a grip of her. She wrenched her arm away from Jean-Paul and hurried towards the bedroom. He chased and caught her in the hall. He swung her round and shook her like a rag doll. He wasn't totally sure if he did it to snap her out of her rising panic or to satisfy his own utter frustration at her complete stupidity. Overcome by his aggression, Clara found herself being dragged back the living room and being slung into a chair.

"What are you doing?" she asked.

"What do you think I'm doing?" he snapped back. "I'm not letting you go to the police. That's the first thing. Secondly, I'm going to refuse to talk to the trembling weakling I'm confronted with. I'll talk to the Clara I knew in the war. The Clara who assassinated Nazis and collaborators and who learned to dispose of the bodies of victims. So, when that Clara is ready to re-appear, I'm here."

Clara stared at Jean-Paul. He was breathless now with the energy he had expended. Carla watched him as he snatched at his breathing in an effort to calm himself. She felt her metabolism beginning to normalise. A strange smile crept onto her lips. She began to feel she recognised herself once more. Jean-Paul pulled the cork out of a half full bottle of red wine. He emptied its contents into two large glasses and handed her one. They sat and drank for a while. Clara's mind was racing. She began to find herself planning the way she would have done in the war. She raised her glass and drained it.

"You're right, Jean-Paul. There's a better way out of this. I'll do whatever you say."

The vicious reprisals the Nazis had indulged in involved the gratuitous murder of hundreds of Parisians. To the Nazis one German life was worth ten French lives. When matters had reached the stage where the French citizenry were turning against the actions of the Resistance in the wake of another mass reprisal, a new tactical plan was handed down in the hope of avoiding more. The aim of creating fear and anxiety amongst the occupiers by leaving corpses where they fell was dropped for a period. Instead, the victims were to be disappeared. If the Nazi authorities couldn't be sure that a missing person had been killed maybe they would hold back on the reprisals. Maybe a missing soldier had deserted. It was a tactic that survived for a few months and was implemented when possible. Because of it, Clara and Jean-Paul had both participated in the disposal of bodies. They knew where the grave sites were.

Fifty-four

"How long will Marc be away for?" Clara's mother was buttering a croissant for Ana as she spoke.

"You know Marc, Maman. I never know exactly when he's coming back." Clara fussed over Ana's milk and intercepted the croissant to spread some apricot conserve upon it. "I just thought now that he's completed the Moreau case, he would have more time at home."

"Maman, if you are hinting you want Ana and me out of here, we can go back to the apartment."

"Don't be silly," Maman laughed. "I was only asking. There's no need to be irritated with me."

"I know. I'm sorry."

"You know I like having you and Ana staying with me. Now get a move on. It's a long ride to Ana's school from here. You need to hurry."

"Okay, Ana. You heard your grandmama. Time for us to get going."

As Ana got down from the table and went to collect her things for school Clara said, "I'm calling to see Jean-Paul after I've dropped Ana at school, so you needn't expect me until later this afternoon."

"That's fine. By the way how is Jean-Paul? That poor man. It breaks my heart when I think of what he went through in the war."

"He's not bad. He has health issues but he is sensible. He takes his medication and he follows his doctor's orders. He will probably outlive us all."

"Well, I hope so. He deserves to."

Fifty-five

Detective Inspector Badeaux made his first approach to Clara by telephone. "Bonjour Inspector. Yes I would be happy to come to the commissariat and speak with you. When would you like me to come?"

After delivering Ana to school the following morning Clara walked to the nearest Metro station and rode into central Paris.

"Come in Madam Durand. Please take a seat. Can I offer you a drink? Coffee? Water?"

"No thank you Inspector. I breakfasted before coming."

"You are married to Marc Durand, yes?"

"That's correct."

"Are you aware that your husband's work colleagues are concerned for him? They have actually reported him missing."

"I am surprised, Inspector. As far as I know Marc is out of town on legal business."

Badeaux leaned back in his chair to enable his left hand to burrow into his jacket pocket. It re-emerged clasping a crumpled packet of Gitanes cigarettes. He flicked one out directly into his mouth and offered the pack across the table to Clara. She shook her head and thanked him with a closed-mouth smile. The match which he struck flared with a whiff of phosphorous and he drew deeply on his cigarette. Exhaling a cloud of blue-grey smoke just over Clara's head, he leaned forward, resting his arms on the table between them, his hands playing with the pack and said, "I was wondering why you have not reported a similar
concern about Monsieur Durand's whereabouts. After all, you are his wife."

Clara laughed. "Inspector, clearly you do not know my husband very well."

"By which you mean?"

"Well for one thing, his work takes him all over France. He is often away for weeks at a time. You will be aware of his involvement in the Moreau case which has just concluded?"

Clara paused to observe Badeaux's reaction. She sensed she had put him at a disadvantage. He reddened and began to fumble with his cigarettes, trying to get them into his pocket. It was a subject he was uncomfortable with. He leaned back in his chair metaphorically dodging her next shot.

"You will have read of the case, monsieur. Moreau has been sentenced to death for his war crimes. Were you in the police force during the war, Inspector? Maybe you knew Moreau?"

Badeaux instinctively knew Clara had seized on his embarrassment and was trying to put him on the back foot by driving the point home. So why, he was wondering, would she feel the need to do that? "So where exactly do you think your husband is right now?" he countered.

"He told me he was going to be working in Marseille for an extended period. I assume he is there."

"Does he not telephone home from time to time?"

"Yes. But not always. There have been times when he has been away for several weeks with rarely a call. Might I ask, do you have worries about his safety?"

Badeaux ignored her question and asked one of his own. "Tell me, do you have an address or number at which he can be reached?"

"No, I'm sorry I don't. But again, that's not unusual for Marc. He often forgets to inform me. He can be away and visit many towns in one trip."

Clara shifted in her seat and her tongue flicked across her lips. She was acutely aware of the Inspector watching every movement she made.

"You seem a little anxious, Madame Durand. Is there any reason for that?"

"I think being here and being interrogated by you has unsettled me, Inspector. You are making me uneasy about the whereabouts of my husband. I am becoming concerned for his safety."

"But you say he is in Marseille, working."

"That's right. But when he goes away you do not normally invite me in to answer questions on his whereabouts, so naturally, I am becoming worried."

"Where do you think he is at this moment?"

"I have no reason to think other than that he is in Marseille."

"For work?"

"Precisely."

"What would you think if I told you that his law colleagues say that they have no work in Marseille at this time and that they have definitely not sent him there?" Clara looked down at her hands folded in her lap. "Have I embarrassed you Madame?"

"I think you know very well that you have."

"And why would that be? Might there be some other reason for his absence at this point?"

Clara did her best to present a straight face. Could it be that the Inspector had an inkling of what had actually happened? "Yes, there could be. It wouldn't be the first time."

"Meaning?"

"Meaning it wouldn't be the first time he had spent time away from our family home without telling me where he was."

Clara got up from her seat. She waved away the cloud of cigarette smoke that the Inspector had half filled the room with. She looked out through the glass pane into the busy office beyond. At separate desks she could see two young women being interviewed. They were women Clara knew Marc had had liaisons with. She turned and faced the Inspector.

"I think you know what I mean. Otherwise, why have you called those two women in for interview?"

"Ah, you see through me Madame. Am I so transparent? Your husband, he has – shall we say – liaisons?"

"I don't need to tell you what you seem to know already."

"Of course not. But it makes me wonder how that makes you feel? Does it anger you that your husband behaves in such a way?"

"I think, Monsieur Inspector, that you know who my husband is. And by that I mean, I think you know his history, his reputation."

Badeaux opened a brown card file which lay in front of him on the desk. "I know plenty about your husband. Who is there in Paris who doesn't? His role in the Resistance is well documented. Children might not have read of him in their history books but they will certainly have heard of him from their fathers and mothers."

"In that case you will know of his reputation in other fields. He is an extremely charismatic man. Some women find him irresistible. What about you Inspector, will the children have heard of your wartime activities?"

The Inspector exhaled a thick cloud of nicotine smoke. He could not be shaken a third time by Clara's crude attempt to unnerve him.

"We all tried to do our duty for France in our own way, Madame." He flicked through the file. "I have to congratulate you also Madame," he continued. "Your war record is also impressive."

"As you say Inspector, we all tried to do our duty."

Badeaux took a fierce pull on his cigarette, exhaled with a sigh as he stubbed it out in a stained ashtray. Perhaps we should leave things there for now, Madame Durand. I take it you have no plans to leave Paris imminently?"

"No Monsieur."

"Very well. You may go. If your husband contacts us, you will let us know?"

"Of course."

Badeaux opened the door and held it for her as she walked into the outer office. She held her head erect and her gaze fixedly in front of her. The other two women who had been called in for interview and the policemen at their desks all turned to follow her progress as she exited.

Fifty-six

"Marc had a thousand enemies who would love to see him below the soil. Badeaux has nothing he can pin on you." Jean-Paul carried the coffee pot to the table and sat down opposite Clara.

"He is having me followed," Clara said. "He must think he has something, or he would not have delegated men to do that."

"He is having you followed exactly because he has nothing to go on. You must relax. Let him play his games. He's not smart enough to catch us out. We dodged the Gestapo for four years. Remember? He's nowhere near as smart or ruthless as they were."

"We didn't all dodge them all of the time, did we?"

Jean-Paul paused in his coffee pouring. Clara immediately regretted hurting him by reminding him of his capture by the Carlingue. "I'm sorry, Jean-Paul. I must be letting the Inspector get to me. Please forgive me." They sipped their coffee in silence for a few moments.

"I knew he was having you followed. He has invited me to the commissariat for an interview. He has seen us together. He will have me down as a suspect or an accomplice. But he's never going to discover Marc's body and without that Marc will continue to be considered a missing person. It will remain a low-level enquiry."

"Come in Monsieur Paquet. Take a seat. Let me get you a coffee. Was your journey here uneventful? I hope so. There are so many road-works in progress now that it is impossible to know if any trip across town will go smoothly."

The Inspector was being almost loquacious, but Jean-Paul remained calm. 'I've been through worse interrogations than this,' he kept telling himself. 'He's not going to charm me into saying something stupid.' The conversation began simply enough. "You know a Madame Clara Durand?"

"I do. We worked together during the war – as I am sure you are well aware."

Badeaux smiled to himself. "You also know her husband, Monsieur Marc Durand?"

"Of course. We were also comrades in the war."

"You led an eventful life in the war, Monsieur Paquet." Jean-Paul saw no need to reply.

"As you know I am investigating the disappearance of Marc Durand."

Badeaux stared at Jean-Paul as if believing he could see inside his skull. Jean-Paul stared back. "Perhaps we can start by you telling me when you last saw Monsieur Durand."

"We haven't been in regular contact. Marc is a busy man. He has been pursuing Moreau for many years and he has just successfully seen his work completed. Let me think. We probably last met about three months ago. I remember having an evening with him in the Latin Quarter. We both have a liking for American jazz and big band music. We met for dinner and then went to listen to a band at Le Club Dynamo."

"But you see his wife more regularly than that, do you not?"

"Yes. Clara and I are good friends. We too shared wartime experiences. I owe her my life. I also owe my life to Marc. We three were very close."

"But you have remained closer to Madame than to Monsieur?"

"I see more of Clara, if that is what you mean. But Clara is always in Paris. Marc's work takes him all over France and even beyond into Belgium, Germany, The Netherlands and so on."

"Let me be blunt, Monsieur Paquet," Badeaux grunted, leaning forward in an impatient manner. "Are you and Madame Durand in a sexual relationship?"

"Absolutely not," Jean-Paul replied immediately. "If that is your line of enquiry you are a bigger fool, than you look."

"I see you do not like that suggestion, Monsieur. I don't see why. She is a very attractive woman is she not?" Jean-Paul said nothing. "Perhaps it is convenient for you that her husband is out of the way."

Jean-Paul made a dismissive exclamation as if the Inspector was beneath contempt. He swivelled in his chair, facing sideways to Badeaux. A long silence ensued. During that time Badeaux proceeded to lay out a series of photographs side by side on the table. "Perhaps you would take a look at these, Monsieur."

Jean-Paul swivelled in his chair to find himself looking at pictures of himself and Clara. They had been taken at various different times around Paris. Usually, they had Ana with them but not always.

"Yes. You have had photographs taken of me and my friend with her daughter. You won't need me to tell where we were or what we were doing at those times. You can ask the photographer instead. In fact, you can ask Marc when he resurfaces. He is very well aware of my friendship with Clara."

"Your friend Marc, he is, how would you put it? A philanderer?"

"You can put it however you choose to. That's none of my business and I would never comment on it. Marc and Clara are very happily married."

"Maybe Monsieur Durand permits your closeness with his wife because you are not a threat. Is that it? Maybe your weakness makes him dismiss you?"

"My weakness? What do you mean by that?" Jean-Paul knew he was being baited but despite himself he was becoming annoyed.

Badeaux flicked open a file and began to scan its contents. "It says here that you receive a war pension for your patriotic endeavours under the invaders." Jean-Paul waited for the Inspector to continue.

"But I see that it says here you receive an enhanced pension for the injuries you received at the hands of the enemy. Maybe you are damaged Monsieur Paquet. Maybe you are incapable of......"

Badeaux let his voice trail off. Jean-Paul's annoyance subsided. It was obvious the Inspector was clutching at straws.

"My weakness?" he smiled. "Resisting the torture you and your fellow collaborators inflicted on me. Is that what you call weakness? You should be ashamed of yourself. You are no Frenchman. You're a coward and a quisling and a Nazi collaborator. You should have been stood up and shot at the end of the war. Instead, you just carried on in your job. No more Jewish children to send to the gas chambers so you waste our time with your stupid questions and insinuations."

Badeaux, watched Jean-Paul. He was disappointed that his probing failed to kick off a stronger reaction. After twenty or so more minutes of attempting to get information out of him Badeaux gave up. He left Jean-Paul alone in the room and walked across the passage to an office facing his. His superior called out in response to his knock and Badeaux entered.

"Well?"

"Superintendent Bertaud, I think I can unsettle this Paquet. I would like to hold him for twenty-four hours. He won't like being locked up in a cell and he might decide to tell us what he knows."

"On what grounds?"

Badeaux knew he had to be careful here. His superior was an unusual man for the police force. Particularly for one who had managed to rise in the ranks. Bertaud had fought with the Free French and was sympathetic to Resistance fighters who might have fallen on hard times and turned to crime. He was well aware of Badeaux's own role in the war as a young policeman under the Nazis.

"We could keep him for refusing to co-operate with the investigation. His nerves are shot. I'm sure he would cave in if locked in a cell."

"Cave in about what? We're talking about the Durand case. What are you investigating exactly? A grown man, a known philanderer hasn't come home. Tell me what crime has been committed?"

"I can't say just yet, but I know there is something fishy about this whole business. Twenty-four hours. That's all I ask?"

"If I understand you inspector Badeaux, you are hoping that by locking this man in a cell for twenty-four hours you will bring back the nightmare of his days in the hands of the Carlingue and that he will have some kind of breakdown. Am I right?" Badeaux made no reply. His face remained expressionless.

"So, I am right. I take it you learned these techniques during your own time with the Carlingue?" Again, Badeaux's face remained impassive.

"Given that you have nothing to say to my questioning I infer that you have nothing more to contribute to the discussion."

Superintendent Bertaud waved his hand dismissively at Badeaux. "Let him go. If you come up with anything substantial come back to me."

Badeaux walked along the corridor towards his office. On his way he beckoned a sergeant to follow him.
"Close the door," he said as the sergeant followed him in.

"Bertaud says we must let this Paquet go. But I'm not altogether happy. I want you to put a man outside his door whenever you can free one up. Let's try to annoy him a little. See if it rattle's him."

Fifty-seven

It took a while but Badeaux's ploy began to work. At first Jean-Paul had been amused to discover that he was being watched, but eventually it began to prey on his nerves.

Clara and Ana had by now moved back into their own apartment. Ana was back at school and Clara, although managing on her war pension, was actively seeking employment. After several excellent interviews for fairly low-level positions with various businesses, from department stores to small manufacturing outfits, she was surprised and increasingly disappointed to receive rejection letters. Sometimes these came along after verbal assurances that she had done enough to secure the post.

One day, having dropped Ana at school, she crossed the city to the site of her last rejection. It was a warm day and so she walked to a nearby park where she strolled for a while and then sat to read the book she had brought with her. Just before the lunch hour she made her way back to the premises and waited. The managing director's personal assistant emerged, as Clara had hoped, and set off along the street. Clara followed her to a nearby cafe and waited outside until the woman had been served with her meal.

"May I join you for a moment?" she asked.

The startled woman looked up; her fork paused on its way to her lips. A faint look of recognition passed across her face but it was as if she was thinking, 'I know you but I can't remember where from'.

"I'm hoping you remember me," Clara said as she slid into the seat opposite. The woman remained puzzled.

"I'm Clara Durand. I applied for a post with your firm two weeks ago."

"Ah, yes. Madame Durand," the woman said shifting uncomfortably in her seat as recognition dawned. "How can I help you?"

"I hope you can," Clara replied. "I don't want to spoil your meal. I will only take a moment of your time. When I had finished my interview, I was led to believe that I had been successful. But two days ago I received a letter of rejection. I only want to know if I am doing something wrong. I am not experienced at interviews and I seem to be making the same mistake over and over again. I get excellent reactions at interviews and then I get rejected.

Please, if you can, help me."

"You did nothing wrong Madame Durand. We were very keen to employ you. Very keen until we were informed that you are a suspect in an ongoing criminal investigation."

Clara nodded, eyes fixed on the woman opposite, as the truth sank in. It didn't come as a great surprise. Badeaux was a persistent opponent. An air of sadness sank around her. In meek resignation, she eased out of her chair, nodded her thanks and left.

The increasing sense of claustrophobia which had been affecting Jean-Paul, now began to impact upon Clara.

"It's pathetic really," Clara said. Jean-Paul was in her kitchen frying sardines with lemon juice. "Badeaux has nothing and will never get anything. He's just toying with us and enjoying the sense of control it gives him. But he's no nearer to proving anything."

"I don't think he cares anymore," Jean-Paul replied. "He just does it because he can. He didn't care for the way we referred to his war record and he's exacting his revenge."

Ana came in. "I wish you hadn't sold the television Maman. I get so bored without it."

"We needed the money, darling. It won't be the only thing I have to sell."

Jean-Paul waited until Ana had gone back into the lounge before saying, "Have you heard about the plans to disinter the bodies of the victims of the Nazis?"

"Yes. What's so important about that? It's a good thing."

"Yes ... but... well..... you know."

"I know what? You don't mean?"

"No, I don't mean that. But once they have done this they could move onto the bodies of the Nazis that we disposed of. And then."

"So is that where.....?"

"Don't ask. But we should maybe think about more than today and tomorrow. Maybe we should make a longer-term plan.

When Clara's application to be accepted into Canada as an immigrant was rejected, it was obviously nothing to do with Badeaux. He certainly did not carry that much weight. It was because of the assault she had made on the G.I. who had attacked Huey. She had been convicted and it remained on her record. It would never go away.

"We'll have to think of something else," she said resignedly. "Or perhaps just give up altogether. You'd better cancel our berths. At least we can get our money back."

"I don't see why," Jean-Paul had replied. "I can get your passport problem solved and you can re-apply under a nom-de-plume. Meanwhile Ana and I can go on ahead to Montreal and get everything ready for your arrival."

A few weeks later he appeared at her door with a smile on his face. It was three days before he and Ana were due to set sail from Le Havre to Halifax. As they stood around the dining table, he unwrapped a brown paper parcel and handed the contents to Clara. She laughed out loud when she saw what he had brought. "You're not serious."

"Why not? They worked well enough during the war."

In her hand Clara held two passports. One for her and one for Ana. Hers was in the name of Camille Paquet. Ana's was for Ana Paquet.

Clara's face deepened in seriousness. "How will this work?" she queried. "Ana's application is under her real name – Tate. That's the name she's been accepted for."

"Don't worry," Jean-Paul placated. "I will use her original passport for entry to Canada, but then, when you arrive, you will have the option of adopting the same name for her as yourself and a passport to go with it."

"You've been working things out, haven't you? Are we expecting them to assume we are a married couple? You've used the surname Paquet for us." "We could be. Or if you prefer, we could be brother and sister."

"Why not?" she said.

This time her application was accepted and a date was set for her emigration four weeks from the date of acceptance. Because of the delay in re-applying, Jean-Paul and Ana had already gone on ahead by the time her acceptance had come through. In the intervening weeks, letters had begun to arrive. She looked forward to their arrival and, under the eyes of the concierge she eagerly checked her mailbox every day. She began to miss Ana like a lost limb, and she suffered bouts of frustration and even melancholy. She worried that she might never see Ana again. The few flimsy blue airmail letters, with their crinkly, crumpled fragility began to delight her and she longed for her own day of departure.

The occasional appearance of one of Badeaux's men no longer concerned her. It had become an irregular occurrence for one of them to appear outside her building. The missing person case was no longer an active investigation, though Badeaux seemed unable to completely let it go. He pursued it whenever he could as a kind of hobby. He would soon be a thing of the past and thousands of miles behind her.

On returning home one day after shopping for an outfit to travel in she was slightly unnerved to see the tall moustachioed figure of Badeaux himself standing outside her apartment block. He lifted his hat to her as she approached.

"Hello Inspector," she smiled. "Are you waiting for me?"

"How are you today, Madame Durand?"

"I am very well, Inspector. Have you come all this way just to find out how I am?" "Not entirely. I was wondering why we haven't seen your daughter recently. And, as a matter of fact, your friend Monsieur Paquet seems to have left Paris."

"My daughter is staying with an aunt of mine in Brittany. She became anxious because of the men you sent each day to harass me. As for Monsieur Paquet, I have no idea. We are friends but I am not his keeper."

"Of course, Madame. Well, never mind. However, I do have something for you. You may not have seen it yet." He reached inside his coat and pulled out a newspaper. "Here is this evening's edition of *Le Parisien*. Pages four and five will interest you."

He handed the newspaper to her, smiled, lifted his hat again and walked away. Clara was shaking when she reached her apartment. She threw her shopping and her coat onto a chair and laid the paper on a table. Turning to page four she found herself face to face with Marc. It was a close-up of him, taken at the end of the war. He was wearing his Resistance medals, a sash of ammunition across his chest and, he held a rifle in both hands. Despite the anger she felt beginning to rise within her, she could not tear her eyes away from the text. A bold two-page headline read – THE MISSING HERO -. After a paragraph posing questions about his disappearance, the article went on to extol his virtues as a leader, a fighter, a hero. Towards the end of the article, which had described in glorious detail several of the actions Marc had taken part in, there were four paragraphs devoted to Badeaux and his suspicions. By the time she had finished reading Clara was in a raging fury. She screamed at the photograph. "Murderer! If they only knew the truth."

Part of her knew that Badeaux must have set this up to unsettle her. Maybe it would make her crack and give Badeaux an opportunity to wheedle the truth out of her. She kept returning to the final three or four paragraphs to re-read them.

"Inspector Badeaux of the Parisian police retains suspicions about, what he refers to as, the 'so-called disappearance' of Marc Durand. The inspector believes that this wartime hero may have been the victim of foul play. Clara Durand, the missing man's wife, has been questioned several times but has been of no help. Marc Durand is Madame Durand's second husband. Strangely, her first husband, a black American G.I. also disappeared. What does Madame Durand know that she is not telling? The inspector appeals to all members of the public to come forward if they have any

information that might help the police solve this tantalising mystery."

While she was thus preoccupied, Clara had not been aware of Badeaux's return to the apartment block. He had re-entered just after she had climbed the staircase to her door. The concierge admitted him and led him to her rooms below the stairs. She offered him a seat and handed him an opened, flimsy, airmail envelope which had been lying beside her recently boiled kettle. The inspector read it carefully whilst sipping the black coffee the concierge handed to him. He nodded appreciatively before re-folding it and handing it back to her.

"Re-seal it and put it back into her box, just as you have with the others."

"I will, Inspector. I hope it has been of use to you."

"You have been very useful, Madame."

He pushed his hand into his inside pocked and withdrew several Francs. The concierge wiped her hands down her flower-patterned overall before reaching out to accept the payments.

"Many thanks, Monsieur. You are most kind. I'm glad I can help the police in their work."

"If any more come open them too. Call me at the station. I will try to come to you immediately. If it is not possible for me to come, I want you to copy out the contents before returning it to her box. It's better if you do that than to keep it from her until I can get here."

"Of course, Inspector. You can rely on me."

Clara screwed up the newspaper and tossed it aside. But during the evening she returned to it many times. Each time she read it she became angrier. It wasn't the insinuations made against her that infuriated her. It was the elevation of Marc to sainthood that sickened her. Knowing what he had done she burned with a sense of injustice. She sat and wept at the memory of Huey and how he had been duped by Marc. How Marc had cold-bloodedly laid a death trap for him. And how he had then mopped up the pieces by marrying Clara and adopting Ana. And now they were turning him into a national hero. In the few remaining days left to her in France she began to conceive of a plan.

Fifty-eight

Clara's last night in France. Tomorrow night she would be in Gerona, Spain. Her train would arrive there in the early hours of Saturday and she would have a long wait, hanging around the station for a late afternoon connection to Madrid. An overnight stay in Madrid would be necessary before commencing the last leg of her journey to Lisbon. Waking up in Lisbon on Monday 21 September she would say her final goodbye to Europe as she embarked for Halifax, Nova Scotia and her onward journey to Montreal where Ana and Jean-Paul were waiting for her.

Her suitcase was packed and had been since the previous weekend. But now she busied herself with the sealing of two envelopes and scribing addresses; one to her mother and one which was addressed to *Le Parisien*. This one was extra-large. Clara had spent a long time compiling its contents. 'Let the world see the real Marc Durand,' she was thinking. 'How will they love their hero when they know what he was really like?' When its contents became known it would become clear, especially to Badeaux, that she had a very strong motive for wanting Marc dead. But that wouldn't matter. By the time it came out she would be long gone and living under a new identity. She knew that she couldn't risk using *La Poste*. If she did, there was a slim chance that her letters would arrive before she had crossed the frontier. She needed to be sure that they would not arrive with their recipients until she was well underway across the Atlantic Ocean. The simplicity of her solution to this problem appealed to her. The concierge had an outgoing mailbox for residents of the block. For a small regular payment, the old lady emptied the box each Monday and delivered any letters or parcels to *La Poste* as long as full postage was already attached.

Her day of departure began with a constant drizzle accompanied by sporadic gusts of wind which seemed determined to wrench Clara's umbrella from her hand. In her other hand she held her suitcase and, across her shoulder, a holdall. Her walk to the taxi rank was only two blocks and the ride to the Gare Montparnasse would take less than thirty minutes. She had not noticed the concierge follow her to the door of the apartment block and watch her progress until she had turned the corner. Hurrying back to her rooms the concierge extracted two packages from the outgoing mailbox, picked up the telephone and called Inspector Badeaux.

The concourse at Gare Montparnasse was crowded. Many of the departures from here were to Spanish destinations and refugees from Franco's regime were often waiting in expectation of relatives who had escaped Spain. Franco's agents prowled the concourse and platforms, seeking enemies of Franco to report back on. There were passport checks at the barriers for trains departing for Spain. Clara shuffled along, hoping to remain invisible. She wore a headscarf and dark glasses. Franco's agents did not bother her. She was more interested in the Gendarmes who patrolled back and forth, constantly scanning the crowds. Badeaux remained a phantom on her shoulder and would, she supposed until she crossed the frontier and was beyond his jurisdiction.

The line she was in stretched twenty metres from the barrier. In front of her was a family of five. Clara could tell from their appearances that they had had a difficult time in Paris, probably staying in hostels and seeking charitable institutions for meals. The father was dressed in a crumpled suit. He wore a white shirt, buttoned to the neck but without a tie. He constantly looked around him as if expecting something unwanted. His wife held a restless, three-year-old child in her arms. She struggled to keep him as he writhed bad-temperedly, desperate to get down and explore the station. The other two children were approximately nine and eleven years old - a boy and a girl, constantly complaining about the wait and their boredom. Their dark features marked them out as unmistakably Spanish, like so many of the others in the line. Clara felt uncomfortable fearing that the family would attract closer inspection by the Gendarmes.

When the family finally reached the barrier, the guard took an age to inspect their documents and then insisted that they open all their luggage cases. The wife protested furiously but the guard was stone-like in his insistence. Clara fought her growing frustration. The people directly behind her were vocally protesting and the gendarmes were keeping a distant eye on the situation.

Finally, the family re-packed their dishevelled suitcases and were shuffled through the barrier. Clara approached the gate. The guard took hold of her passport and ticket.

"Where are you travelling to?" he asked.

"Gerona," Clara replied.

"Will you be travelling onward?"

"No."

"What is the purpose of your journey?"

"I have a sister there who needs my help now that her husband is deceased." The guard stared at her passport for a long time.

"Please remove your scarf and glasses."

Clara did as she was asked. She shook her head to let her hair fall to her shoulders. The guard studied her. Finally, reluctantly it seemed to Clara, he closed the passport with her ticket inside it and stood aside to let her pass.

Arriving at her seat, with her luggage safely stashed on the overhead rack, Clara began to feel safe. But as time ticked slowly on and the train still sat, immobile beside the platform, belching smoke and making random juddering movements, her frustration began to re-emerge. The train slowly filled up. Twenty minutes before departure her compartment was fully occupied and she was gently squeezed against the window by the father of the family she had been next to in the line. Opposite her sat the eleven-year-old son, who stared at her relentlessly.

At last, with a neck-wrenching jolt, the train began to move. An infinitesimal acceleration caused the platform to slide by. Just as Clara allowed herself a silent sigh of relief, everyone on her side of the compartment was thrown forward as the train slammed to a halt. Heads turned to the windows as shouts were heard from the platform. Then boots could be heard running through the train. Compartment doors slammed open and shut. Then it was their compartment. The door slammed open and a gendarme forensically scanned the faces. He turned to the corridor and yelled, "In here!"

As he pushed his way in, two companions joined him and moved towards Clara. Just as she was flinching away from their grasp, the mother of the family screamed. The son burst out crying and the daughter shouted defiantly. The father of the family struggled within the grip the gendarmes had him under. He accidentally kicked Clara as he struggled to free himself. His attempts were in vain. In no time they had him on his face in the corridor and handcuffed. He was then dragged to his feet and led away.

Doors slammed, whistles blew, the train jolted forward and they were underway. The remaining family members were distraught. For the first twenty minutes Clara was in the middle of a cacophony of misery. Eventually, the mother dried her own tears and calmed the children. Without being asked she tried to explain to Carla. "They think he helped the French Catalan sabotage group. It's not true."

Clara did not respond. She could not afford to be involved or implicated. As the train bulleted its way south, towards the foothills of the Pyrenees, Clara managed to snatch a little sleep. She was vaguely aware of the mother leaving and entering the compartment. She saw her pacing up and down the corridor outside the compartment door. The children slept, stretched out on the benches. She did not like herself for it, but she knew she would be glad when her proximity to this family was over.

It was the train slowing that awakened her. Looking through the window she could see that they were approaching the frontier crossing. There would be another passport check here. After a twenty-minute wait, the train jolted forward again, and at a snail's pace it crept along for about three miles. It came to a halt beside a stone building and several officials in frontier guard uniforms climbed on board. The tedious process of checking everyone's passport had been going on for over an hour when, finally, a guard entered Clara's compartment. He collected all the passports and retired to the corridor to scrutinise them with the help of a colleague. After several minutes he returned and handed a bundle of passports to the Spanish woman and then turned to leave.

"Excuse me," Clara called, getting to her feet. "My passport please?" The guard turned. He waved the passport in the air. "I will be back," he said.

329

From her window Clara saw him walk along the platform and enter the stone building. Her eyes remained glued to the door as if willing him to appear. Suddenly he was there. But he was not alone. He was followed by a tall moustachioed man in a thick black overcoat and a trilby hat. Inspector Badeaux. The guard pointed towards Clara's carriage and they both hurried along the platform towards her.

Of course, she knew what was coming. She was to be arrested. But she could not be sure of the reason. Was it just the false passport? If so, there was a chance that she could explain that away before her parcel arrived at *Le Parisien*. But if it was not about the passport, it could only mean that Badeaux had found a way of intercepting the post and reading the contents of the package.

The Inspector was at the door of her compartment. "Will you please come with me Madame Paquet?" he asked in a surprisingly soft voice.

With an abrupt acceptance of defeat, Clara got to her feet, lifted her luggage and allowed herself to be escorted from the train.

Fifty-nine

Montreal, Canada, August 1997

Mount Royal Cemetery began to empty. The hearse was gone and the cars which had made up the cortege now took turns to glide off slowly toward the exit.

Two individuals remained at the graveside. The older of the two women was in her mid to late forties. She was athletically slim with a good figure and an attractive face. She wore a dark blue suit appropriate to the occasion. She was much lighter in complexion than her companion although both women were recognisably black. The younger woman was in her twenties, she was an inch or two taller than the other and she too was suitably dressed, this time in a black suit with a white-collar trim. They stood side by side and read the inscription on the temporary wooden cross that had been planted at the head of the new grave.

Jean-Paul Paquet

1919 – 1997

A hero of the French Resistance

Beloved Guardian of Ana Paquet (Tate)

RIP

"How long before the permanent headstone is erected?" the younger woman asked.

"They won't say for definite. It depends how long it takes for the soil to settle."

"Are you sure you're alright?"

"Yes. I'll be fine. He was everything to me. He was the only family I had but I never felt that I had missed out on something. He filled all the spaces. I loved him more than if he had been my father."

The younger woman reached out and took Ana by the hand. "Come on. We'd better join the others. My husband is waiting to drive us into town." They turned and walked towards the waiting Volvo.

"Ceceline," Ana said, stopping them both for a moment. "Your mom named you after her sister?"

"That's right, I have a cousin called Danika." The women smiled and walked on

"I can't tell you how much meeting you has meant to me," Ana continued. "All of my life it's been just me and Jean-Paul. I never dreamed that I would one-day find a family. I'll be eternally grateful to you for searching me out. And to have you here at Jean-Paul's funeral is so comforting. I don't feel so alone in the world now."

"My mom often talked about you. My brothers and sisters and I grew up with you as a missing part of us. Grandma had told my mom, Danika and Aunts Ceceline and Mary about Uncle Huey's tragic return to Alabama. He was so proud of you. He boasted about how clever and pretty you were and couldn't wait to get back home to France to be with you and your mom."

"I had no idea about my father's family."

"Grandma tried to get in touch but she got no reply. I grew up in Chicago. I only saw Grandma a few times. She died when I was ten."

"It didn't turn out the way Mama and Jean-Paul planned it," Ana ruminated. "We were all supposed to have a life together in Canada. My mother was rejected by the Canadian authorities at first because of a criminal conviction from her youth. They found a way around that but, in a way my mother sacrificed herself so that my father's killer would be exposed. The trouble is it ended up exposing her too. She was either very foolish or very brave. I can't decide which."

"If you hadn't become a published writer, I would never have been able to trace you. But your story about a black resistance fighter was such a sensation. All of my friends were reading it. When I read it, I spotted clues that only someone familiar with our family history could have known about. That's when I decided to try and contact you."

"I'm so pleased that you have. Come on now. The others will be downtown already. The wake cannot begin until we are there. Does your husband...?"

"William......"

"Does William know where Sherbrooke Street is? It's the Hilton on Sherbrooke."

"Back home in Chicago William drives for a living. If he can't find Sherbrooke from here nobody can."

The women laughed and climbed into the car. William touched the accelerator on the idling engine and the car slid gently out of the cemetery.

Sixty

Paris 1967

Le Monde: Friday 18 March 1967 **Female Assassin Executed.**

Madame Guillotine avenges the murder of war hero Marc Durand.

Clara Durand, previously Tate, née Bisset, at the age of 41, was guillotined yesterday morning, March 17,1967, in the courtyard of the prison de la Roquette in Paris by executioner André Obrecht.

Madame Durand was convicted of the premeditated murder of her husband, Marc Durand on the evening of September 22 1963. Marc Durand suffered a fatal knife wound to the heart. The police coroner stated that he would have rapidly bled out and died in a matter of minutes after the fatal blow was struck.

Clara Durand is the first convicted female criminal to be guillotined since the abortionist Marie-Louise Giraud was executed on the morning of July 30th 1943.

The trial has been a sensational controversy throughout the length and breadth of the nation. The accused admitted killing Durand but pleaded not guilty to the crime of murder. Her counsel argued for clemency due to the circumstances. A plea of 'crime passionnel' was attempted but the judge ruled it out declaring it inappropriate for the defendant. Female defendants are rarely permitted this form of defence and the judge in this case declared himself bound by that tradition.

Counsel for the defence had argued that the discovery of Marc Durand's role in the murder of her first husband, Huey Tate, had been sufficient to drive her to the extremity of passion. Tate, an American who had served in the second world war with the Allied forces, and had been involved in the liberation of Paris, was himself murdered in the State of Alabama, allegedly by members of the Ku Klux Klan. The discovery of Durand's involvement in a conspiracy to have Monsieur Tate murdered had been enough to tip the accused over the edge. Despite knowing of the murder of Tate, the victim had hidden that knowledge from the woman who was now his wife. He even kept up this deception before the French civil courts when he and Clara successfully applied for the annulment of her first marriage due to desertion.

Judge Dupuis ruled this claim inadmissible. No case of the murder of Monsieur Tate had ever been lodged and therefore this could not be accepted as a cause for passionate revenge. He also instructed the jury to wipe from their minds anything they might have read in the popular press regarding this case, particularly the sensationalising treatment in *Le Parisien*.

The prosecution successfully proved pre-meditation for the following reasons. Firstly, Madame Durand had made careful plans to have her daughter, Ana Tate, removed from the apartment where she later killed Durand. A wartime colleague of both the accused and the victim, Jean-Paul Paquet, had taken Ana to his apartment at the accused's request and is now, reportedly living in Canada with her. Secondly, she, and Monsieur Paquet, had planned their escape from justice by seeking emigration. Madame Durand had only been foiled in this because of a wartime conviction for assault. There is no doubt that she planned to commit the murder of Durand.

It was noticed in the press gallery how the jury was heavily impressed by the prosecution's account of Durand's war record. Judge Dupuis denied the defence any opportunity to outline Madame Tate's own war record, declaring it irrelevant.

The prosecution produced Monsieur Caron. His evidence claimed that Madame Tate had been involved in *'collaboration horizontale'* and had only been saved from the punishment she deserved by the intervention of Durand.

The prosecution spent a long time examining the accused on her marriage to Huey Tate. Monsieur Fabron for the prosecution, suggested to the accused that her decision to marry a negro was a strong indicator of her deficient judgement. No self-respecting French woman would do as she had done, he argued. Some members of the jury audibly gasped when she replied that she had loved her husband. Turning to the jury, Monsieur Fabron said that it was easy to see how a deficient personality with a dubious moral past could plan and execute a murderous action.

The jury returned with their verdict in just under three hours. In sentencing Tate to death, Judge Dupuis declared that he had no hesitation in ridding the world of such a scheming, devious and evil individual. Her existence had been a rebellion against nature and a betrayal of the innate goodness of French womanhood.

End.

Printed in Great Britain
by Amazon